"Who's there?"

came the voice that had haunted Garret over fifteen years and hundreds of thousands of miles.

He tried to find his own voice, but no words would come. Then the door cracked open, and he saw the long brown tangle of her hair. He tried to grin, but it was hard to grin from down on one's knees, especially when the fever sent another racking chill through his body.

"Oh, my God," Suzanne Montgomery said quite clearly in the night. The door flew open.

"I told you," he managed to whisper. "I told you I'd be back someday."

Dear Reader,

Wow! What a month we've got for you. Take *Maddy Lawrence's Big Adventure*, Linda Turner's newest. Like most of us, Maddy's lived a pretty calm life, maybe even too calm. But all that's about to change, because now Ace Mackenzie is on the job. Don't miss this wonderful book.

We've got some great miniseries this month, too. *The One Worth Waiting For* is the latest of Alicia Scott's THE GUINESS GANG, while Cathryn Clare continues ASSIGNMENT: ROMANCE with *The Honeymoon Assignment*. Plus Sandy Steen is back with the suspenseful—and sexy—*Hunting Houston*. Then there's Beverly Bird's *Undercover Cowboy*, which successfully mixes romance and danger for a powerhouse read. Finally, try Lee Karr's *Child of the Night* if you enjoy a book where things are never quite what they seem.

Then come back again next month, because you won't want to miss some of the best romantic reading around— only in Silhouette Intimate Moments.

Enjoy!

Leslie Wainger

Leslie Wainger
Senior Editor and Editorial Coordinator

Please address questions and book requests to:
Silhouette Reader Service
U.S.: 3010 Walden Ave., P.O. Box 1325, Buffalo, NY 14269
Canadian: P.O. Box 609, Fort Erie, Ont. L2A 5X3

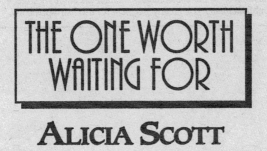

THE ONE WORTH WAITING FOR

ALICIA SCOTT

Published by Silhouette Books

America's Publisher of Contemporary Romance

SILHOUETTE BOOKS

ISBN 0-373-07713-0

THE ONE WORTH WAITING FOR

Copyright © 1996 by Lisa Baumgartner

ALICIA SCOTT

recently escaped the corporate world to pursue her writing full-time. According to the former consultant, "I've been a writer for as long as I can remember. For me, it's the perfect job, and you can't beat the dress code." Born in Hawaii, she grew up in Oregon before moving to Massachusetts. Now an avid traveler, she spends her time chasing after two feisty felines, watching Val Kilmer movies and eating chocolate when she's not running around the globe.

She is currently at work on her latest project in Boston, where she awaits the discovery of true love or ownership of a chocolate shop—whichever comes first.

To my editor, Gail Chasan, for not only
believing in this series, but for improving it.
I can't wait to see what we do next.

Prologue

In the D.C. Dulles Airport, a man who'd seen better days finally boarded the plane. He was the last person on and people looked up with mild impatience at his boarding. One glance at the man's face, however, and all eyes quickly turned away.

His midnight black hair fell past his shoulders, the strands tousled and streaked with what might have been mud. A large lump swelled out from his forehead while a long, angry red welt slashed down the side of his face, neatly slicing through several days' worth of dark stubble on his cheeks.

He wore a button-down dress shirt that was now wrinkled and stained. The gray wool sports coat thrown over it was clearly too warm for the eighty-five-degree night, but there was no sign of sweat on the man's face. In fact, he seemed to hunch inside the coat as if fighting off a chill. Or perhaps he was just trying to conceal the full muscular bulk of his physique, his broad shoulders and massive arms already straining the boundaries of the old coat and adding to his dangerous, disreputable air.

Garret Cagney had developed into quite a man in the years since he'd left Maddensfield.

He weaved a bit as he made his way to the back of the plane, and the people in the aisles instinctively leaned away, trying to put even more distance between themselves and what appeared to be a drunken bum. Even the flight attendants seemed concerned, but none quite had the courage to ask for his ticket stub.

When he finally reached the last aisle seat, Garret sat down abruptly, his face paling with the impact. For one moment, he swayed where he sat, a giant tree about to fall. Then his massive hands clenched the arms of the seat so tightly that his bruised and battered knuckles turned white. He steadied, and the grim expression on his face made his two aisle mates quickly turn away.

With the low hiss of someone releasing a pent-up breath, the huge man finally eased down into the seat. He pushed the seat back in spite of the explicit instructions not to do so, and in minutes, he appeared to fall into a deep sleep.

A flight attendant who had been approaching to ask him to straighten his seat back did a little double take and let the matter go. Somehow, it appeared wiser just to let this one sleep. Around her, people began breathing a little easier.

He slept through the takeoff, muttering every now and then in a language no one recognized. The two suited men next to him exchanged glances, then both shrugged. The man didn't belong on a flight of mostly business travelers, but it was a short enough distance to Charlotte, and they could sustain their discomfort for that long.

Presently, the flight attendants began to move up the aisle with the cart of beverages and peanuts. The two men both ordered beers, looked at the passed-out man next to them and switched their orders to Coke. The attendant smiled as she handed them their beverages, then her gaze fell on the remaining man, as well.

He really did look like someone who'd run into serious trouble. But then she saw the rising color on his cheeks, the beads of sweat forming on his brow. And despite his disheveled, dangerous appearance, she felt the first touch of concern.

"Sir?" she asked politely, the two businessmen watching her with something bordering disbelief. "Sir? Are you all right?"

She reached out to touch his shoulder and instantaneously his huge hand snapped around her wrist. She gasped audibly, and the middle business traveler nearly dropped his drink.

The man's eyes opened, and the feral gleam she saw in their dark depths made her heart leap and explode in her chest.

"I'm sorry, sir," she squeaked. "I didn't mean to disturb you."

Abruptly, he frowned as if seeing her for the first time. His eyes cleared, and he shook his head slightly as if clearing away some hovering mist. The movement made him wince, and the pain brought back the last of his consciousness. For the first time, he looked at his viselike grip on her wrist. He released her hand immediately.

"My apologies, ma'am," he said, the words hoarse and rusty from disuse. "I didn't mean any harm."

She nodded and saw him wince again from the pain of speaking. She drew her hand back, clutching it protectively against her chest, but didn't stop staring at him. Under all the bruises and scrapes, he retained the faint resemblance of a remarkably handsome man. Even now, rumpled and unshaven, he possessed a certain magnetism. Or maybe it was simply the aura of near-tangible danger.

"Can I get you something, sir?" she heard herself asking.

"Just rest," he whispered, his eyes already fluttering closed.

She nodded again, then licked her lips. He really didn't look in very good shape. "Maybe a glass of juice?" she found herself suggesting. "Orange juice would be good."

His eyes opened again, and he looked at her with fresh assessment and new appreciation. He grinned, a slow cracking of his lips that had once made women practically swoon at his feet. Even now, the effect was noticeable. The flight attendant suddenly blushed a little, and she smiled back at him.

"Yes," he managed to croak. "Juice would be perfect, ma'am. And water, too, if it isn't any problem."

In one corner of his mind, he was aware of how strange and foreign the words seemed on his tongue. He hadn't spoken English for a long time, but what he'd spoken instead refused to come to mind. The mist remained, hovering in the back of his brain, blocking out all that had been and leaving him with only a sense of urgency about what was to come. He had to get to Maddensfield.

No matter what, no matter how, he had to get to Maddensfield.

And then, another woman's face came to mind, soft and young with hazel eyes. She was standing at the bus stop, watching him go. And through the rain, he could see the tears streaming down her cheeks.

Suzanne. He had to get to Suzanne.

The attendant set down the two cups in front of him, and before he lost his strength, he picked them up one by one and tossed them down quickly, tasting nothing. He needed the liquid. He needed something to sustain him for the journey still to come. He managed one last smile at the kind woman in the aisle, then allowed the blackness to settle in yet again.

He roused himself again when the wheels of the plane hit the ground with a bucking roll. He felt the jar in his back and had to grit his teeth to keep from gasping out loud with the pain. The good thing was that the pain brought consciousness once more. He was in Charlotte. He forced himself to look at his watch. Nine p.m. He needed to get a car, or maybe a bus, perhaps a taxi.

His mind felt groggy, and he couldn't quite focus on which mode of transportation was best to use. He rose slowly when he could finally disembark, feeling the pain hit him again, and knew he was running out of time.

Sooner or later, the blackness would not be denied.

He managed to grip the seats and used them to help him walk out of the plane.

His mind still wasn't working well by the time he made it downstairs to the car-rental area. Car, taxi, bus. Car, taxi, bus. Think, man, think.

He was supposed to get a car, he thought dimly. He had the license, the cash. But what if he passed out again? He should take a taxi. He had the cash. He could give a fake name. But the destination would be known, and once they saw Maddensfield, they wouldn't need to see his real name to know it was him. Same with the bus.

Car then. It had to be a car. He thought he might black out any minute. He turned, and without preamble, slammed his fist against the brick wall. The pain was brilliant, flashing through his head like an entire Fourth of July fireworks display. Oh, he hurt. He truly hurt.

Hunched and shivering, muttering words he didn't even understand, he rented a car in the name of Robert Fulchino from the shocked-looking desk clerk.

He had to think hard when he got into the car. The mechanics of driving felt slow and rusty, actions he hadn't performed in a long time. At least he could recall them, despite the fact so many other things remained behind the thick mist in his mind.

He turned the car onto the interstate and headed home. He had to pull over twice, the fog grew so thick. He could feel the tremors begin to overtake him and knew a fever must be setting in. He'd lost too much blood, not to mention the nice lump on his head from the time he'd pitched forward onto the sidewalk. The arriving medics had been a little shocked to see the corpse suddenly stand and walk away. They'd been even more shocked when he'd pulled a gun and told them that if they followed him, he'd shoot them both.

Of course, he'd had to ditch the gun to board the plane. He had a feeling he would regret that later.

The second time he pulled over, he knew he'd been out longer. His watch now said it was 3:00 a.m., and it should only have taken him two hours to get to Maddensfield. He wasn't doing very well.

For the first time, he wondered if he would make it.

And then he calmly slammed his mangled fist into the dashboard and allowed the pain to work its magic once more.

He pulled back onto the highway and drove through the North Carolina night. Maddensfield. Suzanne. Maddensfield. Suzanne.

Forty-five minutes later, haggard and half-delirious, he pulled into the town. He had enough sense left to remember to ditch the car in the forest on the edge of town. His brother, Cagney, was the sheriff now and could retrieve the car in the morning.

Two more miles to Suzanne's house.

Garret slammed his fist into a tree, then started walking. The lucid moments were farther apart. The sky seemed to move with him, and his shirt and jacket were soaked to his skin. He wanted to take off his coat, but knew he mustn't. He needed the warmth. Even if he was hot, he needed the warmth.

But then suddenly, he was chilled again, so it didn't matter. It was cold, and the moon was chasing him, and he could no longer get away. Dimly, he knew he was muttering under his breath, mentioning names though the faces remained lost to him.

Zenaisa. Zlatko. Zenaisa.

The porch loomed ahead, and the relief staggered him. He didn't knock on the door so much as fall against it. His two-hundred-pound frame made a loud, heavy thud, enough to wake her. He had a final intriguing thought of Suzanne appearing with a shotgun and shooting him, then collapsed to his knees on the porch.

"Who's there?" came the voice that had haunted him over fifteen years and hundreds of thousands of miles.

He tried to find his voice, but no words would come out. *Zenaisa.* He felt a horrible, wrenching pain down deep in his gut, and this time, he nearly welcomed the blackness.

The porch light flickered on, blinding him with its fierceness. He waited, clinging to the last strands of consciousness. The door cracked open, and he saw the long brown tangle of her hair.

He tried to grin, but it was hard to grin from one's knees, especially when the fever sent another racking chill through his body.

"Oh, my God," Suzanne Montgomery said quite clearly in the night. The door flew open.

"I told you," he managed to whisper. "I told you someday."

Then, his mission at long last accomplished, he plunged forward unconscious at her feet.

Chapter 1

His head pounded, the images swirling in his mind like a looping roller coaster suddenly gone berserk. He thought once he stood in a broiling world of flames. He could feel the fire lap at his skin like a lover, hot and greedy and voluptuous, and he smelled the scent of searing skin and burning hair. He saw the fire grip his arm and knew he'd truly died and gone to hell.

Sometimes, though, the fire disappeared, running away until he had only the ache in his arm as a reminder. And then he was a lost soul, walking through lands he didn't recognize, talking a tongue that held no meaning. He saw the bodies, scattered across the ground, and this time he smelled a death so putrid not even fire could cleanse it away. The weight of an ax rested strange and heavy in his hand. Slowly, he turned his head to see the buzzards circling in the sky overhead.

He knew without feeling that tears washed through the soot on his cheeks.

Then came the rain, cleansing and fresh and pure, smelling faintly of mountains and honeysuckle. He should have loved the rain, but with rain always came the woman. He saw her standing with her hair plastered down her back, her dark eyes somber and accepting in the night while tears flowed quietly down her cheeks. He looked at her, and his chest burned as if he'd been sprinting for a good fifty yards and still had ten to go.

He always turned away from the woman, and it seemed that inevitably, in this sick carnival ride of his mind, the fire found him once more and lured him into its burning grasp.

He bolted up, gasped out, "Mitch," and then the flames claimed him again. Licking, searing, tasting, grasping.

He fought and wrestled and burned. He died and sprang to life. He cried for people he did not know and turned away from the woman he knew too well. He lived, he lost and he warred, bearing out the sickening twists of his mind, seeking again the brief moments of startling clarity. The ride had to end. The roller coaster had to straighten out. He fought for it. He raged.

But mostly, he burned.

The eighth trip through the whirlwind, his eyes opened, and he managed to glimpse the present. He could see the swimming images of a man and woman, heads bent together in serious consultation.

"We have to send for Dr. Jacobs, Cagney."

"I don't know, damn it. He came here shot and alone, obviously running from something. We have to consider that."

"Consider what? Do you know how to fight a 104 degree fever?"

The man shifted on his feet uncomfortably, and Garret struggled for his voice. No one. No one must know.

"No, damn it," the dark-haired man swore. Cage, Garret thought, and tried to reach out for his younger brother.

"Besides," the woman continued, "Dr. Jacobs has been the doctor here forever. You're the sheriff, Cagney. He'll keep quiet if you tell him to. Everyone around here knows Garret's a Navy SEAL and half of his life is so darn classified not even Mitch knows about it."

"What if he says something?"

The woman turned slightly, and Garret saw the face from the rain. He worked harder for his voice, but the flames wouldn't relinquish their grasp.

"Have you understood a word he's said? I don't even recognize the language."

"Mitch."

There. Once more his older brother's name slid out of the void, scrabbling over thick, water-parched lips. Both heads swiveled immediately, and he forced the roller coaster to hold steady.

"Garret?" Cage whispered. Immediately, he was over at the bedside, bending down. "Can you hear me, Garret?"

A water glass was held to his lips from the other side; dimly he recognized Suzanne had come over. But the fire was fierce again, licking tantalizingly close, curling his hair.

"Mitch...has...to go. They'll try him next."

Cage frowned and exchanged heavy glances with Suzanne.

"Who's 'they,' Garret? Tell me who's 'they.'"

"He has to go. Him and Jessica. Everyone knows... brothers."

The roller coaster lurched sickeningly, carrying him closer to the edge and the excited, lapping flames. The heat, the searing heat. Sweat rolled like tears down his cheeks.

"Are you sure?" Cage asked sharply. "For God's sake, Jessica's eight months pregnant." And Mitch would never agree to run from some unidentified danger alluded to in a feverish haze.

Garret's mind lurched once more, a sharp curve in the carnival ride suddenly thundering ahead. He was going to crash. He was going to burn.

With extreme effort born of desperation, his massive fist leaped up to clutch Cage's shirt. "Get them out of D.C.," he demanded fiercely, his black eyes burning bright. "Get them out of D.C."

Then he hit the corner, his mind looping around and around through the blazing, tortured corridors of his shattered memories. The flames, the bodies, the rain. Over and over. His mind exploded and the darkness rushed in.

Cage swore, his gray eyes meeting Suzanne's with stark worry as Garret's hand slipped lifelessly from his brother's shirt. "You're right," he said shortly. "We'd better call Dr. Jacobs." He swore again, an uncharacteristic sound from his normally calm lips.

Mitch's wife, Jessica, was eight months pregnant with twins, her former graceful model's body swollen and ungainly with her burden. Last time Cagney had seen her and Mitch, they'd been reveling in the joys of their newfound love and finally tranquil life. Oldest brother Mitch had eased back from his position as an independent specialist for the witness protection program in the FBI, while Jessica was taking night courses to earn a master's degree in education.

This new interruption would not be welcomed, but Cagney didn't dare dismiss Garret's warning. Cage sighed and massaged his left leg and the old bullet wound that still twinged. Cagney and Garret had always had their differences, and in particular Cagney had never liked how his brother had treated Suzanne Montgomery fifteen years before. But family was family. When push came to shove, if Garret needed a liver, Cagney would be the first in line, and he knew Garret would do the same.

The only problem was that Garret didn't need a liver right now. He needed help with a problem Cage knew nothing

about. All he had to go by were the contents of Garret's
wallet and a stashed money belt. The wallet held a driver's
license and credit cards for a Robert Fulchino, while the
money belt revealed five thousand dollars in cash, another
set of fake ID, a Swiss Army knife and, Garret being Garret, a pack of three condoms. Suzanne had blushed nicely
when Cage had pulled those out.

"You'd better call Mitch," Suzanne said now, interrupt-
ing Cage's troubled thoughts with her own steady voice.
"I'll get Dr. Jacobs over here. It will attract less attention
than Maddensfield's sheriff doing it. Perhaps you should
call Mitch from a pay phone."

Cagney nodded, not surprised any more by Suzanne's
quick assessment of the situation. Assuming that Mitch's
phone line was tapped, a pay phone would be safest. Suzanne's own background as a schoolteacher hadn't prepared her for these things, but she'd spent plenty of time at
the Guiness household as Cagney's closest friend. Certainly in the past ten years, the Guiness brothers had had
plenty of cause for secrecy.

Cagney realized he was scowling and forced his face into
its normal calm expression. "Give me ten minutes," he said,
"and I'll be back." He jerked his head toward Garret's red-
flushed, unconscious form. "Will you be all right with
him?"

Suzanne raised a droll eyebrow. "Cagney Guiness, the
man's been shot. He's unconscious and feverish. He's
hardly going to ask me to dance. Now get to Mitch and let
me take care of things here."

Cagney gave in by throwing up his hands in mock sur-
render. Suzanne took care of half this town anyway, either
raising its children through her kindergarten classes, coun-
seling its marriages through her church groups, or nursing
its sick of her own pure volition. He was a fool even to
doubt her abilities with Garret. Except, of course, Garret
wasn't just anyone. He was the man she'd followed around

like a moon-eyed half-wit fifteen years ago and cried herself to sleep over when he'd boarded that bus and left Maddensfield for good.

Cage found himself frowning for the second time in five minutes and once more chastised himself. Suzanne was a big girl, and fifteen years was fifteen years. Certainly, more pressing issues needed his attention now.

He banged out of the house and limped down off the huge porch to find a pay phone.

Mitch answered on the third ring. "Mitch. It's Cagney. Get to a pay phone and call me at this number." Cagney rattled off the number, then hung up the phone without further explanation. Given Mitch's involvement with the FBI, none was necessary. Sure enough, three minutes later, the pay phone rang.

"What's wrong?" Mitch demanded abruptly. "I've been having that damn feeling again. Tell me no one's dead." Mitch had a history of premonitions before disasters. He'd already boarded a flight for North Carolina when Nick, the husband of their younger sister, Liz, had been shot years ago.

"Garret's here," Cage announced without preamble and heard Mitch's startled silence. "He showed up on Suzanne's porch early this morning, shot in the back and banged up. He's burning with fever, Mitch, but he keeps muttering your name. He wants you and Jessica out of D.C. He says everyone knows you're brothers."

Mitch swore, a low, succinct word that got to the point. Mitch and Garret didn't run with the same crowds, as the FBI and naval operations weren't exactly the same brotherhood. But you could call the two outfits distant cousins, and most of the powers-that-be knew there were two Guiness brothers playing James Bond.

"What happened?"

"I don't know, Mitch. He's not lucid enough to say anything more. Hell, we don't even understand what language he's raving in most of the time. He's got a lump the size of my badge on his forehead. He may be hallucinating, for all I know. But someone certainly shot him, and something drove him to come all the way back here to Suzanne's porch.''

''We'll go,'' Mitch said tersely, then sighed. Behind the sigh, Cagney could hear the dull echoes of cars passing by. ''Jess is going to kill me. Eight months pregnant and I'm going to stick her on a plane. What about Mom and Dad?''

Cage stiffened, then shrugged his shoulders. ''I don't know. Like I said, Garret hasn't said much.''

''If he's worried about someone coming to look for him, after they finish with D.C., Maddensfield's as good a place as any. There may be a reason he didn't show up at home.''

Cage nodded, wishing to hell that he had something more to go on. Mitch was right, however. In the absence of hard information, they should assume the worst. They were not men who led nine-to-five lives, and experience had bred caution. ''I'll have Davey stake out Mom and Dad's house,'' he said at last. ''Just in case.''

''And Liz?'' Their younger sister now lived with her husband, Richard Keaton, in Connecticut. With the change in last name, she would be harder to track down; Mitch and Jessica had once hidden out at their place for just that reason. But Liz had just given birth to a baby girl a few months back, and again, it was better to be safe than sorry.

''I'll tell her to keep an eye out,'' Cage said. ''Just in case.''

Mitch agreed, which left only their brother, Jake, unaccounted for. But Jake moved in the fast track of the entrepreneurial elite, so no one ever knew what country he was in until they read the social pages. Jake was more than capable of taking care of himself, though; Cagney often thought that beneath the dazzling grin, quick wit and brilliant charm, Jake was the most dangerous of them all. You didn't earn millions by being passive.

"You'll check in, then?" Cage said.

"In a few days. I know a place in eastern Oregon that ought to be far enough. Where should I call?"

Cagney digested the question, wondering if he should risk a call to his sheriff's office. "Call Marina Walden," he said at last. "She can get a message to me."

"Marina, hey?" Mitch said, and Cagney found himself flushing dully. "Does she have long black hair with a gray streak and violet eyes, perhaps?"

"Yes."

"So that's who Mom's been raving about."

"We're getting married in October." Cagney said the words steadily enough, but each and every time, they made his chest tighten with the force of his emotions. He couldn't imagine life before Marina anymore.

Mitch was startled into silence for a moment, then Cage could practically feel the force of his proud grin across the telephone lines. "Congratulations, Cage. I always knew it would happen sooner or later. I can't wait to meet her."

"Soon," Cagney promised. "Maybe when this is all over. Mom and Dad's anniversary is coming up." It sounded so normal, he thought vaguely. So rational and sane, as if one of them wasn't shot, and another forced to flee from a danger no one even knew.

"Will do. Keep your eyes open, Cage. I'll tap a few sources of my own, but I'd hate to meet the person who managed to put a bullet in Garret's back. And I'd hate to be that person once Garret heals."

"Mitch?" Cagney was quiet for a moment, then forced the words out. "Mitch, he's lost a lot of blood. We've called for Dr. Jacobs, but I don't know how it will go."

There was absolute silence on the other end, and in his mind, Cagney could see Mitch clench and unclench his fists at his side. Since the time they were born, Mitch had looked after them all, and he was the only one of them who had ever been able to keep Garret in line.

"He'll get well," Mitch said firmly, but Cagney could hear the tension in his voice. "He's too damn stubborn to die. In the meantime, we'll figure it all out. We take care of our own."

Cagney nodded and, after a last exchange, hung up the phone. He understood the intensity of Mitch's voice, and for just one moment, he felt that intensity in his own blood. The four brothers had all chosen risk-filled paths, but that didn't mean they'd simply accept Garret's injuries with a philosophical shrug.

Everyone in Maddensfield knew you just didn't mess with a Guiness.

Garret didn't know how much time had gone by when he next gripped lucidity. There was no sense of time in the burning embers of his mind. Once, he saw himself as a kid, yelling at Jake for making Liz cry. And then water was pouring down his face from the trap Jake had rigged over his door in retaliation. He was moving forward with his teenage fist ready for battle when all of a sudden Jake's face changed. Suddenly, he was sixteen-year-old Tank who was big enough to shave. And they were all standing outside the school and Tank was yelling at some raggedly clothed, hunch-shouldered girl that her mother was nothing but a stinkin' drunk. Her hair fell straight and shiny down her back as she tucked her younger sister's hand in her own, trying to shield the little girl. Garret knew without thinking who she was.

He moved forward immediately and slammed his fist in Tank's smirking, hair-stubbled face. The overgrown brute came up with a howl, meaty hands swinging, and Garret felt his blood begin to sing.

"Multiple lacerations, three bruised ribs, a bullet hole in the back, spiking fever, severe dehydration, onset of malnutrition and a raging concussion. Hell, I've seen crash-test dummies in better condition than this boy."

Dr. Jacobs. Time zeroed suddenly in, like a zoom lens homing in on target. He struggled to open his eyes, struggled to move his fists. He had to tell him that no one must know. No one must ...

"He needs to be hospitalized, Cagney. This boy needs serious medical attention."

No, no hospitals. No one could know. He fought for the words, raged with the muscles in his throat.

"I don't think that's an option," Cagney said quietly, his face stark and pale while Suzanne twisted cloth bandages into tiny knots beside him. "Surely there's something we can do for him here."

Dr. Jacobs sighed and searched through his bag for penicillin.

"You're lucky he's not paralyzed," he muttered, "but then, I always suspected you boys had more lives than a cat."

"What do we do?"

Suzanne's voice, clear and steady. Garret wanted to turn toward it, but his mind still refused to connect with his muscles. The fire was back, licking closer. The heat, the unbearable heat, searing his skin.

"We gotta get the fever down for starters and get some fluids into the man. What he hasn't bled away he seems determined to sweat out instead. I want an IV, and I'm worried about his head, as well. That looks like a hell of a concussion, even for his thick skull."

"I can wake him every half hour." Suzanne's voice again, soft and steady. He could almost feel the rain against his cheek, cool and clean. "I'll check for dilation of the pupils."

"I can do that," Cagney interrupted curtly. "You shouldn't have to be bothered with such things."

"You'll do no such thing, Cagney," she retorted promptly. "This man is lying in my guest bedroom and I know perfectly well how to take care of him. You've got yourself a new fiancée to go home to, so don't you bother me with your presence, as well."

Her hands came down to rest on Garret's forehead, and he fought bitterly to arch up against her cool palms. Soft and gentle against the crackling flames. He wanted so badly to speak. He had to tell them... The thought skittered away again, and the fire roared forward.

"I really don't like the looks of that," Dr. Jacobs said, and Garret felt his hands replace Suzanne's on his forehead. The old, callused fingers pressed slightly, and the pain exploded like skyrockets in his head.

He jerked up, his eyes popping open with feverish clarity. He had to say, he had to say...

Suzanne was in front of him, her hazel eyes round with shock as her hands pressed him gently back to the mattress. He locked his gaze on hers, fighting the flames, fighting the darkness, fighting anything to get the words out. He knew he must say, he must warn...

"Vatra. Svagdje. Vatra!"

"Shhh," she whispered, soothing him with her hands. He could smell the faint scent of roses, and in his confusion he couldn't understand how roses had ever grown amid all the rocks. The blood, he thought, but then he lost that idea, as well.

"Mrtavi..."

"It's okay, honey," she told him quietly, her palms cool on his burning cheeks. "Close your eyes again, Garret. Rest, darling. Cagney and I will take care of everything."

But they couldn't because they didn't know. Because he didn't know. Oh, God, what was it he had to know? He had to...

"Will he be all right?" Cagney's voice, tight with the strain.

"I don't know. The next twelve hours will be critical. We gotta get this fever down before he cooks the few gray cells he has left. Someone had better take me back to my office for supplies."

"Fine. Anything, Doctor. Just tell me he's going to pull out of it."

"I know, son. I know."

"What's wrong with his forearm?" Suzanne asked. He could feel her fingers trace down his arm and in his fever-ravaged state, the motion pained him.

Dr. Jacobs peered closer at the long, shiny scar running as a denuded zone along his black-haired arm. "Scarring, probably from a burn injury, by the look of it." He shook his head. "You boys always did get into too much trouble."

Garret felt cool air as the sheet was pulled back to expose his leg and hip.

"More burning on the legs," Dr. Jacobs reported. "Not that old, either. Where the hell has this boy been?" Cage's face gave nothing away, and Dr. Jacobs sighed with a shake of his head. He peered down at Garret's gums, noticing the pale color and receding line. Then he felt out the distinct outline of the unconscious man's ribs. Dr. Jacobs face grew grimmer. "Definite beginnings of malnutrition. You'd think he thought a body was easy to replace by the looks of all this damage. Crazy fool."

Crazy fool. The words penetrated the fire, echoing inside his thick, tortured head. With a primal groan, he forced his eyes open and beat back the flames.

"Don't tell," he whispered fiercely. "Don't tell. That I'm here."

Dr. Jacobs's white eyebrows shot up over clear blue eyes, then he nodded at Garret sagely. "Sure thing, son. I'm here to save your life."

Garret tried to nod, but the momentum was lost already. He fell back, feeling the fire flare again. Slowly, he searched for her eyes, her hands cool upon his face. Suzanne from the rain. Fifteen years...

He found her hazel eyes, and they met his squarely, the depths level and clear with guarded concern. The fire took him again. From a long ways away, he felt her hand on his shoulder once more. He turned his cheek against her wrist and let the last of his consciousness slip away.

"There's nothing more for you to do here, Cagney, so you might as well go home. Marina will be worried about you by this time."

"But...look at him, Suzanne. He's still sweating away every damn drop of moisture we can get into him."

"Dr. Jacobs says the fever might be breaking now. We got the IV in him, Cagney. It's the best we can do. One of us at least ought to get some rest. Go home, Cage. I can take it from here."

Garret opened his eyes to see them standing in the doorway. Cage was running his hand through his black hair and his face looked tight. Suzanne's brown hair had escaped in long strands from the knot on top of her head. She looked tired, too. How long had it been? He didn't know and found he still couldn't move.

"Are you sure you'll be all right?"

"Now, Cagney, we've had this conversation before."

"Yeah, yeah. I know." Cage sighed as his hand went through his hair yet again. "I've never seen him look like this before, Suzanne," he whispered quietly. "He was always the big one, you know? I still remember him taking on the bullies on the playground and thrashing every last one of them. Hell, do you remember what he did to Tank Nemeth?"

"I know, Cage. I know. He'll get better, just you wait. And one morning, we'll both come to check on him and he'll simply be gone as suddenly as he came. You know Garret."

Cagney grinned but it looked strangely sympathetic. "Yeah, I know. I was just wondering if you knew."

"Fifteen years is fifteen years, Cagney Guiness. You've told me that enough times yourself. Now get home to Marina. This is no way to treat your fiancée."

"Don't you ever get tired of being right?" Cage started to head for the doorway, and Garret struggled to reach out his hand. At the last moment, Cagney stopped. "In three weeks, I'm supposed to be in New York, you know. Marina wants me to meet her folks. Think I should cancel?"

Suzanne shook her head. "Even if Garret's not healed enough to go, he'll still be healed enough not to want anyone's help. 'Sides, I hear Marina's parents are real nice."

Cagney grimaced. "They have a cappuccino maker."

Suzanne patted him on the shoulder. "You'll do just fine."

He grabbed his black cowboy hat from the peg next to the door and placed it on his head. "I'll be back in a few hours."

"You'll be back in the morning," she told him firmly. "And then only for a short while. You start spending too much time here after just getting engaged to the prettiest girl in town and people are gonna talk. We don't want that, now do we, Cage?"

"Damn it, Suzanne, do you always have to be so practical?"

"It's the only way I keep up with you. Now give Marina my best, and get out of my house. I've got things to do."

"Eight a.m.?"

"Whatever works best. I'm going to cancel my meetings for the next couple of days. I suppose I can lie and say I'm sick. It's for a good enough cause."

"Thank you, Suzanne. You've always been the best."

He turned away, and for just one moment, her practical, efficient demeanor slipped. "Cagney?" she asked hesitantly, her easy smile slipping for just a minute. "Why do you suppose that after all these years he came here? Why not your parents' porch? Why not yours?"

Garret saw Cagney square his shoulders, the sheriff's face composing into the quiet, steady expression for which he was known. "Mitch thinks someone may come looking at Mom and Dad's," he said evenly. "But there's no reason for anyone to investigate here."

Suzanne nodded, her chin still high in the air. "I figured it must be something like that."

"Well, hopefully, we'll know more once he comes around."

"Of course. Take care, Cage. And remember, I'll call if there's anything to report."

Cage disappeared through the doorway, leaving Suzanne alone in the bedroom, her rich brown hair curling in gentle tendrils around her face. Garret continued to stare at her, willing his throat to work, but no sound escaped.

Perhaps she felt the pull of his gaze instead.

She turned, and her large hazel eyes connected with his black, glittering gaze.

"Garret?" she asked immediately. He opened his mouth, but no sound emerged. Quickly, she crossed the room to the pitcher of water next to the bed. With slightly trembling hands, she poured half a glass and raised the cool plastic mug to his full, cracked lips.

He drank like a forty-day drought victim, and she poured him half of a second glass, forcing him to take it more slowly this time. At last he leaned back, the sweat still beading up on his forehead and rolling down his cheeks. Without another thought, she picked up a damp cloth and began to wipe down his forehead in quick, efficient strokes. It was much better to keep moving, she decided. Anything was better than the force of his eyes upon her face.

"Roses," he whispered.

She jumped at the unexpected sound, then laughed a little self-consciously at her own nerves. She patted his forehead with the cloth a couple more times, then glanced down to find his burning eyes still locked upon her own.

"Roses," he told her again, the words rasping. "I couldn't figure out why there were roses amid all the stones."

Before she could move, his hand abruptly touched her cheek. The feel of his finger, dry and hot, caused her to flinch, and his hand fell down.

He sighed, the sound like a desert wind upon loose rocks. "I always knew you would still be here."

She jerked upright at that, the spell broken by her immediate outrage. She picked up the damp cloth and resumed her efficient movements. "Of course I still live here," she said primly, her chin up as she dabbed the cloth around his hairline. "This is my house, my home. I will always live here."

He seemed to smile, but his eyelids were already beginning to flutter down. Just as well, she told herself. She didn't want to talk to the insufferable bastard anyway. She nursed him for Cagney's sake and because she always helped the downtrodden—it was her civic duty. But she'd be more than happy for him to get well and leave. After all these years, she certainly didn't want anything to do with Garret Guiness.

She wasn't some sixteen-year-old fool anymore.

He winced, and she realized her movements had grown rather brisk. Immediately, she relented, redipping the cloth in the basin while she took another look at his flushed face. The cloth stilled in her hands, and her expression froze just for one instant.

He did look so sick, and the lump on the corner of his forehead had turned a putrid shade of green.

She wrung out the cloth and returned it to his closed eyes. "Rest up now, Garret," she told him softly. "You hear me? You've got to get well for Cagney and me. There'll be plenty of time to raise hell then."

"*Mrtavi,*" he groaned suddenly, thrashing his head to the side. The movement hurt him. She saw his lips curl back with the pain and the muscles cord on his neck. "*Mrtavi,*" he yelled, thrashing to the other side. His hands clenched into fists, the knuckles turning white, the one scar standing out in rigid relief. *"Mrtavi!"*

"Shhh," she tried, abandoning the fallen cloth to place her hands on his shoulders instead. "It's over now, Garret. It's over."

But the words didn't penetrate, and as she felt his body bow with unbelievable tension, she felt a moment of fear. He'd always been such a powerful presence.

"Garret—" she began.

He snapped, his body suddenly sinking back into the mattress like a marionette whose strings had been abruptly cut. His head rolled limply to the side, and she knew he'd fallen unconscious once more.

Gingerly, she collected herself, finding her hands trembling violently against his shoulders. Fifteen years ago, she'd stood in awe of him. Because he was tall, dark and powerful, and because he could do things to Tank Nemeth she never would. Somehow, with the passing of time, she'd gotten herself to believe the impressions were only the exaggerated memories of a sixteen-year-old girl. After all, once she'd thought he was her white knight, as well. She'd dreamed that he would come back to save her from her dreary, lonely life.

How mistaken she had been.

But it appeared some things about Garret remained true. He was still huge, and he could still make her hands tremble. And he still left her with more questions than answers.

She laughed suddenly, a small, rueful sound, as she dampened the washcloth again and spread it on his bruised forehead. So here was Garret Guiness, shot, feverish and unconscious.

Leave it to Garret to actually return but give her no satisfaction in it whatsoever.

Chapter 2

As usual, Suzanne woke up with the daybreak, the first few strands of the sun's glimmering rays peeking through the simple white eyelet curtains on her window. She lay there for a long moment, feeling unusually groggy and disoriented. Abruptly, the memory surfaced: Garret was back.

She frowned, and found herself staring at her motionless faded curtains while the July heat wrapped around her, warm and velvety.

Generally, she didn't lie around in her un-air-conditioned room contemplating her decor or the warm scent of roses in the morning air. Instead, she'd wake like an arrowshot, sliding out of bed and changing quickly while she contemplated meetings to attend, chores to do and people to call. She would put on her walking clothes and spend a brisk five miles every morning walking and plotting her day. Sometimes, if the day wasn't too hectic, after walking and showering she would take her tea out on her back porch, admire her roses and bask in the sultry morning for a rare twenty-minute break.

But mostly she moved and ran and plotted. She went to bed with her list of things to do formulating in her mind, then awoke with her thoughts already halfway down the list. No one got things done like she did.

But now, she remained sitting in her sleeveless cotton gown while the morning settled hot and humid around her. Because Garret had returned. Shot up and half-dead on her doorstep. What was a woman supposed to do with that?

She'd checked on him each hour as she'd promised. And each hour, he'd responded with his name, even as the moments of cognizance had faded in and out. Sometimes, he'd looked her straight in the eye, and whispered words she didn't understand. Other times, he'd thrown his head back and forth, the muscles on his neck cording like a wild stallion caught in the throes of a primal rage.

The few words she did recognize were something about a car in the forest and whispered warnings about his mom and dad. At least during the last hour the color had gone down in his cheeks. Perhaps today the fever would finally relinquish its hold. She hoped so; he was sweating away a dangerous amount of fluid, and there were times she was sure he would tear the fragile IV needle from his hand with his fever-induced wars.

But it appeared he'd survived the night. Which brought her, of course, to the day. She felt her stomach tighten, and a strange, light tingling filled her. Anticipation. Abruptly, she punched her pillow, and swung her feet to the floor.

Darn it, she wasn't going to feel such things. She was going to tend to his wounds like a good nurse and see to his health as Cagney's best friend. She was going to be a good citizen, and not think of anything else. She was practical and strong, and she'd paid dearly for both those qualities. If she ran around like some efficiency machine, then the approach had served her well through the years. Everyone in Maddensfield respected her. And no one, *no one,* ever mentioned her mother or all those years before.

She drew her nightgown over her head and stepped briskly into the shower. To prove her conviction, she turned her mind expediently to its lists of daily tasks. She had a meeting about the upcoming August parade at eleven, then the Maddensfield Fair at two. Choir practice began at eight tonight, and it was her turn to supply refreshments. Of course, tomorrow night she was due down at the Y as part of the literacy program.

They would all have to be canceled. She frowned in the shower, lathering her long hair briskly as the thought of lying settled low and uncomfortable in her stomach. She really wanted to curse Garret Guiness. She would have to say she was sick, she thought finally, rinsing out the last of the soap from her hair. At least it would explain why Dr. Jacobs continued to visit her house. Perhaps Cagney's, as well.

She stepped out of the shower and quickly toweled off. With a comb, she impatiently attacked the knots in her long brown hair, her fingers working automatically while her mind wandered free. She'd never liked her hair. It was fine and straight and completely unruly. Other people with long hair seemed to have thick, luxurious strands that shone after a brisk brushing. But, she thought, hers remained dull and lifeless, a color she'd come to call dishwater brown. Ruthlessly, she gathered it up into a knot on top of her head, and pinned it into submission. Over the course of the day, strands would escape to curl hot and uncomfortable down her neck. She'd discovered there was little she could do about that, except console herself with the knowledge that at least at the beginning of each day, she'd won the battle.

She only ever wore a touch of brown eyeliner and mascara, so when she found her hand hovering inexplicably over some ancient eye shadow, she felt the first stirrings of anger. She absolutely, positively, was not going to change anything for the man downstairs. It didn't matter that he was Garret and had once beat up Tank Nemeth for her and her sister. It didn't matter that he'd once flashed those special grins for her and walked her home. He'd left fifteen years ago, damn it. And not once had he ever looked back.

Not even all those nights she'd lain awake, and prayed that he'd come take her away at last.

The ache that appeared suddenly was rusty and deep. She turned away from it completely, and sought out her closet instead. Fifteen years was fifteen years, and so help her God, she was not going to suffer one moment of feeling for Garret Guiness.

She grabbed a skirt and blouse out of her closet without allowing herself a second to reconsider, threw them on and left without even a backward glance at the mirror. It was bad enough she'd given up her morning walk and afternoon meetings for the man. She wouldn't give up anything more.

The resolution lasted as long as it took her to get downstairs to the guest bedroom.

Here, she'd left the window air-conditioning unit running all night, and the air remained cool, prickling light goose bumps along her bare arms. But more to the point, the climate finally seemed to have reached Garret; he now lay quiet and still amid the twisted sheets, his chest falling with the even rhythm of sleep.

As she looked at him, tanned and rugged against the pale sheets, images from the past hovered at the edges of her mind. Garret had always been larger than life, not only because of his size and strength, but also because of the crackling air of raw energy that had surrounded him everywhere. When he'd grinned at her, she'd felt her heart explode like a fresh-bloomed rose in her chest.

It had seemed to her that he'd grinned for her alone.

Sometimes, when her mother had passed out drunk on the living room sofa, and her sister had cried herself to sleep in the room next door, she'd lain in bed and replayed each and every one of those grins in her mind like a precious treasure. And that day he'd taken on Tank Nemeth and all the other kids who'd made fun of her and her sister, she'd barely been able to sleep with the pure joy. Someone had stood up for her. Someone had actually cared.

It didn't matter that he rarely spoke to her, after all, he was two years older and the hero of the school. It didn't matter that the few times she saw him, she couldn't get a single word past her lips. All that mattered was the fact that he'd grinned at her, and each grin was a spark of color firing into the black-and-white solitude of her life.

She'd loved him passionately and purely and never expected him to feel anything else in return. Until the night she'd appeared at his house to walk with him to the bus stop.

She swallowed heavily, her hazel eyes blinking back to the present and the sight of a wounded Garret lying in her guest bedroom, an IV needle stuck in his hand.

And she forced herself to recall the other nights, the ones after the bus stop, when she'd lain wide-eyed into the early-morning hours waiting for him to appear. The nights she'd heard her mother's drunken mumbling, and thought that this night, this night he would surely appear and take her away at last.

This night he would save her. Night after night after night. But each morning she opened her eyes to her own bed and the sound of her mother's groans echoing down the hall.

She pushed away from the doorway, walking squarely into the room. Immediately, Garret's dark eyes opened.

"How do you feel?" she asked quietly, automatically pouring him a fresh glass of water from the pitcher beside the bed. Her hands trembled only slightly.

He didn't say anything, but his gaze latched onto the cold, tantalizing water. In response, she brought the glass to his lips and let him drink deeply.

His head fell back when he was done, a small sigh escaping the parched tightness of his throat. He felt like a stone, trying desperately to absorb water before it evaporated away from the searing heat. She placed the back of her hand against his cheek, and he closed his eyes against the coolness of her touch.

"Better," she murmured, "but still hot." A thermometer appeared in her hand and was unceremoniously stuck between his lips. His dark eyes glittered, but he didn't say anything.

In his fever-soaked visions, he felt he'd seen her a million times and in a million different ways. He'd seen her as the serious girl, walking the halls with her hunched shoulders and long brown hair. He'd seen her at the bus stop, her hazel eyes so luminescent in the rain, her pale face accepting. She always looked sad and strong in his mind, and those eyes had haunted him across more miles and more years than he'd ever intended.

She plucked the thermometer from his mouth and held it up to the light. As her gaze found the red mercury line, she frowned and tiny lines appeared around her eyes.

"A hundred and one," she declared. "Better, but we have a ways to go."

"The bus stop," he said, the words gravelly and low as they rumbled across his cracked lips. Her eyes met his warily.

"Water?" she asked smoothly.

He closed his eyes and searched along the fire-seared edges of his mind. "Do you remember the bus stop?" he whispered, knowing only that he had to know. So many things eluded his memory, buried behind the impenetrable mist. But he could see Maddensfield clearly, the house he grew up in, the faces of his brothers and sister in turn. He remembered high school, remembered scoring the winning touchdown to advance the team to the state play-offs. And recalled the bus stop the night he'd left home.

"Come now, Garret, don't waste your energy on words," Suzanne said briskly, though her heart was already pounding in her chest. The strange tightness returned to her stomach, and she felt anger thread into the weave of anticipation coursing through her blood. She edged away from the bed, and began to tidy things on the table. "You should sleep," she continued, proud of the steadiness of her voice.

"There are so many things I don't remember," he went on, his head rolling restlessly. "Last week, the weeks before that. The year before that. All I see is the mist in my head." He looked up. "So why do I remember the bus stop? Why do I see it again and again in my mind?"

His gaze caught her this time, pinning her like a helpless butterfly while her hands fluttered uselessly over the table-top. The anger and tension weaved tighter, her spine turning brittle and rigid. Why was he asking her these things? Why was he looking at her like that? "You've had a nasty bump on your head," she grated out under the onslaught of his glittering eyes. "You need some rest, Garret. That's all."

He frowned, and at once, she could see the telltale creep of color under his darkly tanned skin. "Do you remember the bus stop?" he demanded again, the words hoarser and edged with feverish determination. The air around him began to crackle with the pent-up electricity of his need.

She set her jaw, her gaze approaching mutiny. But the intensity of his gaze refused to be denied. Damn feverish fool.

"Yes," she admitted suddenly. Her hands unconsciously clenched the edge of the nightstand, while his eyes flared brighter.

"Do you remember what you said?" The fever flushed his cheeks, lacing the words with urgency and fire. This time, she managed to shake her head.

"You said you loved me," he said abruptly, his body shifting with the restlessness of the encroaching flames. Hot again, he could feel the hint of the fire pressing against his mind, the heat just beginning to roll forward. Once more he fastened upon the picture of the bus stop, the rain cold and cleansing on his face, the tears slow and desolate on her cheeks. He could still see her lips soundlessly forming the words, while something strange and inexplicable wrenched his chest. He could still feel the phantom ache, and it drove him mad in his heat-sensitized mind.

His gaze latched onto hers even more fiercely, the glittering depths tortured and cornered and possessed. His bandaged fists began to slowly twist the sheets at his side.

"I was sixteen," she managed to blurt out, the beat of her heart painful against her ribs as his eyes bore into her own. "And you were . . ." She faltered, hating the weakness and hating him for dragging her through his fever-ridden memories. Her lips thinned, and she stared him straight in the eyes. "And you were James Dean."

He grinned suddenly, a slow cracking of his heat-parched skin that turned to a wince. James Dean. Of course, he'd been James Dean. But had James Dean's head ever felt as if it had been stuck in a vat of boiling tar? Did James Dean remember nothing but the woman he was supposed to forget?

"And now?" he demanded urgently with a sickening lurch of his head, feeling at once lost and desperate. Flames leaped at the corners of his memory, his body bowing with rigid intensity. "And now?"

His gaze burned so dark, she felt a moment of panic. He was feverish, she realized dully. Sick and lost in his ravaged mind, saying words he didn't even comprehend. The knowledge lent her strength, and gently, firmly, she laid her hands on his shoulders. With steady determination, she pressed him back down against the mattress.

"Fifteen years is fifteen years," she said quietly, stroking her cool hand across his cheek. "Rest now, Garret. You need your strength so you can leave again." There was a hint of irony and an edge of bitterness in her voice, but at least she knew she still understood the situation.

He seemed to sigh, the tension escaping him with a whisper until he sank like a rag doll into the sheets. The muscles in his neck relaxed, his fists suddenly opening at his sides. His eyes closed, and he slipped away from her completely.

Her hands lingered on his cheeks, feeling the heat burn and ebb. Unconsciously, she brushed back the black strands of his hair and smoothed the sheet up around his neck. One hand retrieved the damp washcloth from the waiting basin and she gently stroked it down his face.

Her hands still trembled.

With a tightening of her lips, she forced her movements to become brisker. She wasn't sixteen anymore, she reminded herself. Fifteen years was indeed fifteen years. And she didn't lie in bed anymore, wondering if this would be the night he would magically return and save her from the dreariness of her own existence. She didn't dream of his spark-filled grins, didn't recall his somber gaze as he'd touched her cheek in the rain and whispered, "Someday."

Now she was the thirty-two-year-old kindergarten teacher, community leader, churchgoer and volunteer. She tended children, cultivated a garden, worked in the community and maintained her legacy home. She was brisk and practical and efficient, and no one in this town ever commented about the hunch-shouldered girl she'd once been. And no one ever mentioned her mother.

Working now on the autopilot she knew so well, she picked up the basin in one hand and the pitcher in the other, and carried them both into the kitchen. She would fix a light breakfast, then see to her garden. Then there were the phone calls to make, the meetings to reschedule, Garret to check. If she had the time, the bathrooms needed to be cleaned, the linens washed. She should probably plan on a casserole for dinner for herself.

Plenty to do. Always plenty of things to do.

Cagney appeared promptly at eight a.m., his face tense and his question immediate. "How is he?"

"Better," she assured him, hazel eyes compassionate. Knowing he wouldn't be convinced until he saw Garret with his own eyes, she led him straight down the hall to the bedroom. "Fever's down to 101, and I've gotten more liquids into him. I still don't understand half of what he says, Cagney, but there's something about a car and your folks."

Cagney stiffened immediately in the doorway of the bedroom, and his lips thinned for a minute. Then with a forced sigh, he relaxed his stance. "I hate this not knowing," he said low and even.

Suzanne placed a calming hand on his shoulder and offered him a reassuring smile. "Give him a day or two, and he'll be able to talk. You've already taken care of Mitch and your folks. It will be all right."

She didn't mention Garret's selective memory of their own interactions. No reason for anyone to know about that.

Cagney remained for an hour, hovering around the bedroom and the living room until she handed him a trowel and told him he could at least make himself useful if he was going to insist on hanging out. But just as he was about to give in and return to the sheriff's office, Garret opened his eyes.

"Cagney," he said immediately, the word thick. Well-trained by now, Suzanne automatically fetched another glass of water. "The car," Garret rasped. When he was done drinking, his eyes focused on Cagney, leaving her in peace for a change. It was just as well. Her hands had started trembling the minute she realized he was conscious.

Cagney hunkered down beside the bed, the concern in his face evident as he stared at his brother. "What car?"

"In the woods," Garret whispered. "I hid it. Rented to Robert Fulchino. No one must find it."

"Why?" Cagney pressed. "Who are you running from, Garret? I need to know more."

Garret frowned, and his bandaged hand groped aimlessly on the sheet as if he was looking for something he couldn't find. "I don't know," he said at last, his head tossing restlessly once more. "I can see my team, and we're diving. We're training. I see Austin and the others. Parachuting, deep reconnaissance, it's all there...until suddenly, the memories just disappear into the fog. I just see the flames. Beautiful old buildings consumed by the flames ... and the sound of gunfire." He shook his head at the confusion, then winced at the motion. A last whisper escaped from his lips. *"Mrtavi..."*

Cagney's jaw tightened, his impatience barely restrainable. "What's that, Garret? What's ... *mchabi*?"

Garret frowned again, and Suzanne could see his growing agitation. Immediately, she placed a reassuring hand on his bare shoulder, where the sheet had slipped down. "It's okay, Garret, sweetheart," she said evenly, her eyes boring pointedly into Cagney's. "There's no reason to rush it. It will all come back with a little rest."

Cagney's eyes narrowed but he got her message. "The language, then?" He tried one last time. "Can you tell me the language, Garret? Where you've been?"

Garret's dark face twisted, and darting among the burned ruins of his memory, he could see pictures, one and one hundred. Flames and guns and shell-pocked buildings. Sniper fire and people darting quickly across the streets. And the searing heat of the wall of flames rising before him as he yelled out commands to the faceless men beside him hefting the ax in his hands. Gunshots, fire, ax. Again, only one word filled his mind.

"Mrtavi," he whispered. He felt pain, he felt rage, and once more he knew the ax rested in his soot-covered arms.

"What is *mchabi*?" Cagney roared, ignoring Suzanne's warning look with the force of his worry. "Tell me what the hell is going on, Garret!"

"The dead," his brother whispered, and his eyes filled with flame and fire and loss. "The dead."

Cagney's face went pale, and Suzanne felt her own spine tingle with the hushed power of the word. Slowly, she drew the sheet up, patting it around Garret's neck, and feeling his cheeks for fever. "That's enough now, Garret," she said, her voice remarkably level. "You go back to sleep. Cagney will take care of your car. Don't you worry about a thing."

Cagney nodded, his gray eyes regaining their steadiness even if his face remained pale. Taking his hand, Suzanne led him from the room.

She spared one last glance at Garret, but he finally seemed to have fallen asleep, his face still drawn against the sheets. Outside the room, Cagney muttered a few choice words about the situation.

"I don't know where Mitch is anymore. I don't know what to do about Mom and Dad," he grumbled low with frustration. "I don't know where Garret's been and I don't know who's safe to ask. I don't know a damn thing."

Nodding reassuringly, Suzanne placed a comforting hand on his arm. "It'll all work out," she drawled, hating to see the usually calm Cagney worked up. He turned, and looked at her with his darkening gray gaze.

"We don't know that," he said flatly. "Hell, Suzanne, you could be in danger right now for helping him. I'm family, but you shouldn't be dragged into this."

Lips thinning, she shook her head with determination. "Your parents have always been more than kind to me Cagney. You think Garret is safe here, so that's all that matters. We'll just take it one day at a time."

Cagney sighed, his face still troubled. "Where the hell do you think he's been, Suzanne? And what in the world is he talking about."

Her own gaze faltered, her hazel eyes soft with worry. "He'll heal," she said at last, "and then he'll remember, and you and he can take care of it. Just wait and see."

The following days, however, proved her wrong.

Cagney returned the car to the airport, and Garret's fever came down while the strange words disappeared completely from his mutterings. Dr. Jacobs grew more satisfied with his general health although he was still concerned about the persistent loss of memory. But after several days of probing and prodding, they concluded that Garret could recall most of his more distant past, and certainly had no trouble retaining new memories since he'd arrived at Suzanne's. On the other hand, he couldn't recollect events of the past two years, only images of fire and bullets. Dr. Jacobs finally diagnosed it as a traumatic memory loss. Hopefully, the memories would return as he became able to deal with them.

In the meantime, the IV disappeared, and Garret slipped into long days of sleeping, sleeping and sleeping.

Suzanne grew used to those days. With Dr. Jacobs's help, she tended to him, his sleeping form passive and characterless. From time to time, she had to fend off earnest offers from friends to come assist her with her own supposed illhealth, but lies seemed to come more readily to her tongue nowadays.

By the fourth day, she didn't give the situation much thought anymore. Until she walked into the guest bedroom with a fresh pitcher of water, and found Garret standing naked in the middle of the room.

He swayed slightly where he stood, his body pale but impressive with his feet planted on her old hardwood floor. Her eyes flew open, the color draining from her face. And in her shock, she couldn't quite avert her gaze.

She saw muscle-bound, darkly haired legs with zigzagging scars down one side. She saw a black-furrowed chest with a narrow line darting through a washboard stomach to areas that made her eyes grow even wider. For a moment, the pure shock made her sway on her own feet.

"I want clothes," Garret snarled.

Her wide hazel eyes riveted up, the heat of her cheeks more searing than his fever had ever been. "Wh-what?" she sounded out breathlessly. But he just stood there as if his nakedness meant nothing, and pinned her with his dark, glittering eyes.

"Clothes, damn it," he repeated impatiently. "I want my clothes back."

She recovered enough to set the pitcher down on a side table, her hands shaking enough to make it a small feat. Her pulse still pounded in her neck, but she forced her scattered thoughts together. Efficient and practical, Suzanne. Remember?

But all of sudden, she was feeling lips on hers in the rain, her young body pressed against the solid, muscled mass, before he whispered, "Someday."

"Come on, damn it, I need my clothes."

He took a step forward with his scarred leg, and that spurred her thoughts back together. She stiffened her spine and forced herself to meet his burning eyes even as her cheeks flushed darker.

"We threw away your clothes," she said simply, her chin unconsciously setting.

He scowled, the expression dangerous and disconcerting in his unshaven face. "I need clothes," he growled again. His eyes bore into her own, as if from sheer force of will he could make the desired garments appear in her hands.

It took effort for her even to swallow. "I have a few skirts that are a tad on the large side," she returned squarely. "Perhaps you'd like to give them a try." He scowled even more, but she simply shrugged defiantly. "I'm telling you, we threw away your clothes. They were blood-soaked and filthy."

His face set, and underneath the thick covers of his whiskers, she could see his skin pale. He took another step, and this time wavered perceptibly. The damn fool was most likely going to faint on her floor. And naked no less.

"Back into bed," she announced briskly, using her best kindergarten teacher's voice. To prove her point, she walked sternly forward, looking at him with thin, determined lips. He, however, did not back away.

"I have to leave," he grated, though some of the heat had gone from his voice, and the strain was becoming more noticeable in his face.

"All in good time," she assured him. She'd reached his side now, but still he didn't step back. And all of a sudden, she was aware of how close she was to his naked length. She could feel the heat roll out over her, intense and beguiling.

Once, she'd felt those arms wrap around her, strong and solid and fierce. She'd pressed herself against that body, feeling his muscled contours against her own soft frame, calling his lips down onto her own. And she could still feel the warmth of that kiss, caressing her skin through the cool spring rain. She'd never forgotten how he'd held her in those last few moments. Offering her something no one else ever had. And she'd never forget how he'd boarded the bus right after and never looked back.

"Get into bed," she said stiffly, her face unconsciously shuttered and hard. "You're sick and you're weak. You want to leave, then do it when you're not going to pass out on my bedroom floor."

He grinned suddenly, the smile unexpected and spine-tingling in his unshaven face. Without warning, he reached out a finger and lightly touched her cheek. She flinched noticeably.

"You sound like a kindergarten teacher," he said softly, switching tactics. He'd learned long ago that where force sometimes failed, charm could still prevail.

She glared at him mutinously, nevertheless, her shoulders more set than he'd remembered. She'd come a long way in fifteen years, he thought abruptly. She wasn't a scrawny kid anymore. Now she was nicely rounded in all the right places, her long hair pinned up in one of those knots that made a man wonder how many pins he could slide out before it all came tumbling down. Not his type at all.

He generally went for slender and athletic types, women who could take care of themselves and who understood a week meant a week and a night meant a night. Suzanne, however, in her cream lace tank top and long, crinkled blue skirt, looked feminine and provincial, all the things he avoided in a woman. She looked like the kind of woman who might walk a guy to the bus stop in the rain. The kind of woman who might cry in the rain and make a man remember long after he'd sworn to forget.

"Back into bed," she reiterated sternly, pointing at the rumpled pile of sheets.

Her expression was so firm, her lips pressed together so tightly, he found his gaze lingering there. And fought the unholy urge to pull her into his arms and kiss her thoroughly. His gaze grew dark and he felt the restlessness gnaw sharply and urgently at his gut.

He had to get out of here, damn it. He had to get on his way, escaping from whatever shadowy thing was holding him captive. Another wave of darkness swept over him and he swayed slightly from the sudden exhaustion. He saw her hazel eyes soften with concern, and it was more than he could stand.

"I always checked up," he whispered suddenly. "I always made sure you were all right." Silly, stupid words, and he hated himself for saying them the minute they were out.

Immediately, her hazel eyes grew hard and her chin shot up. "Of course, Garret. And how kind of you. I'm sure I was doing grand when my mother died. The years of medical bankruptcy weren't hard, either."

He frowned, knowing that wasn't what he'd meant and cursing himself yet again for saying anything. "But I knew there was someone here to look after you," he added instead. It only buried him deeper.

"Drop the distant-protector act," she told him bluntly. "I'm not Cinderella and I'm not looking for a fairy godmother. You went off to play soldier, Garret. That's who you are, that's who you've always been. Don't try to dress it up now."

His eyes narrowed dangerously, but just as he was going to open his mouth, another wave of weakness washed over him. He felt his knees go suddenly loose, and the next thing he knew, she was beneath his arm, guiding him toward the bed.

"Big stupid fool," she muttered the whole way. "Big stupid fool."

She had him back in the bed and covered up as fast as possible. She didn't want to look at his naked legs with their mysterious scars, and she certainly didn't want to see the rest of him. She wanted him well, and she wanted him gone.

"Tomorrow," he whispered as if reading her thoughts. She glanced up to find his eyes staring into hers with an intensity she didn't like.

"Cagney can bring some clothes," she said after an uncomfortable minute. She remained standing at the bedside when she really should be moving away. Garret awake was not an easy man to handle.

He nodded, his dark eyes still not leaving her alone. Suddenly, he grinned again, this time the twisting of his lips at once bitter and mocking. "So anxious to see me go?"

"Never knew you liked to stay," she stated right back.

His grin widened. "You always did understand me."

For one moment, she couldn't say anything at all while the words twisted her stomach into tight little knots of old aches and new pains. She forced herself to take a deep breath, and smooth her hands over her vintage skirt.

"Where will you go?" she asked calmly, congratulating herself on sounding so composed.

His grin, however, wavered. He turned away, and for a long moment, he closed his eyes. And though he didn't say a word, she knew he was remembering the words he'd once spoken but now didn't seem to want to recall. The ragged holes in his mind allowed him to know about her and the bus stop, but denied him what happened to his back.

"I'm sure I'll think of something," he said at last, his big body moving restlessly beneath the worn white sheets.

"It's all right," she found herself saying, the words creeping out on their own. Defensively, she raised her chin. "Cagney's my best friend, Garret, and you and I, we go way back, as well. You can stay as long as you need to. Cagney thinks maybe you're safe here. If that's the case, you should stay. At—at least," she faltered, "at least until you know more."

He gave her a little smile, but it wasn't pleasant. "You always did take care of everyone," he said softly, his frustration directed at once at himself but making him lash out at her anyway.

Her hands stilled on her skirt, then she forced herself to shrug. "Charity is never wasted."

"Little Suzanne, the kindergarten teacher," he whispered, his dark eyes sweeping over her. "Always raising everyone else's children. What will you do when they grow up, Suzanne? What will you do when this batch is gone, as well?"

For a moment, she couldn't move, his words cutting too near all those deep fears she only acknowledged late on rare nights. She made herself continue to breathe, but even then, her voice trembled when she finally spoke. "I remember you as being many things, Garret Guiness," she whispered at last. "But I never remembered you as being so cruel."

She turned, her skirt swirling around her legs, and even as he reached out to her, she swept from the room. The door shut firmly behind her, and he was left only with the frustration burning his gut and the soft waft of roses in the air.

Chapter 3

Garret had healed enough to roar.

Standing in the hall outside the closed bedroom door, Suzanne could hear his raging demands interspersed with Cagney's quiet, steely replies. Garret wanted his clothes, a car and an immediate departure. Cagney informed him his clothes were burned, the car returned, and he might as well stay put until he fully regained his memory.

In the hallway, Suzanne found herself nodding her agreement, then quickly suppressed the movement with narrowed eyes. She didn't care what Garret did, she reminded herself sternly. Garret was Garret. His leaving was not an if, only a matter of when. To listen to his grumbling retorts to Cagney's arguments, she'd do well to remember that.

The door opened abruptly, and she started self-consciously where she stood, trying to make it appear as if she'd just arrived there. Cagney's gray eyes met hers with a knowing look and she flushed immediately.

"So who won?" she asked as innocently as possible.

Cagney's jaw tightened, and she didn't have to look down to know his fists were clenched with the tension. "He'll stay for now. At least until he remembers what the hell he's running from, or Mitch learns enough to fill in the blanks. You'd think we were trying to kill the man rather than save his miserable, stubborn hide." Cagney shook his head and took a deep breath. "I'll be back in an hour or two with some clothes. In the meantime, he's all yours. I'd suggest that you stop feeding him. He gets much more of his strength back and we won't even be able to tie him down."

Suzanne's hazel eyes opened wide as she wondered if Cagney was joking or not. By the look on his normally calm face, probably not. Then abruptly, Cagney's gaze narrowed in on her dress.

"Today's not Sunday," he said suddenly.

Suzanne's cheeks flushed a little darker, but she managed to hold her head up even as her hands fidgeted with the beautiful, tiny-flowered folds of the dress's flowing skirt. The dress had been a Christmas present from Dotti and Henry Guiness, and was one of the few pieces of original clothing she possessed, everything else having been prudently purchased from resale shops. The flowing lines smoothed over her rounded form, while the earth tones brought a glow to her skin and warm color to her eyes. Generally, she saved the Laura Ashley dress for church.

"Everything else needs to be washed," she said a trifle defensively, then attempted a casual shrug of her shoulders. Cagney's gaze narrowed even more, but the moment he opened his mouth, she held up a restraining hand. "Don't you have some errands to run?" she asked pointedly. Her heart was pounding loudly in her ears, but she refused to back down. It didn't matter what Cagney thought. She *had not* put this dress on for Garret. She simply liked the way it felt, and there was nothing wrong with a woman enjoying the feel of fine fabric against her skin. Besides, at thirty-two years of age, she did not have to justify her choices to anyone.

"I give him two days," Cagney said abruptly, his gray eyes steady on her face, "and then it won't matter what you or I say. He'll just leave if for no other reason than he doesn't know how to stay."

"Then he goes," she said blithely, her hands crinkling the folds of her skirt while the disturbing images of Garret's naked body flashed through her mind. "Time to get going, Cagney. Give Marina my regards."

Cagney continued shaking his head even as she led him to the door. She'd no sooner closed the door than she heard footsteps behind her. She turned to find Garret standing ominously in the hallway, a thin cotton sheet knotted ridiculously around his waist like a toga.

"Done talking about me yet?" he said scowling. His dark eyes raked up and down her figure, and she found herself automatically holding in her stomach. His scowl deepened. "Do you always wear dresses?"

"Of course," she retorted dryly, attempting to scan his half-naked frame as casually as he'd done hers. "But only because I don't look nearly as good in a sheet."

And he did look good in the sheet, like some wild pagan with his long black hair and week's worth of beard. The thin white cotton contrasted vividly with his darkly tanned, black-furred chest. His ribs still stood out sharply, a testimony to wherever he'd been but couldn't remember. And on his arm she could see the burn scar, mirroring the one on his leg. She found her eyes lingering there and had difficulty swallowing. He had strong, well-muscled thighs.

She'd thought about him all last night. Lain there on her bed, the hot, humid July wrapping around her while images of his naked, muscular build branded themselves into her mind. She'd found herself wondering what it would be like to run her hands through that crisp, dark matting of hair, what it would feel like to lay her head against his solid, well-defined chest.

The restless, inexplicable ache in her stomach had been almost unbearable.

"I, I gather you're staying a bit longer," she stammered, leaning farther back against the door.

"A bit," he replied darkly. His gaze wandered restlessly around the entryway, and she could see his fists clench and unclench at his side. Garret was the most physical man she'd ever known, more at home with football, track and baseball than in the tight confines of the classroom. From the bleachers, she used to watch him practice, captivated by the sheer beauty and grace of his power. Dreading returning home.

"Maybe I could show you around," she said breathlessly, trying to think of anything to keep herself distracted. "I don't think you were ever inside the house."

He shook his head and abruptly his scowl faded. She knew without asking what he was thinking because she was remembering it, as well. Her mother, long hair unkempt and skin bloated from the alcohol, lolling against the sofa. From time to time, people had come over and sat on the huge, wraparound porch of the old house. But no one had ever come inside, and no one had ever asked to, either.

"How's Rachel?" Garret asked suddenly, his eyes watchful.

Suzanne shrugged at the reference to her sister. "Married now," she said simply. "She lives in Charlotte."

Garret nodded. "You get to see her often?"

Suzanne paused, then shook her head. "Rachel swore never to come back," she said squarely, her gaze momentarily resting on his face. "You ought to know something about that. But then, you at least went off to do some good instead of serving as a human punching bag for a drunken lout."

Garret stiffened, his dark brows drawing together into a fearsome line. "Her husband beats her?"

Suzanne arched a fine brow. "It happens, you know."

"Well, damn it, you ought to do something about it!"

"And what would that be, Garret? Kidnap her, maybe shoot him? She's a grown woman. She makes her own choices."

Garret glared his disapproval, but she met his dark gaze unflinchingly with her own steady eyes. She didn't need him to lecture her about her sister. She'd spent the first twenty years of her life trying to raise Rachel, trying to protect and shelter her from the burdens of their life. She didn't need Garret to point out her failure, and she didn't need Garret to voice all the worries that continued to age her before her time.

"Men shouldn't beat women," Garret said curtly. He began prowling the small square of the entryway again, the folds of cotton swishing around his thighs as he walked.

Suzanne didn't say anything, just watched his relentless pacing.

He whirled around abruptly, just a few feet away, and pinned her with such dark eyes she forgot to breathe.

"I can go have a talk with this guy before I leave," he offered suddenly.

Suzanne smiled, a small, twisted smile, and shook her head. "This isn't high school anymore, Garret. Conway isn't Tank Nemeth. You did what you could once, and God knows I've tried. Maybe someday..." She shrugged. "I put aside a little money here and there. If she ever gets up the courage to leave, I'll help her. It's the best any of us can do."

He nodded, but he could see the tightness around her eyes, the press of her lips. He'd upset her, and he'd always hated to see Suzanne Montgomery upset. Then she squared her shoulders in a gesture he knew too well, and he felt his muscles tighten beyond restraint. It was all he could do not to take a step forward. As she moved away from the door, he caught the scent of roses, and he had to clench his teeth not to abruptly draw her into his arms.

Damn, but he'd never understood himself around her. And damn again that he was here in this ridiculous sheet, barely able to remember his own name.

He wanted nothing better than to throw his fist through a wall, or worse, catch her in his arms and kiss her senseless. How many pins before that proper hair came cascading down? How many kisses before that tight look left her face and she melted against him, moaning his name.

He whirled around and began pacing the confines of the entryway in earnest. If he had to stay cooped up much longer, he was going to lose what was left of his mind.

"I'll show you around," Suzanne offered softly.

He nodded without meeting her eye, and followed her gratefully into the next room. Her hips swayed softly when she walked, the deep brown folds of the dress swishing seductively around her ankles.

His body went hard, and he decided he truly was a depraved S.O.B.

At least the living room was big. He immediately veered away from her, crossing to the wide expanse of bay windows. Through the white-rimmed panes of glass, he could see the hot July sun seeping through tall maples and deep green firs. At the edge of her lawn, golden fields swayed with the force of an invisible wind. If he stood outside now, he would smell honeysuckle and heat and freshly mowed grass. In the mornings, there would be a hint of cool pine, drawn down from the mountains, and in the evenings, the hum of the crickets' lullaby. Hot, languorous days and soft Southern nights, meant for lounging on porches with sweating glasses of minted iced tea in hand.

It had been a long time since he'd been home.

"People come by often?" he heard himself asking curtly.

Behind him, he could feel more than see her shake her head. "The house is set back a bit, and I don't get too many visitors."

"Good."

He forced himself away from the window and continued his prowl. The living room was everything he'd expected, he decided. The worn hardwood floor was well oiled and partly covered by an old gold, crimson and blue Oriental rug. Rather than a normal-size couch, she had one of those antique love seats with faded gold fabric and curved legs he didn't trust to support a child, let alone a full-grown man like himself. Everything was old and worn, but she'd tried to dress the place up with vases of roses and brightly flowered pillows.

If you looked closely enough, though—and he always did—you could see the fraying of the fabric, the thin lines etching up through the plaster of the walls. The house was simply damn old, its contents, as well. Maybe too old for a single woman on a schoolteacher's salary.

He filed that away in the back of his mind and wondered why, once her mother had died and her sister had moved away, she continued to stay. From the perimeter of the room, he spared her a quick glance. She stood in the center, trying to appear nonchalant, while her hands slowly crushed the hell out of her skirt. He found himself grinning.

Old TV, not even with a remote. But she'd come into the nineties enough to purchase a VCR, and shelved neatly beneath it was an alphabetical selection of a dozen movie titles. He scanned them quickly. *An Affair to Remember, The African Queen, Casablanca, From Here to Eternity.* He threw her a cocked eyebrow, and her chin came up primly.

"I like classics," she said. He kept looking at her, and she crunched her skirt a little more. He began to feel like the big bad wolf confronting Little Red Riding Hood.

It wasn't such a bad description.

"The dining room's through here," she told him, her voice light. He could still read her agitation, however, in the quick rise and fall of her chest. The pretty, tiny-flowered fabric of her dress molded her breasts nicely, highlighting the soft, feminine swell with an enticing trim of lace. She walked through an archway into another room, her skirt swirling around her, and he followed her with the hunger still burning in his gaze.

The dining room was dominated by a large oval table, and she took refuge behind it.

"It's not much," she said quietly. The table was old, and once it had probably been beautiful, as well. But her ancestors hadn't been good caretakers, or perhaps back then they'd had enough money not to care. At any rate, the formerly rich cherry wood was now warped with water damage and the table was wobbly from years of neglect. Nicks and scrapes, filled in from her futile attempts at refinishing the piece, rimmed the outside edge.

It seemed to her that Garret's sharp eyes saw every flaw, and she kept her shoulders rigidly straight. She'd fought so hard to save the house that simple possession had seemed enough. Now, for the first time, she was looking at her rooms through a stranger's eyes and seeing all the blemishes on her prize—the old furniture she couldn't afford to reupholster, the rug she didn't have enough money to replace. She'd wanted to repaint the rooms last year, but the roof began leaking in the spring, taking up all her money instead.

Garret came to the marked-up buffet, and a traitorous blush crept unwanted up her cheeks. Behind the protective glass rested her one true indulgence: her dolls.

She flitted over, more nervous than she ever wanted to be, and opened the glass doors as if it didn't mean much to her at all.

"I started collecting them ten years ago," she said, her voice only slightly breathless. He stood right beside her now, and she could smell the warm masculine scent of sweat and soap.

"When your mother died," he filled in softly.

Her hands stilled for a moment, then she willed them back into motion. She forgot sometimes how smart Garret was, how easily he could fill in the blanks. "Yes."

She drew out the first of the ten dolls, a beautiful, porcelain girl with long brown hair falling in silky ringlets. She had wide blue eyes, blushing cheeks and a feathery hat. An exquisite creation, she was draped in a lovely dress of rose-flowered cotton, gathered with lace and bows. Suzanne lifted the doll up, feeling the full porcelain body rest like a baby's weight in her hand. As she raised the doll, the delicate eyelashes fluttered up, her jointed arms coming down.

"She's fully jointed porcelain," Suzanne tried to explain briskly. "She has pierced ears, detailed clothing down to the shoes and twenty-four-carat gold painted around her wrist."

All careful considerations when contemplating buying a doll. And none of them explained why she'd actually bought the first doll ten years ago. Maybe because she didn't like to recall the tightness that hit her chest when she'd seen the beautiful little girl staring back at her with china blue eyes. She didn't like to think of the pang of loneliness that struck so suddenly and so sharply that tears had sprung into her eyes as she stood in front of the store.

The dolls were everything beautiful and innocent and cosseted. Everything that as a child she'd never been, and as an adult would never be. And sometimes, in moments of weakness, she could picture herself handing the dolls to a phantom daughter and whispering with her about the beauty of their shared treasures.

Now, she fussed with the doll's hat, her hands trembling, while she tried to keep her emotions under control. "They're good investments," she said evenly. She could feel Garret's eyes boring into her face and didn't dare look up.

"They're pretty," he said roughly. She nodded, but he felt the nervousness rolling off her in waves. Her face was pale, her hands shaky as she fidgeted with the fragile doll. And suddenly, he could see her in the rain, dressed in the ragged jeans and worn T-shirt she'd always worn back then, her hair long and lank around her thin face. He'd never completely understood why she'd walked him to the bus stop until those last moments when the bus had been pulling away and he'd seen her lips form those three silent words in the rain.

Funny how he'd never forgotten that image. Funny how over the years, in all the wars and battles, in times of crisis, it was always her face that came to mind. Now here he was, standing in her house with its antiques and roses and dolls, and he felt suddenly eighteen again.

He felt hungry and raw and strange. More than anything in the world, he felt like he wanted to take the doll from her nervous hands, draw her into his arms and kiss her.

He found himself leaning forward, and at the last moment, her hazel eyes swept up to meet his own. Immediately, she froze, a deer captured by headlights, and her gaze fell instinctively to his bearded lips.

He leaned closer, catching the faint scent of dried roses and apple shampoo. He watched her lips part, full and pink and trembling with the anticipation. His body was rock hard again, and he only knew that he wanted her.

His large, callused hands drew the doll from her nerveless grasp and rested it carefully on the ledge of the buffet. Then he cupped his hands around her shoulders, feeling the soft, polished cotton of her beautiful dress and pulled her toward him. She came willingly, her eyes still round and glazed as they fastened upon his face. For a long moment, he didn't move, but let her feel the heat and hardness of his body pressed against her soft, giving curves. His bare, muscled leg pressed between her own, rubbing her intimately.

She gasped softly, her cheeks coloring, but she still didn't pull away. His thumb caressed the softness of her cheek, following the curve to her tender earlobe, finding the throbbing blue pulse in her neck. She shifted restlessly, the movement brushing her suddenly swollen breasts against his furred chest. His gaze darkened, his eyes heavy lidded as they fell once more to her lips.

"Suzanne," he whispered huskily, "kiss me."

Her hazel eyes opened wider at the command, and for the first time, he saw the war in her eyes.

"I—I can't."

His thumb brushed across her soft lips, feeling them tremble. "Yes, you can."

Her eyes closed, and a deep shudder ran through her body. She could feel the muscled heat of his thigh, the rough caress of his thumb, the crisp arousal of his chest hair. In all her practical, efficient existence, she'd never felt like this. Deborah Kerr had probably known these sensations when Cary Grant had kissed her that first time on the cruise. But then Cary Grant had called it love, and Garret promised no such thing.

"You're leaving," she whispered.

His thumb rasped again over her lips, so soft, so seductive. "Yes."

"It's not right."

His left hand ran down her spine, following the curve to her buttocks. She shivered once more, instinctively arching against his granite body.

"All you ever have to do is say no."

Her eyes opened, and she peered at him through dark, dazed depths. He was seducing her with touch, with words, with feelings. And she was letting him, like the small-town, provincial fool that she was. Hadn't she learned anything fifteen years ago?

And why did his body have to feel so good pressed against her own, just as she'd imagined it would last night when images of him tortured her into the early-morning hours?

Her hands came up of their own volition, flattening themselves against his bare chest. Tentatively, she combed her fingers through the dark matting. It was crisp and silky and nerve-tingling against her fingertips. She pressed her hand flat again, and absorbed the heat of skin, the feel of his pounding heart.

She closed her eyes and, because she'd dreamed about this man so much, allowed herself one moment of weakness. Slowly, hesitantly, she leaned forward and pressed her lips against the base of his throat. Very tentatively, her tongue came out and tasted him.

Immediately, his hands tightened on her shoulders, a shiver racking his tall, muscular frame.

"Suzanne..." he whispered thickly. His fingers were strong on her shoulders. Strong and needy.

And all at once, she was afraid.

"This is crazy," she muttered frantically, pushing herself away and taking quick steps back while her cheeks flushed a desperate red and her knees threatened to give out completely. She banged up against the head chair and clutched the antique for dear life. "I'm saying no. No, no, no."

It was probably more than adequate, but she was too flustered to care. Her cheeks were bright from burning heat and acute embarrassment. What had happened to the practical and efficient woman she'd become? What had happened to all that backbone she'd fought so hard to build?

Before her eyes, Garret swayed a bit, then steadied himself with a quick hand on the old buffet.

"Aye, aye, Captain," Garret said, his knuckles turning white on the buffet edge with the effort of holding himself up. As Suzanne watched in wide-eyed shock, his face paled, his arms beginning to tremble as his regained strength suddenly fled.

The buffet shook dangerously, and he immediately reached for the table.

Instantly, Suzanne was at his side, concern for him sweeping away her embarrassment. Without hesitation, she wrapped her arm around the wounded man's waist, pulling out a chair for him. "Sit," she commanded. "For goodness' sake, Garret, you've got to take better care of yourself."

Out of habit, she felt his forehead, then brushed back his hair, peering into his dark eyes. For a change, he didn't look devilish or intimidating; he simply looked like a man in pain. He shifted a bit, and his face winced with the effort.

"Garret, you must try to take it easy."

"Seduction never used to be difficult," he muttered. Suzanne's cheeks colored immediately, but she kept her chin in the air.

"You need more water," she declared primly. "I'll bring you a tall glass and I want you to drink it all down. Perhaps we should try a light lunch, as well. You'll need your strength."

Instantly, she remembered Cagney's comment from earlier, and she halted midmotion. If the past five minutes were anything to go by, she certainly didn't want Garret to recover any more of his strength, either. Or worse, maybe she did.

With a mental kick, she thrust herself back into action, bustling toward the kitchen. She was the nurse and the hostess, she reminded herself. She would keep it on those terms.

Some of the color had returned to his bearded cheeks by the time she returned. This time, she kept her gaze off his chest and busied herself with putting the doll away while he drank. That accomplished, she kept her eyes decorously on the wall.

"Better now?" she asked after a bit.

He nodded.

"Hungry?"

"Maybe. Tired mostly."

"You should lie down, then. Cagney will be back shortly with your clothes. I can fix a small meal for later."

He nodded once more, and absently spun the glass in his fingers. It felt cold and slick and wet. And looking at the shiny droplets condensed on the outside, he remembered absolutely nothing about the past two years. Shouldn't water trigger some sort of recollection for a SEAL? God, it seemed he'd lived in water since joining the navy at eighteen. Shallow dives, deep dives, open-water dives, night dives. He'd done it all. Until . . . until . . . the picture eluded him, dipping behind the black haze of his amnesia.

As if reading his thoughts, Suzanne piped up hesitantly, "Do—do you remember yet the language you were speaking? Or maybe where the burn scars came from?"

He frowned darkly, feeling his exhaustion even more intensely, and shook his head. A man suffering malnutrition, who bore marks of fire. Where the hell had he been?

Suzanne sat down at the head of the oval table and looked at him curiously. "What do you remember?"

He glanced up, finding her eyes still cautious, but sincere with their concern. He hated to see that concern in her eyes. No one should ever have to worry about him, but himself. Disgusted at the whole turn of events, he let the glass go and drummed his fingertips impatiently on the table.

"I remember Hell Week," he said suddenly, his fingers fast and rhythmic. "I remember training." The jogging with green fatigues and heavy boondocker boots through seven days and nights of sand while the extra twenty-eight pounds of his wet kapok life vest practically dragged him to his knees. He remembered the sheer exhaustion of being allowed only two hours' sleep a night, and the temptation to give in that might have been too strong if Austin hadn't always been right there at his elbow, egging him with his golden, surfer looks.

"That's good," Suzanne encouraged him. "That was fifteen years ago?"

"Thirteen."

"What about five years ago?"

His fingers stalled momentarily, and more images poured into his mind. Creeping low through jungles with his tiger-striped team, MP-5s carried low, but safetied. The XO motioned ahead, and Garret responded immediately to the silent command, falling into flanker position with Austin at his side. Into the clearing, target in sight. The first shot rang out, and the yells began. "Early contact, early contact." MP-5s were switched to full-fire and the SEALs released the jacketed hollow-point bullets in controlled three-shot bursts. His arms vibrated with the motion as he raked the submachine gun around, sweeping the four-to-six position. He didn't feel anything though. In the chaos of combat, he was only aware of the singing of his blood and the dull roar of adrenaline in his ears.

"I remember," he said.

Suzanne nodded, but her eyes were more intent on his face now. His fingers had stopped drumming, but his shoulders moved instead, as if he was reliving a scene hidden to her eyes.

"Three years ago?" she tried.

"Parachute," he responded promptly this time. In his mind, he was at eighteen hundred feet and fighting with two collapsed cells of his silk chute while the altimeter clicked away precious feet. At the last moment, he wrenched the cells enough for them to suddenly catch the air and he buoyed sharply up. Several hundred feet off course for the LZ, but at least in one piece.

"Two years?"

His brow furrowed, and suddenly he wasn't so sure. He could feel the weight of a Beretta in his hands, ringing off a quick two shots as he rocketed up through the hatch of a plane. Or maybe it was just training, and those weren't terrorists at all but the three-by-five note card he had to hit with both shots on all occasions. Then he had escape and evade training, E&E, and he was under water, holding his breath as the sound of a ferry passed by. Two more minutes, his lungs burning more and more as the seconds ticked off. Until just when he thought he couldn't possibly take it anymore, he lifted his head up and saw the three-man craft finally turning away.

Training. He'd been participating, part teaching. And then . . .

He'd left, he thought for the first time. At the end of the two weeks, he'd left and gone—

"Garret?"

He shook his head, the pieces slipping away as before. "I don't know." Suddenly, he couldn't bear it, and he jerked back his chair to stand. He swayed immediately, but this time he didn't care. He hated being sick and he hated being weak. Damn it, his SEAL team was out there somewhere. Austin and Luke and Charlie and C.J. and the others and what the hell was he doing sitting in some dining room not even sure of his own memories? *Where in hell had he been? And what had gone wrong?*

"I should check in," he muttered. But the minute he said the words, other images filled his mind. The fire consuming the building while he frantically swung his ax, trying to save what he could while bullets whizzed behind him and the distant sound of shelling penetrated even the roar of the flames. Working with a team of faceless men to fight the fire, men not in camouflage or even fire-fighter uniforms, but men in denim and cotton, all covered in soot and sweat, all still fighting the fire while the snipers tried to pick them off one by one. And walking back to the camp with those shadowy men, his new team.

Then, coming to the rocks, the ax in his hand, the birds circling overhead, he saw the bodies.

"No," he muttered, low and frustrated and fierce, pounding his fist abruptly on the table. Hot pain lanced down his side, but he didn't even mind the piercing slivers. He just wanted to remember. For God's sake, he had to remember.

His fist rose again, and for one savage moment, he really wanted to slam it through the wall. But at the last instant, he saw Suzanne's face and knew he couldn't do that to her house. He raked his fingers through his hair instead, and his whole body shook with the effort at control.

"Garret?" Suzanne whispered. She remained poised at the end of the table, her face pale as she watched his face contort and his muscles practically scream his fury. For a long minute, she didn't dare move, afraid the slightest startlement would send him over the brink. Then, as she watched, he slowly reined himself in inch by inch with a tremendous effort. He sat like a stone, and his face looked grim. "It'll come back, Garret," she murmured, her hand reaching out a little on the table, only to flounder halfway and fall limp. "Give yourself a little time."

"I don't want time," he said lowly. "I want answers."

She shrugged helplessly, not sure what to tell him. "You have to get your strength back anyway," she returned. "You can at least work on that now."

It seemed to help, for his obsidian gaze drifted up to find her face. Slowly, he nodded. "I can do that."

She offered him a small, hesitant smile. "It'll work out."

"Always an optimist, Suzanne. You know, you really ought to make me leave."

She stiffened a little, her eyes automatically wary. "What do you mean?"

"I don't know what's happened, Suzanne. Until I do, I can't very well protect myself, let alone you. You deserve better."

"Cagney said you would be safe here."

"With all due respect, Cagney's a small-town sheriff. What does he know?"

Suzanne frowned and her lips thinned. "Just because you always thought you had to leave doesn't mean there aren't some pretty neat things and people right here in Maddensfield. You've been away a long time, Garret. With all due respect, what do you know?"

Abruptly, Garret grinned, and just like it did fifteen years ago, the grin made her heart leap in her chest. All at once, he was the old, wild Garret. And for no good reason at all, she felt reassured.

"Point well taken, schoolteacher," he drawled. "Point well taken."

Chapter 4

Suzanne crawled behind the wheel of her old Ford and breathed a sigh of relief. She was back to her routine. Everything would be all right now.

She'd risen with the dawn, her mind promptly full of all the things she had to get done today. People to check up on, the car wash to set up, groceries to buy and other various errands to run. She'd breezed through her morning walk aware of only the sun shining through the trees and the hint of blackberries in the air. Shower, change, and then she was on the back porch with her chamomile tea to admire her roses.

Nothing stirred behind the door down the hall, and that's the way she wanted it. After finishing the tea, she'd grabbe her purse and, at 8:30 a.m., finally rejoined her hectic life. She had to check up on eighty-year-old Mrs. Alston and probably restock her pantry and write a letter or two for her. At eleven, Suzanne was due down at the church to organize for the car wash. She'd oversee that until four, then most likely take the kids out for pizza and congratulate them on

their fund-raising efforts. Of course, she should stop by the
bank, buy more bandages at the pharmacy and pick up
some groceries.

With all those things to do, she'd be very busy all day.
Busy and hectic and happy. Definitely too busy to think
about some wounded man in the downstairs guest bedroom of her house. Or the way he looked in just a sheet.
And certainly the way he looked suddenly clean shaven and
freshly garbed at her dinner table.

This was much better, she assured herself as she pulled
into Mrs. Alston's driveway. She'd been shut up in her house
for the past five days, and that had made it hard for her to
keep things in perspective. But now Garret was well enough
to fend for himself, and as Cagney pointed out, she needed
to return to her routine or people would be suspicious.

So now she was back to business and life would return to
normal. She'd be her old efficient, practical and busy self.

It seemed to work. Mrs. Alston, sweet but fretful after a
week with no company, required sincere attention. Then the
kids, with all their exuberance, had forgotten to bring
sponges, which Suzanne volunteered to fetch. Accustomed
to the summertime car wash by now, plenty of locals
stopped by with their pickup trucks and large sedans. She
had her hands full trying to exercise quality control and
manage the cash. By four, everyone was rosy cheeked, wet
and happy. That left pizza and errands.

With all this activity, the day seemed to just fly by. It
wasn't long before she was walking out of the grocery store,
two bags in hand, and noticing the growing dusk. As she got
into her car this time, her shoulders were tighter, her stomach tense.

The last of her errands was done. And now she could return home, where Garret had been sitting and waiting all
day. Her shoulders set even tighter.

The dusk was thick when she finally turned into her own
driveway, but no lights shone from her bay-windowed

house. Instead, the three stories yawned gaping black windows, silent and still.

She killed the engine and sat there for a moment.

Maybe he'd already left.

He now had clothes, and a few minor toiletries that Cagney had produced. Except for general weakness and his lack of memory, he wasn't doing too badly. She imagined it took more than general weakness to stop Garret.

She clambered out of the car and retrieved the groceries.

It didn't matter, she reminded herself as she climbed the steps of the front porch and began juggling the bags in search of her keys. She wasn't some sixteen-year-old kid looking for fairy tales anymore. She didn't lie in bed at night dreaming that this night he would finally come and sweep her away from all the despair.

She'd outgrown all that simply by waking up each morning and finding herself in the same lumpy bed. Night after night, morning after morning, until Garret had been no longer gone for weeks or months, but years. She'd buried her mother and said goodbye to her sister. She'd saved her ancestral home and built herself a new life.

She didn't believe in rainy promises anymore, and she certainly didn't believe in white knights. She knew how to take care of herself. Actually, she knew how to take care of everyone.

Which, right now, seemed to include Garret. Or maybe it *had* included Garret.

She finally managed to get her key in the lock, and with another quick adjustment of the grocery bags, she opened the door.

The dark brought back memories, as well. He was gliding along, smooth and easy beneath the heavy, silted depths of the water. They weren't down that deep, but the river was so thick it choked out the light. He moved with strong, rhythmic kicks, gliding through the water as soundlessly and gracefully as the SEAL name implied. His swim mate, Austin, guided them both with a flat compass that cut through the algae, while Garret kept his eyes focused on the depth gauge and counted kicks. Two people moving as one, they slid through the water effortlessly, the algae glowing as it parted like a thin line of forged steel.

He'd spent a lot of time in water and knew it intimately. *The fire, the rocks, the bodies.*

They had nothing to do with water, and over the course of the day he'd nearly come to terms with that. At least, he was trying to. He whirled around and paced the perimeter of the living room once more. It had been like this all day. The tight, cramped feeling of helplessness. The house looked big, but he'd decided sometime around noon that it was still too small for him. He felt like a damn zoo exhibit, roaming the ground floor and waiting for someone to toss him peanuts.

He didn't want to remain in the damn house. He wanted out. He wanted water and wet gear and a good knife. He wanted to know what was wrong, then to seek and destroy. He'd been trained to evade and escape, to hunt and kill. The SEALs weren't renowned for their discipline; instead, they were the cowboys of the armed forces, known for their incredibly toned bodies, long hair and new and ingenious methods of accomplishing SpecWar objectives. Garret had fit right in.

He'd never believed in patience.

Yet as much as he probed and prodded his brain, all he could recall were flashes and shards of memory. Every now and then, if he stopped walking, he even felt a sliver of fear.

Fear was not bad, he reminded himself for the tenth time, and switched walking directions yet again. Fear was a matter of basic instinct and primal survival needs. As SEALs, they all faced fear sooner or later. He'd encountered it deep underwater, inhaling through his Draeger a potentially lethal mix of oxygen and carbon dioxide so that no telltale bubbles escaped to mark his progress. As the saying went, "no bubbles, no troubles." There was, however, one drawback to the highly effective means of infiltration: a prime symptom of overdosing on the lethal inhalation, O_2 toxicity, was the extreme fear of imminent death.

It had happened to Garret once. He and Austin were almost upon their target when his mind had blacked out and imploded back in with virtual neon signs of impending danger. Abruptly, he abandoned his hold on Austin's weight belt and clawed his way back up to the surface. Self-control shut down; logic shut down. All he knew was that if he continued, he would die.

He'd recovered after deep breaths of fresh, sticky air, Austin bobbing up beside him to keep guard. After he pulled himself together, he and Austin had continued. But the incident taught him of fear, the primal reaction to the need for self-preservation. He'd never felt it as sharply as he'd felt it then, but it had pricked his spine a time or two since. And now, if he stopped moving, he could feel the fear creeping up the base of his skull.

In the shadows of falling dusk, he finally halted before the huge expanse of the bay windows. He leaned upon the windowsill, contemplating the deepening night while he reflexively tightened his biceps. He glanced down at his arms, checking out the bulge of muscles, and shook his head. At his physical peak, he'd been able to bench press 450 pounds, slightly above average for his SEAL team. The extreme upper-body strength was necessary for hauling oneself and small arsenals out of the water and up hundreds of feet of rope to the desired deck of the infiltrated ship. Now, he tested his arms and figured if he could manage three hundred pounds, it would be a miracle.

He was fit, but not SEAL fit.

So what the hell kind of fit was he?

His stomach tightened, the fear tingling, and he felt his frustration soar.

Where the hell had he been? And why couldn't he remember?

He squeezed his head with his hands, but it didn't help. He could remember his E&E training, the UDT—underwater demolition team—training, and even the six months in spy school. He could remember most of his SpecWar assignments and his teammates. He could remember, actually, quite a lot.

Until about a year and a half ago. Then, suddenly, there were just the images of fire and foreign buildings. Austin and the rest of his SEAL team disappeared, leaving another cast of shadowy men he couldn't bring into focus. They fought the fire with him; later, they all walked together across the river, out of the city, where the terrain grew rocky and birds abruptly appeared to circle overhead.

Ant then, in faint, distorted snapshots, he saw the bodies and felt the tears creep down his soot-covered cheeks. *Zenaisa.*

Who was *Zenaisa?* Where had he been?

His hand clenched in a fist, and for one long moment, the frustration and helplessness made his muscles stand out in rigid relief. He swore, low and bitter and harsh, and wondered for the millionth time if he'd truly lost his mind.

Maybe the strain had been too much. Maybe he'd cracked up.

He would give anything for a punching bag right now. Or any kind of distraction at all.

Where the hell was Suzanne anyway?

When Cagney had recommended last night that she return to her normal activities, Garret had agreed. But the woman had been up at dawn and creeping out of the house by eight-thirty in the morning. It was after nine at night now. Was she ever planning on coming back? Maybe he'd scared her away for good.

He at once grinned and grimaced.

He really should just leave. He knew he made her uncomfortable. After the afternoon's little episode, she hadn't even been able to look him in the eye. He'd had to ask her to help him with his bandage at night, and she'd skittered around so nervously she'd even made him jumpy. Or maybe his own nerves came from the soft scent of roses that followed her, the gentle touch of her trembling hands on his bare back.

At least his libido still worked.

He shook his head and returned to his pacing. He'd stride around the living room one way until his head seemed to spin, then sharply check himself and go the other direction. Hamsters must feel this way in their constantly rotating wheels.

A car door slammed, breaking the tension, and his sharp eyes riveted abruptly to the door. Suzanne. It was about damn time.

Or was it her?

Immediately, he moved, a silent shadow floating past the bay windows. Right before the entryway, he paused, flattening himself against the wall as his senses strained. The metallic grating of a key finding the lock. The sharp click of a bolt retreating home. The door handle turned, and the door swung inward.

Moonlight followed her through, revealing the golden highlights of her brown hair, accentuating the elegant line of her alabaster neck. He forced his breath out quietly.

"It's about time," he said.

She jumped and whirled at once, groceries tumbling from her arm as the very wall disconnected before her eyes and materialized into a man. Her heart leaped into her throat, and for a moment, she was so terrified she couldn't even breathe.

"I didn't mean to scare you," Garret said.

She opened her mouth, but sound still refused to come out. She struggled for another deep breath, while her round eyes fastened onto his face. He looked dangerous. She lost her grip on the second bag, and produce tumbled across the hardwood floor.

He came forward without a sound, bending down as gracefully as a dancer. His hand was large and calloused, swallowing up the first green apple that rolled across the entryway. As his fingers curled, she could see tendons ripple across his forearm, then disappear as he casually dropped the apple back into the sack.

Clean shaven, his chiseled face looked hard and expressionless. Worse, his underfed, hollow cheeks gave him the lean, hungry lines of a predator.

Her gaze dropped back down to the entryway floor, and she focused on trying to retrieve a few apples herself.

"You scared me half to death," she managed to blurt out at last, her hands latching onto a head of lettuce.

"Old habits die hard," he said simply.

She nodded, not daring to meet his eyes. She didn't like to remember who he was, because who he was had nothing in common with her universe. She lived for her children and for her community. He lived to fight wars none of them would even read about.

And soon enough, he would return to them.

"I—I thought you might have left," she found herself saying, then immediately bit her lip. She quickly shrugged nonchalantly, drawing his eyes to the smooth expanse of her exposed shoulders.

His jaw tightened, his gaze lingering. "Soon."

She nodded, not able to meet his eyes. "Hungry?"

Wordlessly, he nodded, his eyes drifting to the curve of her neck and the faint pounding of her pulse. He'd followed that curve with his fingers, felt that strong, regular rhythm with his thumb. Just as fifteen years ago, he'd tasted her lips with his own, felt her cling to his shoulders and whisper his name. He rose and shut the door.

She straightened on the spot, the hairs on the back of her neck rising inexplicably. Garret always brought a certain edge with him, a wound-up feeling of crackling electricity. But now the tension had risen a notch above even that. She was no longer on the fringes of an electric storm.

She was in it.

She swallowed hard, her chin rising. Unconsciously, she held the two bags of groceries in front of her as a feeble defense.

"I'm—I'm going to put away the groceries now," she said nervously.

He nodded, his black eyes never leaving her face. And though he never said a word, never even moved, she knew exactly what he was thinking. Clutched in her arms, the groceries shook slightly.

"I really have to put them away," she whispered again.

Again he nodded.

With a mild oath, she tore her gaze away, scampering off to the kitchen before she could lose any more of her composure. There, she turned on every light as if that could chase away the impending storm.

Her hands still shook as she began to put away the groceries, her ears attuned to the sound of footsteps in the hall. But minute after minute dragged by without his approach, and she finally allowed herself to draw in a long gasp of air. For one moment, she simply gripped the edge of the counter and allowed the tension to shudder out of her.

Good Lord, she was losing her mind.

She took another deep breath and steeled her defenses. Then with quick, efficient movements, she returned to attack the groceries.

She was a thirty-two-year-old woman, she reminded herself as she loaded the crisper. She did not have fluttering little attacks every time she saw a man. She was a practical, logical woman, she reiterated to herself as she pulled two steaks out of the sack. Her life rotated around the community, her roses and her house. She was very busy and very fulfilled. She was well respected and well liked.

She wasn't missing anything at all, and the only reason Garret was even around was because Cagney was her best friend, so she was willing to help his brother. That was it.

Logical, efficient, practical. She took care of people; everyone knew that. So she'd helped tend Garret's wounds and fixed him a meal or two. Any day now, he would be gone, and that would be the end of it.

She sliced some cheese with more force than was necessary, quickly spreading the slices around the perimeter of the plate, interspersing them with crackers. A cut-up apple filled the center, making a pretty and simple arrangement.

A late-night snack, then she'd retire to her room, another day completed. Tomorrow, she'd work in her garden. She lifted the plate, took another deep breath and pasted on a polite, relaxed smile. Feeling a bit like a general going to war, she marched into the living room.

All the lights were still out, just the moon streaming in through the bay windows to bathe her living room in a silvery light. It made things soft and velvety, and immediately, she hesitated. The electric tension still charged the air. Attracted as if by a magnet, her eyes went straight to the man responsible for it all. He was leaning up against a thin strip of wall between the bay windows, the moonlight behind him so that he was completely cast in shadows, his face totally unreadable.

She wondered if perhaps he hadn't planned it that way.

Slowly, she lifted up the plate and forced her voice to sound steady and unconcerned. "I brought some cheese and crackers if you're hungry," she said simply. Then squaring her shoulders, she marched to the coffee table and set down the plate. She could feel his eyes on her and kept herself purposefully distant. If he wanted to play his games, well, let him. She was tired of acting the fluttering, provincial fool.

"Thank you," he said quietly.

Darn if the words didn't throw her for a loop. Since when was Garret polite? She found herself wavering while the sane corner of her mind whispered that politeness was only a new kind of bait he was using in his trap.

"What... what did you do today?" she asked, standing stiffly in the center of the room. Suddenly, the air between them crackled with unseen frustration.

"Nothing." He whispered the word like a curse, and the quiet vehemence immediately touched her. Of course he'd be tense. She'd known all along that Garret Guiness was not the kind of man to be kept locked up. But here he was, wounded and without his memory, confined to her house while she gallivanted around on her merry way. She worried her lower lip. They were definitely going to have to find something for the man to do. Otherwise he would simply go insane.

"Come here," he said roughly. Still working through her thoughts on this new dilemma, she simply picked up the cheese and crackers and obeyed. It wasn't until she was an arm's length away that she was jolted back to attention. And that was when he reached out and without warning, took the plate from her hands.

He didn't appear to want any cheese and crackers because he set the plate on the floor instead. Suddenly, she knew.

Already his hand was on her wrist, firm but gentle as he dragged her toward him. Eyes wide, she followed the unquestioning force of the direction. The tension was back, and she half expected to see sparks of lightning in her living room.

She stopped just inches away, her breathing suddenly tight and quick. She still couldn't see his face clearly, but she could feel his gaze burning into her. Abruptly, his thumb caressed the exposed skin of her shoulder, and she jumped.

"I like your dress," he said in a low voice. Dumbly, she nodded. She'd told herself this morning she'd picked the dress for comfort, but with his hands branding her bare skin, she couldn't shy away from the truth. It was a simple broomstick dress in a dark pine green. The V-necked tank top left her long arms uncovered while the Empire cut fell to a crinkled skirt that flowed around her ankles. It should have been shapeless, but when she moved, the light fabric followed the contours of her body with sensual suggestion.

Now Garret's eyes skimmed down her figure, seeming to find each of those round curves fascinating. Slowly, his large hand slid to the base of her throat, his calloused fingers resting delicately around her graceful throat.

"Was it good to get back to your routine today?"

Hardly able to breathe, she nodded, feeling his fingers rough and strong against her skin.

"Meetings?" he asked silkily. His hand lifted, tracing the outline of her ear. She shivered at the light, tantalizing touch. "I bet you're the volunteer type," he whispered. "Maybe church bingo. Fund-raiser. Definitely garden club material."

She tried to muster indignation at his words, but it was hard to command her own muscles when he kept touching her. Besides, he wasn't saying anything that wasn't true. Then he leaned down, and she found herself holding her breath in anticipation.

"And men?" he whispered, so close she could feel the motion of his lips. "Does getting back to your routine mean you'll be staying out late with men?"

She licked her lips and tried to think of a suitable answer. The correct one would be no, but she hadn't so lost her senses that she'd admit that to him.

"Of course," she managed to reply finally. The words lacked force, and their meaning was probably undermined by the way she arched her neck closer to the warmth of his lips. "By—by the dozen," she added hesitantly.

In the dark, she could feel his grin. "I bet they all play bingo," he drawled.

She nodded, her mind seeking out a sharp retort while her lips still tingled from the teasing proximity of his lips. "Yes," she said at last, not able to think up anything else to say about these nonexistent men.

Abruptly, he leaned back, and she felt the sharp pang of disappointment. His thumb rasped up her neck, a corresponding shiver sparking up her spine. He didn't lean forward again, though. Instead, he seemed to be looking at her with something close to contemplation. Then, he shook his head.

"You should keep away from me," he said in the shadows. She nodded, but didn't move. "I don't like being caged up all day," he continued. Whatever war he'd been fighting, he lost, because suddenly his hand moved, smoothing up to find the knot at the top of her hair. While she sucked in her breath, he drew the first hairpin out. "I just want to know how many," he murmured. His strong fingers found the second slender pin and slipped it out as well. Slowly, her long hair unwound and cascaded down.

She had to bite her lip against the soft sigh that nearly escaped. At the end of a long day, there was nothing quite like the relief of her long hair finally falling free. The cool, fine strands brushed against her shoulders and neck. Unconsciously, she arched back her head.

He didn't say anything, but buried both of his hands in the mass of her hair, combing through the silky tresses, massaging her scalp with slow, sensual strokes that made her lean closer. He picked up a handful of the brown strands, letting them spill over his hands to fall halfway down her back.

His dark eyes gleamed.

The restlessness surged and soared again in his veins. He needed a distraction. And here she was, her eyes already heavy lidded and half-closed while her hair tangled around his hands like a silken net. He should walk away. She wasn't his type, and she certainly deserved better than him. All he had to offer were goodbyes; she'd do better with the bingo folks.

But then she looked at him again, her gaze golden with simmering anticipation and barely suppressed passion. He stopped thinking and started feeling instead. Want. Need. Desire.

He leaned forward sharply, catching that beguiling scent of roses and shampoo. His hands stayed entwined in her hair. His lips found hers.

She trembled at the first touch of his lips brushing across hers. He felt the tremble, and it filled him with primal satisfaction. One hand snaked around her back, curving around her warm, slender waist, and without deepening the kiss, he drew her up hard against his frame. Her breasts pressed against his chest through the thin fabric of her dress, her hips tantalizingly close.

With schooled discipline, he slanted his mouth slightly and deepened the kiss. His tongue touched her lips, tracing them suggestively. She jolted at the contact, skittish and untamed in his arms. He continued soft and slow, willing her to respond.

Tentatively, her arms crept around his neck, and he congratulated her with a teasing nip at the corner of her mouth. Breathlessly, her lips parted, and his tongue slid between her teeth, delving into her mouth with long, sure strokes.

She gasped, her muscles turning to liquid as she melted against his hard frame. Suddenly, her arms were clinging to his neck for support, while his mouth did wild and wonderful things that flushed her cheeks and heated her blood. He tasted dark and masculine, an exotic temptation she didn't completely understand but wanted to have. She found herself pressing closer, her lips parting wider while she unconsciously arched her neck.

His hand drifted down to cup her buttocks, and then he was pressing his hips intimately against her. She gasped again, and he took the opportunity to tangle his tongue around her own. Shivers raced down her back, and she tentatively returned his ministrations.

He growled low in his throat. "Yes, sweetheart. Do that. Kiss me back, honey, just like that."

The power was heady and strong, nearly as beguiling as the kiss itself. She could feel his hard, hot body pressed against her own, his corded neck beneath her hands. And his tongue dueled with hers, plunging and plundering, only to draw back and tease her mercilessly. She tasted his lips, firm and hot and masculine. She explored the corners of his mouth and heard him groan while his hips rubbed against her own suggestively. She could feel his heated length through her thin dress and she was at once breathless and needy.

Her thighs grew damp, and she hadn't known her own restlessness until now. Suddenly, she was the one pressing against him, her fingers tangling in the long, jet strands of his wild hair.

His hand brushed forward, cupping her breast. She arched back, her eyes closed while hot, exotic need boiled through her. She wanted his hand on her breast just like that. And when his fingers found her nipple, rolling it seductively, she bit her lip against the unbearable pleasure. She wanted his hands everywhere. She wanted him to find her, to torment her and end the wonderful torment with something that was sure to be even better. His hardness pressing, rubbing against her. His rigid, burning length, plunging into her...

His hand slipped inside her dress to find her breast, and she didn't protest. She wanted simply to let herself go and turn herself over to this new world unexpectedly exploding in her veins. She wanted him to make her feel all the things she'd never known.

But then she opened her eyes, looking at the shadowed man she really couldn't see in the darkness of the room.

And all of a sudden, she felt the fear. She didn't even know him. He was just someone she had worshiped all those years ago when she'd been too stupid to know otherwise. He'd left her at the bus stop with a rainy promise that had become the center of her world. And how many nights had she lain there praying he would come back? All those nights she would have sold her sixteen-year-old soul if only he'd return and take her away.

The shattering mornings when she'd awaken in the same bed, with her mother's drunken snores already filling her ears.

He wasn't holding her in his arms then; he wasn't calling her sweetheart and honey. He was thousands of miles away, playing the soldier he always wanted to be, while she struggled with the same small-town life she'd always led.

Now, he was merely the stranger passing through town. A stranger who traveled with three condoms in his wallet and knew a whole lot more about the world than she did. A stranger who would inevitably return to that world without ever giving her another thought.

Without warning, her eyes filled with hot tears. And even as his lips nipped at her own, she thought she might hate him.

Before he could react, she pushed herself away with all her might. And as he reached out reflexively for her, she drew back her hand and cracked it across his cheek.

The room grew deathly silent, and for a long moment, the only movement was the rapid rise and fall of her chest. His hand came up and gingerly touched his cheek. Still, he didn't say anything.

"Next time you need a distraction," she snapped, her voice low and furious, "there's an exercise bike on the second floor. Why, with it you might get your strength back even faster so you can leave that much sooner."

He rubbed his jaw again. "Suzanne—" he began, but she wouldn't let him finish.

"You're just passing through, Garret. I know that, Cagney knows that, we all know that. So don't waste my time with any lines, and don't you touch me again. I'll be your host. I'll be your nurse. You want something more, go look elsewhere."

His eyes darkened dangerously, and once more, the air around him began to crackle. "If that's what you want. But about thirty seconds ago, I could've sworn you wanted something completely different."

She gasped, her mouth opening and closing, then opening again. But no words would come out, no answers for his blatant accusation. Her cheeks flushed red and fiery, and she didn't know where to begin anymore. Her body trembled traitorously at the mere memory, and her cheeks burned even more brightly. At that moment, she hated the both of them.

"I'm going to bed," she announced stiffly, clenching her hands in an effort at composure. "I'd suggest that in the morning, we simply start fresh. This never happened, and certainly won't happen again."

"As you wish."

She nodded, though his choice of words sounded ominous. She pivoted sharply and, before she could do herself any more damage, marched down the hallway toward the stairs.

She did not want Garret Guiness.

She managed to keep that in mind until she made it up to her room. Then she closed the door and felt the hot tears of frustration roll down her cheeks.

Chapter 5

*H*e was back at the rocky outskirts of the foreign city.

Around him, he could see the makeshift tents and wooden lean-tos of a temporary camp. Cooking fires smoldered within small circles of rocks, logs set up as benches. Right now, however, no one sat around the campfires.

Instead, the center of the camp riveted all attention. There, an old, tottering school bus rested with idling engine. A man and a woman were directing the flow of activity, and as Garret watched, the younger children in the camp slowly climbed onto the bus. Dimly, he heard orders being issued in French and understood the commands because he knew French from his Cambodia days.

Abruptly, he was aware of all the other sounds: the weeping of the women, letting their children go, the wails of the children, frightened by their mothers' tears. And finally, the distant, constant sound of shelling.

Every now and then, one of the weeping women would look toward that sound and the distant sight of the city. The shelling had grown closer just this morning.

Then Garret's eyes found her.

He recognized her right away, and in the depths of his mind, he already knew her name. Zenaisa. She bent over, her long, honey blond hair half hiding her face as she straightened the collar of the young, somber-faced child in front her. Behind her, her husband, Zlatko, looked on with a grim expression.

The first tear trickled down her son's face, and with a feeble smile, she wiped the tear away. A matching tear trickled down the other cheek. She found that tear, as well, and then she smoothed his threadbare coat with a mother's touch, her hands lingering briefly on her son's thin shoulders. The EquiLibre L'Entreprise Humanitaire would take the children away to safety. Most likely they would remain in an orphanage for the months to come. Some might be adopted. Perhaps some might even manage to find their parents after the war.

No one knew.

As Garret watched, Zenaisa reached into the folds of her overcoat and pulled out a small package. Even from his position at the perimeter of the camp, he could see her hands tremble. And even from this distance, he recognized the carefully tied bundle as the remnants of their last UN package, containing tins of beef and fish, half a box of cheese and one bar of soap. Zenaisa had stood in line five hours to get the supplies.

Sudic began to cry in earnest now, his pinched seven-year-old face crumpling into a mask of raw terror and desperate pain. For one moment, Zenaisa gave in and crushed her last living child close to her heart. Her hands shook as they smoothed his dark hair, her shoulders trembling as she rocked his tiny frame and prayed for strength and hope in a time when there appeared to be none. Zlatko placed a hand on her shoulder, and she loosened her grip on the child.

There were tear tracks on her cheeks, but she still smiled at Sudic, soothing him with soft words as her hands lin-

gered on his shoulders one last time. With a sigh of determination, she stood and brushed off her dusty skirts. Then she took her son's hand and led him to the bus.

She stood there for a long time as the bus pulled away. The women around her sobbed, some tearing at their hair with the force of their grief. But Zenaisa just stood there and watched her son's face disappear into a haze of dust.

Zlatko came up behind her and placed his large, callused hands on her shoulders. She turned then, looking at him with a wide Slavic face that once had been beautiful, but now was worn and tired. Abruptly, she threw her arms around her husband's shoulders, burying her head against his neck.

And right before Garret had to look away, the emotions burning his own throat, he saw her shoulders shake with the force of her tears.

"Darn it, Cagney, the man needs something to do! We can't just keep him locked up in my house all day."

Cagney eyed her with his calm gray gaze and arched an eyebrow. "Is there something I should know?" He'd never seen practical Suzanne so flustered before. It was only eight a.m., but half her hair had already escaped from its customary knot, and her cheeks were flushed.

"That's none of your damn business!" she snapped, raising his brow even higher. "Just help me figure out something for him to do!"

Cagney sighed, rising from the corner of his desk to stretch out his leg while he contemplated her words. It was too early in the morning to be worrying about Garret again. He was a newly engaged man with a beautiful, passionate fiancée. What in the world was he doing arriving at the sheriff's office at eight a.m.?

He dragged a hand through his rumpled black hair and gave Suzanne another thoughtful look. Garret always did wreak havoc on her nerves.

"How's his back?" he asked presently.

"He gets around all right. He still sleeps quite a bit, but I think he's about to eat me out of house and home."

"Sounds like Garret."

"You're not helping."

Cagney threw up his hands in self-defense and tried to fend her off with a disarming grin. "I'm working on it, I'm working on it. But for goodness' sake, Suzanne, I haven't received much more than a couple of phone calls and post-cards from Garret in the past ten years. How do I know what he likes to do?"

"He's your brother."

"Guilty as charged, I'm afraid." Cagney pivoted, and unconsciously began rubbing his left leg. His limp was much better these days, since he'd started doing the doctor's stretching exercises. Still, if he moved too suddenly, the old bullet wound plagued him. "Dad just overhauled his shop. I suppose I can ask him for his old tools."

"Furniture tools?" Suzanne looked unconvinced, but pondered the idea. "Where would we put them?"

"Don't you have that shed by your garden?"

"Yes, but my garden supplies are in there."

Cagney gave her an exasperated look. "Surely you can move your garden tools for this. Remember, it'll get him out of the house."

That seemed to convince her. "Will they all fit?"

Cagney shrugged. "Only one way to know. Look, I'll talk to Dad this afternoon and tell him I'd like to play around with his old tools. He's never said anything, but I think he's always wished one of his kids would show an interest in craftsmanship." Cagney frowned, looking unhappy. "I hate lying to him, you know," he said suddenly. "I hate having a deputy watching my own parents' house and not being able to tell them."

Suzanne's gaze instantly softened, and she nodded her head. "It can't be much longer," she said quietly. "He really is recovering remarkably fast. Sooner or later, it won't matter if his memory has returned or not. He'll simply leave out of the pure frustration of not knowing what to do.''

Cagney looked at her for a moment, then gave in to his impulse to tell her everything. "I heard from Mitch," he said abruptly. "He did some minor checking from the road. Garret's considered AWOL."

Suzanne's eyes opened wide. "Garret would never desert. He just wouldn't."

Cagney nodded his head. "I know, I know. He would never deliberately desert. But let's face it, Suzanne, he came here covertly. Obviously, they don't know where he is."

"Do you think maybe he should contact someone?"

Cagney frowned, his face looking troubled once more. "I don't know, to tell you the truth. But Garret always did have uncanny instincts. I used to think both he and Mitch were throwbacks to the old warriors. Mitch always knows when something bad is about to happen, and Garret...Garret just seems to know what to do. Think about it. He was shot in the back. Most people would have gone straight to the hospital, and most men back to their unit. Garret came here, told us to tell no one and ordered Mitch out of D.C. Until he remembers more, I think we have to trust that."

Suzanne nodded, but her face was as troubled as his own. "How's Jessica?" she asked, changing the subject.

"Eight months pregnant with twins, so she's mad as hell to be on the road. Mitch says she's going along with it for now, but if Garret had them leave for no good reason in the end, she'll skin him alive. Hmm. That could be interesting. The Ice Angel taking on Garret."

Suzanne gave him an exasperated look. "I'm sure Garret had them leave for a very good reason," she insisted. "So you'll get the tools?" she prodded, returning to the original subject.

Cagney nodded. "I'll see what I can work out. Most likely I can bring them over this afternoon. I'll try to stop by the lumberyard as well. Maybe we can figure out something constructive for Garret to do rather than eat all your food.''

Suzanne's mind unwittingly flashed to what other activities Garret had been doing, and she felt her cheeks flush. "Fine," she squeaked, and immediately headed for the door. If she blushed much darker, Cagney wouldn't need her to say a word to know what was going on. And she'd just as soon keep her foolishness to herself.

Maybe she had been living alone for too long, and that made her, well, susceptible to Garret. But she was over that now. The efficient Suzanne was back. She'd gotten up first thing this morning and called Cagney to get something worked out. Now Garret would work in the shed, and she'd have her house back. It was exactly what she wanted.

She marched primly to the door, ignoring the small flutter of disappointment in her stomach.

"Just come over when you have the tools," she called over her shoulder as she opened the door.

"Will do. And Suzanne, it'll take more than a hobby to keep that whisker burn off your neck."

Her cheeks turned positively scarlet, but she didn't say a word. Not even when she slammed the door on Cagney's droll gaze.

Her house still looked like her house when she pulled her old Ford back into the driveway. The wraparound porch was becoming warped in places but could probably survive another year before being replaced. The white paint at least looked good; she'd awakened the morning after her mother's funeral to find her fellow church members on her front porch, armed with paintbrushes and pails of fresh paint. After the strain of the past few years, their actions had brought tears to her eyes. Now, every three years, they all reappeared on her lawn, ready to help yet again. When she died, she would leave the house to the church. Rachel didn't want anything to do with Maddensfield, and there were no other Montgomerys left.

She climbed out of her car and took a deep breath. This was her home, and she was proud of the life she'd built. And darn it, she'd come far enough to be able to deal with a simple man.

She marched up the porch into her house, this time looking immediately behind the front door so she wouldn't be scared witless again. There was no sign of Garret, however. She combed the first floor, but it was empty. Slightly puzzled, she climbed up to the second floor. But the four bedrooms were empty, with nothing stirring but old cotton curtains she'd sewed years ago. Frowning, she went up to the third floor. It was much too hot up here during the summer, so the three bedrooms were used only for storage. Garret wasn't here, either.

The first prickle of unease snaked up her spine.

She climbed down the stairs much faster than necessary, her lips pursed and her brow furrowed as she found herself searching the second floor yet again. But nothing—no one—moved. The house was simply empty.

He'd left.

She'd known it would happen, had told herself quite logically that the day would come. But that realization didn't quite prepare her for the sudden sinking feeling in her stomach, the new tremor in her hands. All at once, she felt empty and not herself at all.

Then in the next second, she heard a sound from the backyard. Bunching her loose skirt in her hand, she bustled down the remaining stairs and along the back hall. She came to a heart-stopping halt in front of the back door, her eyes opening wide. Through the window she could see an ax arch up in the hot July sun, then come whistling back down into a small log. It split cleanly and toppled to the ground.

Without breaking rhythm, Garret placed a new log on the stump and hefted the ax once more. Bare muscles glistened in the hundred-degree heat and high humidity. Sweat rolled down his biceps and chest, disappearing into his black

furred chest as the ax arched up and swung down with relentless precision.

She felt her mouth go dry and her legs begin to tremble.
She placed her hand flat against the window for support, her
eyes still glued to the man in front of her. With a bandanna
tied around his forehead, his jet hair spiked with moisture
around his shoulders, he looked wild and reckless. And he
looked comfortable and efficient with an ax in his hands.
She opened the back door.

Garret didn't know how long he'd been chopping, and it
didn't matter. He'd found the old ax in the shed and the tool
had called to him. From his earlier memories, he knew he'd
used an ax to chop wood as a teen. In the fire-seared corners of his mind, he knew he'd carried an ax for far more
serious purposes. He'd picked up the old tool out of fasci-
nation, and the comfortable feel of it in his hands had sent
chills up his spine. It was like coming home.

He'd followed his instincts after that, finding a pile of logs
outside the shed and setting them up on the stump one after another. In the beginning, the movement had tested rusty
muscles. Now, a fourth of a cord of wood later, he moved
like a well-oiled machine. He felt the sweat and the heat and
the thirst. He felt the slow burn of tired arms and the tingling pain of his wounds.

He felt good. And as he moved through the pain and heat
and thirst, he could remember the sign every SEAL saw
from the first day of training: "The more you sweat in
training, the less you bleed in combat."

He hefted the ax above his head, and let it whistle on its
way back down.

"What in the world are you doing?"

Suzanne stood on her back porch in a yellow twenties-
style dress, her hands on her hips. She looked lovely, her
hair rolled into a bun at the nape of her neck. She looked
angry.

He swung the ax up and felt his blood sing. He slammed the ax back into the wood, watching it split with instant satisfaction.

Suzanne, however, wasn't put off. Out of the corner of his eye, he saw her come bustling down the porch steps, her lips thinned into the kindergarten-teacher look he was beginning to know so well. But rather than stop in front of him, she went immediately to his back. He heard her gasp, but even then it took him a few minutes to put it all together.

He flexed his back muscles, and without the distraction of the ax, felt the instant burn. He'd torn open the wound, of course.

"Would you just look at this?" Suzanne said promptly. She stomped in front of him with such an enraged look, he could only grin. It fueled her anger even more. "You've torn open your scab," she reprimanded him sharply. "All of Dr. Jacobs's hard work gone, just like that. Your back is a horrible mess. And for what? I don't exactly need firewood in the middle of July!"

"Well, firewood never does go bad."

"You're proud of yourself, aren't you? You've ripped open your back and by all rights should be in a heck of a lot of pain, and you're proud of yourself!"

"Right on both counts." He grinned, finding himself intrigued by just how flushed her cheeks became when she was angry. He liked her hair like that, too; it looked much softer than when she had it pulled all the way up on the top of her head. All the loose strands waved around her face like a delicate frame. He was almost tempted to wrap some of them around his finger, except that she was indeed correct. His back suddenly hurt like blazing hell, and movement no longer sounded so appealing.

He didn't mind the pain, though. Physical pain he understood. And he certainly liked it better than the dreams he didn't understand. *Zenaisa.* Zenaisa and Zlatko at the outskirts of Sarajevo. He recalled that much now. But what was a Navy SEAL doing at a camp in Sarajevo, and why did just the thought of both those names fill him with feelings of pain and loss?

His face darkened, a frown crinkling his brow.

"What is it?" Suzanne asked instantly. Her eyes narrowed. "Did you remember something?"

He shook his head, then negated the movement by half nodding. "No. Yes. I don't know. Nothing I understand."

Suzanne was quiet for a long moment, the anger draining out of her. Generally, she wasn't that emotional a person. Garret just got to her somehow. And his back really was a mess, the blood mixing with the sweat to stain the edge of his jeans. Still, a part of her could sympathize with his frustration. It must be horrible not knowing what had happened to him.

"We should get you back inside," she said at last. "See what we can do about bandaging that wound. You're not going to get well if you keep treating yourself like this."

He nodded, his eyes still troubled and looking out in the distance at something she couldn't see. "I like the ax," he said abruptly.

She nodded, not understanding.

"I shouldn't, you know," he continued on. "I had training in guns, explosives, diving and parachuting apparatuses. I know the difference between C-4 and C-5a. I know about altimeters, MP-16s and Draegers. So why the hell do I keep remembering an ax? I think I was a fire fighter, Suzanne. Now why would a Navy SEAL be a fire fighter? What happened to my team? Why doesn't anything make any sense?"

His words ended starkly, and his dark eyes bore into hers with deep frustration and raw need. Her hand came up to rest lightly on his sweat-covered shoulder.

"It'll come back to you," she said quietly, her hazel eyes steady and calm as they found his. "Dr. Jacobs said to give it time, and it's only been a week. That you're remembering things is a good sign. Sooner or later, they will all fall into place, and then you'll know what to do."

He nodded, but his face was still grim.

"Garret," she said after a minute, her voice hesitant. "Garret, Mitch found out that you're listed as AWOL."

He stiffened immediately, and she wished she could recall the words. But he deserved to know what was going on with his own situation. His hands clenched at his sides, the muscles in his neck cording with frustration. She stood there wordlessly, waiting for him to work through his feelings. Still, she jumped when he abruptly kicked a piece of wood halfway to the porch.

"Damn, damn, damn," he muttered darkly, then threw in a few other words that instantly colored her cheeks. He managed an apology, but his eyes weren't in it.

"It's okay," she told him stiffly, her chin coming up. "I know you, Garret. I know you would never desert from the navy. As soon as you get your memory back, you'll be able to explain everything."

He glared at her. "Why do you believe in me?" he quizzed her irritably. "I've never done anything but leave you at a bus stop."

"You're a Guiness," she said simply, though her heart was beginning to hammer in her chest.

There was some truth to his words, except that Garret hadn't exactly run out on her, or anyone else for that matter. He'd always said he would leave when he was eighteen, and he'd done exactly that. He'd always wanted to be a soldier, and he'd done exactly that. She just couldn't imagine him running away from anything.

"Come inside," she said at last, when he continued to stand there, still and glowering. "We'll take care of your back before you cause any more damage."

After a brief hesitation, he followed her in. It seemed the only thing to do. The navy thought he'd gone AWOL, and he supposed he had. He'd been shot in D.C. yet he'd come directly here instead of returning to his unit, all because he simply felt he had to.

Hell, maybe he had lost his mind. Maybe he had deserted. He couldn't remember a damn thing that suggested otherwise. And he didn't dare do anything until he knew more. Like who would shoot him in the back, and why was he so certain the person was still out there, looking to finish the job.

His back burned with a leaping flame as he climbed the porch steps. Then exhaustion and thirst hit him like a freight train, reminding him suddenly of his weak muscles and the blazing heat. He wavered on the last step, and without asking, Suzanne slipped an arm around his waist.

He wanted to pull away, knowing he was blood-covered and sweat-soaked and entirely too filthy for her beautiful dress and graceful manners. But she simply thinned her lips and looked at him with stubborn eyes that challenged him to say anything. He accepted her help and cursed himself for his weakness.

In the guest bedroom, Suzanne made him stand in the middle of the room while she used a damp cloth to wipe down his bare chest in quick, efficient swipes. The cloth trailed around the waistband of his jeans, causing his stomach muscles to contract. But she didn't seem to notice, her face grim and her hands busy. She stepped around to his back and shook her head at the sight.

The minute she dabbed at the wound, she felt him stiffen, and knew it must hurt like the devil. She tried to be gentle, but the scab tangled with the terry cloth, tearing the wound slightly more. Garret didn't move, but sucked in his breath.

"I'm sorry," she said softly. "I'm being as gentle as I can."

He could only nod, unable to say a word as the sweat beaded on his brow with the strain. Suzanne disappeared into the bathroom across the hall, returning with a fresh, damp washcloth and a roll of bandages. She pressed a gauze pad over the wound for several minutes, stopping the bleeding. Then, head bent low over the task, she taped a new gauze pad over the wound.

Then the bandaging was done, the damage fixed, and suddenly she was so close to his bare back she could almost taste the salt on his skin.

She rose abruptly, wavering from the sudden movement. But straightening only put her at eye level with his golden shoulders, the muscles sharply defined from hunger and exercise. She breathed in the hot flavors of July and sweat and wood, and the smells tickled her senses. Even lean from hunger, he was a powerful man. And in just a matter of inches, she could flatten her palm against his bare chest, feel the heat of his skin and the texture of his hair. She could run her finger down his arm, following the curve and indent of his biceps down to his scarred forearm and massive hand. His fingers and palms were callused and rough, a working-man's hand. They'd felt tantalizing and masculine on her skin.

Her eyes drifted up, finding his dark eyes watching her with glittering depths. The awareness sparked between them swift and electric as always. Her body remembered the feel of his hard, sweat-slicked torso pressed against her own soft curves. Her lips remembered the tantalizing caresses of his tongue, the tingling burn of his whisker-roughened cheeks. Her scalp knew the arousing feel of his callused hands tangling with her hair.

Her pupils dilated, the gold flecks in her hazel eyes deepening into the amber, sensual gaze of a cat purring over a saucer of cream. He caught his breath at the power of her gaze and felt his body instantly respond. His jeans were suddenly tight and confining, but he didn't move. He still remembered her words of last night, and they hung between them as sure and solid as a steel wall.

Then her gaze fell once more on his full, sensuous lips, and her tongue darted out to lick her own lips with anticipation—

The doorbell rang, and before either could react, the front door unceremoniously opened and footsteps rang out on the hardwood floor. Suzanne was jolted harshly back into reality, staring at Garret with panicked eyes as the footsteps drew closer.

Without wasting a moment, Garret pushed her out into the hallway and flattened himself against the wall behind the door. The pressure on his back made him wince, but no sound escaped as his senses honed in immediately on the approaching stranger.

"There you are," Cagney called out impatiently . "I brought the tools— What the hell happened to you?"

Too late, Garret remembered the blood and sweat that now stained Suzanne's beautiful old dress.

"I was just helping Garret out with his back," Suzanne replied smoothly enough. There was only the faintest trace of tremors in her voice, and Garret found himself grinning. Not bad for a schoolteacher. "The damn fool tore open his wound again." Garret's grin disappeared.

The door swung inward, the doorknob nearly hitting Garret in the gut as Cagney passed through. Cagney's gray gaze settled on his brother behind the door, and he shook his head.

"Next time, I'll announce myself as I walk in," Cagney said dryly.

"It would be helpful."

For no explicable reason, tension filled the air between the two. It wasn't helped by Suzanne's entry and her obvious need to avoid Garret. Cagney looked at her sharply, his shrewd eyes taking in the heightened color on her cheeks. His eyes swung back to Garret, narrowing dangerously. But Garret returned the look just as steadily, neither of them saying a word.

After a long, strained moment, Cagney broke the silence by tersely explaining he'd brought their father's old wood working tools. As their father had completely redone his shop, starting with the purchase of a Delta Unisaw, Cagney was now the proud owner of a table saw, six-inch jointer, router, wood lathe and planer. Some of the tools were temperamental with age, but it was a fairly robust set. To make sure Garret didn't have an excuse for not being able to begin, Cagney had also wheedled some cherry wood out of his father. Henry was happy with his son's new interest, and Cagney had enough guilt to age him before his time.

And he certainly wasn't in the mood for any more of Garret's antics.

After a curt discussion, the two brothers went out to the shed to set up the shop. Watching them go, Suzanne allowed herself to release a pent-up breath. This was exactly what she'd wanted. Now Garret would spend his days in the shed, and she would be free to return to her usual schedule of busy, busy, busy. No more tense moments in the living room and certainly no more of that chopping wood.

As she'd told Cagney, Garret really was healing remarkably fast. She imagined that now it was really only a matter of days. He already appeared to be remembering some things. Probably just a couple more days.

She looked down at her vintage dress, seventy years old and now stained with blood and sweat. She shook her head and reminded herself again how grateful she would be when Garret left. On the way back to her room, however, her fingers remained pressed against her lips.

He hovered on the edge of the dream, at once fighting it and urging it on. He needed to remember; he hated the memories. His hands wrapped unconsciously around the sheets, his huge body straining as his sleep-drugged lips muttered words his waking mind didn't want to know. Then instantly, he was there.

* * *

Fire leaped around him, clutching at his skin, licking at his face. He could feel the searing heat rippling like waves around him. The smoke stung his eyes, and the water creased down his heat-parched cheeks without his notice. His attention was all on the flames, and once more the ax rested in his hands. He lifted it hacking his way closer to the fire.

He could hear the voices of people pleading for help, hear the whiz of gunfire at his back. Somewhere to his left, a man cried out and he knew without looking that a bullet had hit its target. Suddenly, as if feeding off the pain, the fire leaped in front of him. He had reached out a determined arm to shove the burning wood aside, then heard the warning creak above his head. Too late he realized the real danger, the trap the fire had laid.

The burning rafter crashed down upon his head, burning his arm, melting his clothes into his skin. His throat corded with his roar of pain, but no sound penetrated through the wicked crackle of the laughing flames.

The next thing he knew, he was out in the open, the sky clear and star-studded above him. In the distance, he could hear the nightly sounds of mortar fire and the corresponding explosions of walls toppling down, windows shattering. Here, the sounds were as familiar as a cricket's song, and only silence caught you off guard. He tried to move, and the pain that rocketed up the side of his body made his lips curl.

Abruptly, a woman's face appeared, her cheekbones wide and slanted through her long, dark blond hair. Zenaisa. She fretted over the bandages of his arm, then all of a sudden realized he was awake. She sat back then and smiled at him with her eyes, her whole face softening. Zlatko appeared, placed an arm around her shoulders and peered down at Garret.

"The patient heals?" he asked.

"The mule heals," she replied and once more she was smiling at Garret. He felt a painful grin crack his lips.

"Takes more than fire to stop me," he croaked out.

Zlatko waved a dismissive hand. *"Bah. It's only because your hide's so thick not even flames can penetrate."*

He sounded gruff, but Garret had known him too long not to see the concern around his soot-rimmed eyes. He offered his friend another grin. *"I told you someday it would be your turn to pull me from the flames."*

Zlatko merely shrugged. *"I only saved you for the women's sake. I didn't want to hear their tears all night if their favorite pet died. Besides, Zenaisa would beat me."*

At the last minute, the man winked at his wife, a gesture completely at odds with his stoic face and oversize hands. As she smiled back at her husband, Garret could see the exhaustion fall away from her face and a glimpse of the woman she'd once been shine through. Just for a moment, he felt like an intruder between the two, and as he did so often, he turned away.

Then he remembered the last sound of sniper fire.

"The Chetniks?" he whispered.

The laughter fled from Zenaisa's face, and Zlatko looked down at the ground. Garret knew the rest without being told. *"Kemal"* was all Zlatko said, and in an instant Garret could see the intense, brooding nineteen-year-old in his mind's eye. He nodded, and his burned limbs flared with anguish.

"The funeral?"

"Yesterday, my friend. You have been unconscious for a while. You are big man to drag from a building, no?"

Garret nodded and felt the pain in his chest. Another gone, another part of the team dead. If only he'd had more time to train them. If only they'd had better supplies...

"You rest," Zlatko said softly, and Garret opened his eyes long enough to see the quiet sadness in his friend's eyes.

"Zenaisa will take care of you, and you will heal. We need you, friend. For all the fires to come."

Once more he nodded and felt the blackness of sleep descend even in his dreams. His last thought was of Zenaisa standing in Zlatko's arms. She comforted his friend, as she comforted them all. In her hands, he would be all right, and one day soon, he would again lead them all into the flames....

Garret jolted awake, Zenaisa's face still fading out of his mind. At once he was aware of the burning in his back mixing with ghostly pains in his arm and leg. His heart pounded in his chest, while the sweat rolled down his cheeks.

Zenaisa and Zlatko. He'd worked with them in Sarajevo. Worked with them, lived with them, and for a while, been part of their world. Because...

The reason ducked again behind the fog in his mind.

Until...

The black mist clutched the next scene tightly, leaving only the dread to pervade his mind.

And he knew deep within his stomach that whatever came next, he really didn't want to know. But even as he thought it, he saw the faint, abstract images of the ravaged camp, the circling birds... the bodies.

And he felt once more the weight of the ax in his arms.

Chapter 6

Suzanne was just coming down the stairs in the morning when she heard the telltale sound of banging cupboard doors. She froze on the staircase, her hand going self-consciously to her rumpled hair and old clothes. It was only five-thirty in the morning, early for Garret to be up. She worried her lower lip, glancing down at the baggy sweatpants and oversize T-shirt she always wore for her five-mile walk. She'd never really worried about how she looked in the old clothes, but then, she'd never encountered a man like Garret this early in the morning, either.

She squared her shoulders and descended the last two steps. It was ridiculous to consider her appearance now, she told herself sharply. She looked like someone about to go exercise. End of story.

Still, she was holding in her stomach when she walked into the kitchen. Garret glanced up with a scowl, then did a quick double take at her outfit, which didn't help matters. Her chin came up another notch.

"Rather early for you, isn't it?" she asked primly, getting down a glass from the second shelf as casually as possible. Stretching up made her stomach flatter, but she quickly disregarded that as a reason for her actions. She poured herself a glass of iced tea, even though she rarely drank before walking.

"I couldn't sleep," Garret said tersely. "You got anything to eat around here?"

She looked at him closely, noticing for the first time the shadows beneath his eyes and the tightness in his face. He moved like a man on a wire, pacing the old kitchen with too much energy for five-thirty in the morning. His hair was still disheveled, his blue chambray shirt unbuttoned and open over his new denim jeans. For one moment, Suzanne's gaze rested on the golden expanse of his bare chest, and she found herself thinking he looked considerably more sexy in a rumpled state than she did.

Quickly, she averted her gaze to the safer site of her old, cracked kitchen table.

"There's cereal in the pantry," she suggested.

He nodded and headed straight for the walk-in area. After muttering and cursing under his breath, he emerged with her lone box of raisin bran. Experimentally, he shook it and heard the sound of a nearly empty box. He scowled once more.

"There's eggs if you want to fry 'em," she said with a shrug. "Or maybe SEALs drink them raw."

The look he gave her explicitly registered his thoughts on her sense of humor. She merely returned it with a calm, arched eyebrow, finding his uncharacteristic frenzy an intriguing change of pace. But then he reached up for a bowl and instantly winced as the motion pulled the scab on his back. Immediately, she was at his side.

"Here, let me get it for you."

"Damn it, I can get the bowl myself!"

She handed it to him anyway and felt her skin practically blister from the heated anger in his look. "It's just a bowl, Garret," she told him quietly, her hazel eyes soft.

The rage drained from his face, leaving his eyes suddenly looking haggard, haunted. He held the bowl against his bare stomach, then without saying a word, turned away.

"You remembered something?" she guessed.

He picked up the box of cereal and dumped the last of its contents into the green ceramic bowl. He looked at the pile of bran flakes and sugar-dusted raisins then finally, slowly, he nodded.

"Want to talk about it?"

He shook his head. "There's nothing to talk about."

"Talking sometimes helps," she said casually, placing her glass in the metal sink. With a practiced touch, she banged the faucet twice and was rewarded with hot water.

"I'm fine," Garret said tightly. He opened a drawer with more force than was necessary, then grumbled a few harsh words when it didn't reveal any silverware.

"As you wish," Suzanne said simply. She opened the drawer beside the sink and handed him a spoon.

He took it, but his jaw was clenched and his eyes glittered dark fires of futility and anger. "I'm not one of your damn charity cases," he muttered. "Don't forget that."

Her hand stilled on the cracked Formica countertop, his words wounding. She turned around slowly and gave his cereal a pointed look. "As you said."

His face darkened, a vein pounding dangerously in his forehead. But now, she was angry, as well. She hadn't asked for any of this. She hadn't asked him to leave her at the bus stop, just as she hadn't asked him to return even more attractive than she remembered and just as determined to go. To hell with him anyway.

"It bothers you, doesn't it?" she found herself saying, unable to hold back. "It bothers you to need someone, to need me."

Suddenly he moved, and she took an automatic step back against the kitchen counter as he stalked forward. He swiftly placed his hands on either side of her, pinning her with his body and with his eyes.

"Sounds like the pot calling the kettle black, to me," he said with deceptive softness. His jet eyes gleamed with unholy fire.

Her hands began to tremble, but she kept her eyes level on his face. "Just what do you mean?"

"Need, Suzanne. We're talking need here. You say I don't like to need you. But I'm not the one searing you with hungry glances all day, then backing away the first time you make a move. Let's talk about that need, Suzanne."

"That's entirely different," she retorted flustered, her cheeks burning bright red. One of his hands came up to caress her soft skin and she flinched. His eyes mocked hers.

"It's need, Suzanne. Pure and basic and primal. And when you look at me like you looked at me yesterday, hell yes, I need you."

"That's not what I mean," she explained again, but the breathlessness of her words wasn't helping matters. "That's just, just..."

"Lust? Desire? Animal attraction? Primitive passion?"

She nodded furiously, her cheeks burning.

He traced the curve of her cheek with a rough finger. "You're thirty-two years old, Suzanne. Surely you don't need to dress it up anymore. And surely you can admit to something so simple, so basic, as human need."

His words were softer now, beguiling, but no less dangerous. They cut the ground right out from under her, shaking her to her very foundation. Because suddenly she was thinking of how she'd looked at his bare chest and felt the need all the way to her stomach. Worse, she was thinking of the bus stop all those years ago and how much she'd needed him to give her something to believe in. How much she'd needed him to stay. What was so basic, so simple about that?

She licked her lips and fought for the rigid backbone and steely strength that had gotten her through the years. "Maybe that's exactly the point," she challenged boldly, keeping her chin up and her hazel eyes steady. "It's basic, and it passes. You'll admit to lust, Garret, because it doesn't tie you down. There are no obligations. I know how much you like that."

Her words must have hit home, for his jaw clenched. If she thought she had him, however, she was mistaken. Garret had always been sharp. And he'd always seen more than she'd wanted.

"And what about you, Suzanne?" he prodded, his eyes hard. "The kindergarten teacher, the community adviser. You took care of your mother and your sister. Now you take care of the whole damn town. But who do *you* need, Suzanne? Who do you ever allow that close?"

Unexpectedly, her throat tightened, and she had to fight against the sudden burning in her eyes. But she'd be damned before she'd ever let him know the answer to that question.

"I have friends," she said stiffly. "I belong in this community."

"But who do you need, Suzanne? Who do you need?"

The intensity in his voice caged her in, making her feel trapped. At the last minute, she lashed out fiercely, her hazel eyes suddenly snapping fire. "I don't need anyone, all right, Garret? And I certainly don't need you pacing my kitchen like a damn beast simply because you've had a bad night! Lots of us have bad nights!"

Immediately, he backed away, but his eyes were assessing on her face. Her eyes had turned a molten gold, her cheeks a healthy red. That prim, efficient look was gone, and suddenly she no longer reminded him of rain, but of fire. It suited her more than he would have guessed. "I like you angry," he said.

"I like you unconscious."

He grinned, the mercurial change in mood catching her off guard. "You look good in sweats, too. Gives you sort of a soft, rumpled look."

"You're trying to drive me crazy."

"If you can't beat 'em, sweetheart, you might as well join 'em." He laced the flippant words with a fine irony she immediately understood. Her stance relaxed. She placed a hand on his arm.

"Give it time, Garret. Give it time."

"Yeah, well, it seems I don't have much choice in the matter. Wonder if any of the tools Cage and I hooked up actually work."

"Probably. But please don't burn down the shed."

"Don't think I could, sweetheart. Seems I might know something about fires."

"What do you mean?"

He laughed, a dry, humorless sound, and raked a frustrated hand through his black, wavy hair. "If only I knew. If I only I knew."

He turned and simply walked away, leaving her alone in her kitchen and very confused.

When Suzanne came back from her walk over an hour later, she found Garret facedown on the tiny love seat, his lumbering body splaying off onto the floor. The discomfort of the position underlined his exhaustion, so she crept past the living room archway as silently as possible. Perhaps sleep would dull his relentless edge and provide her with a measure of peace.

Upstairs, she showered quickly and, with a sigh, donned her gardening clothes. As a child, she'd never had any dresses like the other girls. Her and Rachel's clothes were cast-off jeans from the other schoolchildren, and a constant source of shame. From the time she started making her own money, she'd also started acquiring her own collection of beautiful dresses and skirts. However, there were definitely activities where only pants made sense. Walking was one, gardening the other. So she pulled on an old pair of brown polyester pants she'd bought from Goodwill and matched it with a long, pale yellow man's shirt that was splattered with white paint. With black rubber boots on her feet and an old straw hat on her head, she looked like a gardener.

Or maybe a scarecrow.

Funny how she'd never given the outfit much thought before. Cagney had seen her in it; most of her friends had caught her wearing it a time or two. But the thought of now going downstairs left her staring gloomily in the mirror. With a determined sigh, she set her shoulders. She was not going to care what she looked like. She was not going to alter her plans one whit for Garret Guiness. He was simply an old acquaintance, and by God, she wanted to work in her garden and so she would.

That, of course, didn't quite explain why she crept so silently back down the stairs. In the back hallway, however, right as she was reaching for the doorknob, he caught her.

"Garden?" came his low, masculine voice from the doorway behind her.

Without turning, she nodded her head.

"Need some help?"

She heard the sound of his approaching footsteps and quickly shook her head. "You should rest," she blurted.

"Nah. I've slept enough already. Besides, I checked out the garden yesterday. The raspberries are definitely ripe." She whirled around to find him grinning at her nonchalantly, his shirt still unbuttoned. "Nice hat," he added.

"Have you been eating my berries?" she accused, her eyes narrowing dangerously. Her garden was her territory. Everyone knew that.

He held up two hands as if to ward her off, then tried another grin. When it had no impact whatsoever, he switched to the somber approach. "Sampled would be a far kinder word. Just one or two." Or three or four. "I swear."

"I'm going to make jam with those berries."

Her face was so intense, he found himself grinning again. His mother had been the same about her garden all those years ago. Not that she managed to salvage much from five wild children. Of course, Jake was the one who came up with all the best infiltration ideas—though dressing up like a scarecrow might have been a bit much.

"Honest," he said now. "I'll help. We'll consider it a raspberry tax."

She wasn't sure she wanted him in her garden. She wasn't sure she could handle more time in his broad-shouldered presence. But he looked sincere, and perhaps it was rude to turn down a genuine offer of help. Finally, she relented with a nod. "But we're picking berries," she reiterated. "Picking, as in putting the berries in a bucket, a plastic bucket."

"Aye, aye, Captain," he affirmed, smiling as she muttered something less than complimentary under her breath. Whistling tunelessly to himself, he followed her out the door.

If Suzanne was possessive about her garden, she had a right to be. The broad expanse took up most of her backyard and was a delightful mix of beautiful roses and fruits and vegetables. A brick wall ran along the back, covered now by the pink American Pillar climbing rose. The left border was a carefully cultivated mix of cream-colored Alba Maxima roses and the deep crimson Tuscany Superb. Last year, the Tuscany had won grand prize at the Maddensfield Fair. Lower-growing roses such as the Gallica rose, Complicata, surrounded the base of her blueberry bushes, and the far right border unveiled loose, fragrant clusters of red, pink and white Autumn Damasks.

In the middle of the floral explosion, she'd laid out neat, orderly rows of strawberries, asparagus, carrots and squash. Next to the blueberry trees, wire frames supported the raspberry bushes' climb toward freedom. She'd splurged heavily on the garden, importing rich soil to support her efforts, and rewarding the soil with carefully considered blends of chemicals and natural fertilizers such as ash and compost.

When her mother had been dying in the hospital, her stomach swollen, her skin loose and yellowish green, Suzanne had also fertilized the roses with her tears.

"You have a beautiful garden," Garret said behind her.

"I like fresh fruit."

She led him over to the raspberries and tried not to think about his eyes on her back. For a while she left him at the raspberries with a pail and wandered alone among her roses. She clipped off dead blossoms with a practiced hand, testing the soil for moisture. She liked the way roses smelled, fresh and sweet and delicate. Sometimes she would come out here and close her eyes and dream she was in some faraway garden like the Empress Josephine or the Princess of Wales. In the early morning hours, she would watch the blossoms open, shimmering and moist with dew, and allow herself to marvel in their simple beauty.

There were parts of her life she didn't like to dwell on. But in her roses, as with her dolls, she'd at least found some measure of contentment.

"Hey, I didn't know I was a one-man crew."

She turned toward Garret's plaintive words, finding him watching her with speculative eyes. She summoned a smile to her face and crossed back over to the raspberries.

"The roses must take up a lot of time," he said, his eyes still steady upon her face.

She nodded. "They're coming along well this year."

"When did you start the garden?"

She just shrugged. "Oh, years back, I suppose. Dotti actually gave me the idea."

Garret nodded at the reference to his mother and pulled a ripe raspberry off the vine. "I think your garden has surpassed her efforts, though."

Again, Suzanne shrugged. "I have more time, I think." Her efficient fingers rippled through the vine, plucking the soft berries with practiced precision. From time to time, she'd squeeze a little too tightly, and the sweet, warm juice would stain her fingers. She moved on, not noticing.

But her sharp eyes did catch Garret surreptitiously popping a quick berry into his mouth. At the last minute, he caught her look and grinned boyishly.

"They're best fresh," he mumbled through a full mouth.

She arched a fine eyebrow. "I have kindergarten pupils who exercise more self-control."

"Yeah, well, we all have our talents."

He popped another berry, but this time she was faster. With quick reflexes honed by outwitting exuberant five-year-olds, she snatched the berry from his lips.

"Mine," she declared triumphantly. But before she could chortle further, his hand snapped around her wrist like a steel vise. Just as her eyes were opening round with the shock, he seized the warm raspberry from her fingertips with his mouth, licking the juice from her fingers at the same time.

"Mine," he corrected huskily.

Her hazel eyes turned gold, her mouth parting from the tingling impact of his tongue on her fingertips. His dark gaze followed the movement of her lips, then swept up to challenge her openly.

"Are we back to need, Suzanne?"

Mutely, she shook her head, but her golden eyes remained on his lips. He bowed his head and trailed his tongue slowly up her index finger. Her breath came out in a little gasp, and he closed his mouth upon her finger fully, sucking it with sweet, sensuous promise.

"We're definitely back to need, Suzanne."

This time, she simply nodded.

"So what is it you need? Tell me, sweetheart. Tell me what you want."

Peace, sanity, safety and security. Long, lonely nights with her beautiful dolls and classic black and whites.

"Kiss me," she whispered.

He smiled, slow and promising. "With pleasure, sweetheart."

Even as his lips were descending, her arms tangled around his neck. Suddenly, she didn't want prim or proper. She wanted his lips, full and masculine, tasting of stolen raspberries and the hot July sun. She wanted his body, hard and demanding, pressed against her own. She wanted his tongue, skillful and sure, plundering her mouth and stirring sensations she hadn't known existed.

And she needed. She needed his hands, smoothing down her back, cupping the curve of her buttocks. She needed his palm, rubbing against her breast, making her breath come in hot, urgent gasps.

Her hat fell back, revealing her skin to the caressing sun, but she only arched her neck farther back without protest. She opened her mouth wider, welcoming him in, finding and dueling with his tongue as he'd taught her just two nights before. He tried to go slowly, but she gripped him all the tighter and made him go faster.

In the fragrant heat of her garden, he was hard and callused and male. His cheeks rasped with twenty-four hours of beard, his fingers and lips sticky with raspberries and forceful with desire.

She needed his touch and his taste, until the very force of the need burned her eyes, and then she was dragging him down to the soft, rich ground while his tongue plundered her mouth.

He grazed his teeth down her neck, finding her earlobe and nipping sharply while she gasped beneath him. He buried his face between the valley of her breasts, rubbing his cheek against her soft curves while her hands tangled in his hair. Nuzzling aside her shirt, his fingers found the first few buttons and released them with a deft touch. He exposed the white cotton of her bra with its simple pattern of pink-tipped roses and peeled back the thin material to find her ripe breast. He closed his lips over her nipple. She arched back against the rich soil, moaning her compliance as he feasted on her sensitive, swollen flesh, his lips strong and sucking.

"Miss Montgomery. Oh, Miss Montgomery..."

The call penetrated the warm haze, a harsh splash of cold water. One moment, Garret's mouth was warm and moist on her breast, the next, he was simply gone, bolting up like an arrow while his eyes quickly scoured the backyard.

"Miss Montgomery," called the voice, now from the side of the house.

"Oh, bloody hell," Garret said. He reached down and quickly redid the top buttons of her pale yellow shirt while she frantically brushed the dirt from her hair.

The footsteps sounded closer.

"What do we do?" Suzanne demanded to know, her face shell-shocked, her hands still trembling with raw desire and sudden fear.

"The shed," Garret said immediately. He took a step forward, then realized the person was walking down that side of the house.

"The roses," Suzanne breathlessly corrected. She grabbed his hand and pulled him over to the thickly blooming Alba Maxima and Tuscany Superb. "Duck," she squeaked, and practically pushed him through the thick bushes. He hissed sharply, then rolled through to the other side.

"Miss Montgomery, there you are." She whirled sharply, pasting a smile on her face while her left hand tried to pick the last few twigs out of her hair.

"Deputy Davey," she called back, her voice a couple of octaves higher than usual. "What brings you here?"

The young deputy strode strongly toward the garden. Belatedly, she smoothed her shirt and moved to cut him off. "I'm looking for Sheriff Cagney, ma'am. I was told he was on his way here. Have you seen him?"

Suzanne shook her head, retrieving her hat at the last moment and plopping it unceremoniously on her head. Perhaps it would at least partly cover her flaming cheeks. "Why, no, I haven't. Is there something I can help you with?"

"Oh, no, ma'am. Sorry to interrupt your gardening and all. It's just he's asked us to watch his parents' house, and last night someone broke in."

Suzanne faltered, and behind her she was certain she heard a muttered curse.

"Why don't you come inside?" she said quickly. "I'll fix you a nice glass of iced tea and I'm sure in another minute or two Cagney will arrive."

"That's mighty nice of you, ma'am."

She managed another smile and wondered if Deputy Davey could hear the loud, guilty beats of her thundering heart. He simply followed her into the house, his young face its normal benign self.

She'd no sooner poured two glasses of iced tea than the sound of an approaching car filled the air. Standing at attention, Davey solemnly debriefed Cagney the minute he walked in, then handed him a note that had been left on the dining room table of Dotti and Henry Guiness's house. The note was addressed to Garret.

"Mom saw this?" Cage quizzed the young man.

"Yes, sir. She gave it to us, sir. Said she reckoned you would know what to do with it."

Cagney swore softly under his breath. Knowing his parents, he figured they'd cottoned on to the fact that the deputy was watching their house after the first five minutes. At least they were familiar enough with their children's lifestyles by now not to ask too many questions.

"I'll take care of it from here, Deputy," Cagney said at last. "Any chance of prints?"

"No prints, sir. The window was forced open in the back. Not very professional, sir."

That was interesting. "Anything stolen?"

"No, sir. At least nothing has been reported missing yet. Just this note was left on the table."

Cagney's scowl deepened, then he abruptly released his pent-up breath with a sigh. "You did well, Davey. I want you to keep an eye out for a few more days, just to make sure nothing else happens. Keep me informed."

"Yes, sir." Davey headed for the door, turning at the last minute as if he wanted to ask a question. One look at Cagney's steely gaze, however, and the young deputy snapped his mouth shut and marched smartly through the door.

Cagney watched him go, shaking his head. "A sheriff shouldn't have to lie to his own deputies," he muttered under his breath. Then his sharp eyes took in Suzanne. "So where did you hide him?"

"Behind the roses."

She turned and led him down the hall, her shoulders finally beginning to relax even as her mind raced through this new turn of events.

"Suzanne, there's dirt all down your back."

"Gardening's dirty work," she called back over her shoulder.

"Yeah, I bet," he replied, his tone ironic.

This time, however, she couldn't quite stop the secretive smile that touched her lips.

Garret emerged the minute she and Cagney appeared on the back porch, his expression intense. "What happened?" he demanded to know instantly.

Without speaking, Cagney held out the folded slip of white paper. For a moment, Garret just stared at it. Then slowly, he reached out and took it from his brother's grasp.

In the hot sun, he unfolded the paper and read the two simple lines scrawled in pencil.

The waters of Miljaka still flow red. The river remembers, prijatelj, *and so do I.*

And suddenly, he was back in the ruins of his mind.

He was walking, and men were around him. They were all covered with soot, and some still moaned with the fresh pain and old weariness. The ax rested in his hands, the blade fire-seared and bloodstained. They had been gone from the camp for longer than planned, days and nights of fire without end as the Olympic stadium had burned before their eyes. Now, their stomachs rumbled with hunger, and fresh wounds sharpened their rage.

Above him, the birds circled, and even as his exhausted eyes took in the motion, he did not understand.

They came over the hill, and then they all stopped.

Bodies. Everywhere. Bodies and the smoldering tents of a ravaged camp. Not even the smoke could cover the sweet, putrid odor of death.

Behind him, the first man fell to his knees and began to moan.

Like a man in a nightmare, Garret walked into the ruins of the camp that had once been formed by the survivors of a small rural village. Though the village had been mostly Croatian, there had been Serbs, as well, people who had married into the village or simply settled there. Before the war, no one had really cared. And even after the war had begun, they had still stuck together, drawing upon ties of marriage and community once politics had gone insane. Now the Serb and Croatian women lay abandoned with equal disregard.

He walked through the remains, and soundless tears traced through his soot-covered cheeks.

To the last tent he walked, the toppled canvas already smoldering with flames of despair. There, he came to the final unbearable sight, and his eyes would not look away.

Zenaisa. Oh, God, not Zenaisa.

Garret closed his eyes, but it didn't help.

He heard the footsteps behind him, and even as he moved to shield her from Zlatko's sight, he knew he was too late. The lumbering man behind him staggered, then like a giant oak, he toppled to his knees. His massive, scarred hands rose to his head and he gripped his temples as he fought to block out the sight. And he began to rock back and forth on his knees, wailing the pure, keening cry of a man's anguish, the howl of the desert wind and the baying wolf, the cry of toppling mountains and receding seas.

Garret tried to reach out a hand to his friend, but his muscles would no longer move.

"Garret. Garret, sweetheart." Suzanne cupped his cheeks, tilting his head up until he looked at her with shocked, horrified eyes. Then he caught her hands on his face, clutching her wrists as if she was his last anchor in a violent storm. "Garret?" she whispered shakily. "Garret, are you all right?"

He relinquished his grip abruptly, turning his head away because he couldn't stand the sight of so much compassion in her eyes. He fought to breathe, he fought to function and he fought to pull himself back to reality and away from the scene he could no longer salvage.

"I need to be alone," he said hoarsely.

"Garret—"

She reached out again, but he batted her hand away.

"No!" His body was racked by a deep, shuddering breath, then he looked at her, his eyes pleading. "Please," he whispered. "Please just give me some time."

He started walking for the shed and didn't look back.

Suzanne and Cagney let him go, standing behind him in the sun and exchanging worried glances.

"I'm scared," Suzanne murmured softly, turning to Cagney with pensive eyes.

"Yeah," he told her honestly, still staring at the retreating figure of his older brother, "so am I."

Chapter 7

When Suzanne returned from her parade committee meeting late that afternoon, Garret still had not returned to the house from the shed. With pursed lips, she set down the pile of mailings she was now in charge of getting out, and contemplated what to do.

Cagney had tried to talk to Garret before going and had met nothing but angry resistance. In the end, Cagney had stormed out of the shed muttering uncomplimentary things under his breath, and Suzanne had decided maybe it was best just to leave Garret alone.

But it was four now. And seven hours in that shed should be too much for a man still recovering from a bullet wound. With a resolute set of her shoulders, she poured two glasses of iced tea as a peace offering and walked outside.

She could hear the sharp buzzing of the table saw as she approached, the high-pitched squeal sending shivers down her spine. There was something about the noise she'd never learned to like. Taking a deep breath, she waited for a moment of intermission, then banged on the weathered door with one of the glasses.

"Garret. It's Suzanne. I thought you might like something to drink." There was another moment of silence, and she found herself holding her breath. Then slowly, the old wooden door creaked open. She had to blink several times to adjust to the darker interior, then her eyes focused on the man before her.

He had stripped to the waist, his chest sweaty from the un-air-conditioned room and dusted with fresh, tangy sawdust. An old white rag was tied around his forehead, giving him a renegade look that suited the grim, unrelenting lines of his face. She managed to keep her hand from shaking as she held out the tall, wet glass.

"Iced tea?"

He took it from her with just a nod, his eyes, completely unreadable, scouring her face. After the past week in his presence, however, she could read his tension in the corded muscles of his neck, the stiff set of his shoulders and the renewed forcefulness of his stance. As she watched, he arched his head back and drank down the entire glass of rose-cinnamon tea in one gulp. Moisture beaded at the bottom of the glass, one cold drop jumping boldly onto his chest and sliding recklessly down his washboard stomach. He didn't seem to notice.

"May I come in?" she finally asked, her voice slightly breathless. "Just for a minute or two," she thought to add.

He studied her with dark eyes. Then finally, he stepped aside. Even so, her shoulders brushed his bare chest as she stepped into the cramped corners of what was meant to be a storage shed.

Given the short notice, he and Cagney had done a good job. The table saw rested in the middle of the shed, while the walls held the additional tools. Overhead, they'd strung three extension lights up on nails. While they didn't give off the strongest illumination, they could easily be moved to focus on whatever particular tool he'd selected. Everything was powered through heavy-duty extension cords running to the outside outlets of the house.

At the moment, Garret appeared to be edging two semi-circles. With a nervous hand, Suzanne ran one finger along the first circle's smooth, beveled edge.

"A table?" she guessed. Behind her, he nodded, setting the empty glass down on the nearest surface. As she turned, he hefted up the semicircle and clamped it onto a side table. Almost as a secondary thought, he replaced the yellowed goggles over his eyes.

"Stand back," he said tersely. She obliged quickly, holding one hand over her glass of iced tea. Still, she jumped when he flipped the router on. For the first time, she noticed the penciled line curving a two-inch border along the wood. He followed the line now with the router, moving with a slow and steady patience she wouldn't have associated with him.

Wood shavings curled up and around the thin router blade, filling the air with the sharp hot odor of fresh-cut wood. Garret's right arm bulged as he steadied and guided the tool along the groove, sweat beading up and trickling down his back, staining the white patch of his bandage. Her eyes followed every shimmering drop, the scent of sawdust and sweat filling her nose and tightening her stomach. She had to curl her hands around her slippery glass to keep from reaching out and following one of those tracks with her finger.

Garret snapped off the router and examined his work with a critical eye.

"Did...did you help your dad out in the shop often?" she finally asked. He didn't even turn and look at her.

"Some."

"What's the groove for?" she tried asking again.

"Decoration. I thought I'd hammer in beading, maybe a black walnut."

"That sounds nice."

Again, only the nod.

"Garret? What's wrong?"

His hand stilled on the wood, then slowly resumed its tracing of the quarter-inch groove. "Why, Suzanne? Looking for another soul to save?"

"Maybe." She kept her chin up, refusing to be put off by his apparent surliness. Every time she offered, his answer was the same. Seemed like after all these years, Garret still liked to play the lone rebel.

"Well, don't worry about mine," he said expressionlessly. "I'm sure there's a special place reserved just for SEALs, one filled with guns and booze and big-breasted women." He could almost feel her lips thinning into that disapproving line behind his back, but he didn't retract his words. The more she understood the type of man he was, he thought grimly, the better. He kept his eyes on his work and his concentration on keeping his hands steady. His back hurt like bloody hell, and if he wasn't careful, more stray memories flashed through his mind like stark black-and-white news photos. He could almost imagine reading the captions.

Innocent woman brutally slain.

Women and children killed in senseless slaughter.

In Sarajevo, the savagery continues . . .

"Garret—"

"Get out, Suzanne."

"No, darn it, I won't. Garret, I'm your friend."

He turned swiftly, slamming the wood down and causing her to jump at the sharp, ringing noise. He pinned her with eyes that were suddenly filled with a black, unholy rage.

"Friend? Why, Suzanne, why the hell be my friend? What the hell is in it for you?"

She swallowed hard, the glass of tea trembling in her hands. "Friendship isn't about that," she whispered.

He gave her a look of disgust. "You really are so provincial," he sneered. "You still think you can take care of everyone, don't you? Don't you, Suzanne?"

"No."

But he didn't seem to hear her quiet denial. "You can't, you know. You can't save anyone, and you can't save me. You women are all caught up on redemption. The worse the man, the more you want him. Well, I'm not looking for redemption, Suzanne, and I'm not one more of your little pet projects. Stick to your students and your sister. Leave me the hell alone."

"What did you remember?"

"Damn it, I didn't remember a thing!"

"What did you remember, Garret?"

Suddenly, he grabbed her glass and threw it against the door. Crystal shards and amber pearls of tea sprayed across the wall, streaking over her skirt. "Nothing. Get out."

"Garret—"

"I remembered nothing!"

"You remembered something!"

"Damn you, Suzanne. Damn you." And without warning, before she could move, he grabbed her trembling arm and wrenched her against his granite form. His mouth came down, fierce and bold and angry. He crushed her lips, splitting their tender fullness with his power. She pushed against the solid wall of his chest, but it was like arguing with concrete. His sweat mixed with her blood, stinging her lips and bringing tears of fright and pain to her eyes.

Then just as abruptly, he drew back and practically pushed her from him. She barely caught the wall to hold herself up, then slid down trembling from shock.

"Just stay away from me, okay?" he grated, his breath ragged, his eyes hard. "I leave in the morning, okay? Just give me until then."

Slowly, she pulled herself up using the wall. Her legs felt weak and watery, and her hair was tumbling down around her face. She looked at him with wary eyes and dragged in a deep, shuddering breath. Tentatively, she touched one finger to her lip and brought it away to see the blood. His eyes followed the movement, his hands clenching at his side when he saw the damage he'd done.

Her round hazel eyes met his dark, condemned gaze. This was Garret, who never liked to see girls cry, she reminded herself. This was Garret, who took on Tank Nemeth for her and her sister. This was Garret, who never liked to admit to needing anyone.

She pushed herself away from the wall. And before he could stop her, she stood on tiptoe and wrapped her arms around his neck, pressing herself fully against his hot, sweaty length. "It's okay, sweetheart," she whispered into his ear. "It's all okay now."

And then he was trembling in her arms, his large hands clutching her back as if she was the only shelter from the storm. He pressed his head against her hair, and she felt another shudder rack his granite frame.

With soft, soothing words, she rocked him in her arms, her hands combing through the ends of his hair. She felt beads of moisture fall against her cheek, tangy and salty. And from somewhere low in his throat came the soft, lonely cry of a man's anguish.

He tipped her head up, seeking to find her lips with his own. The kiss was no longer harsh or forceful; instead, his tongue plundered her mouth with aching need and desperate hunger. He soothed her cracked lip with his tongue, then delved deep into her mouth once more. She arched back, clinging to his shoulders and returning his kiss just as passionately. The slow, skillful seduction was gone, and she responded far more wildly to his raw, shuddering need.

He hoisted her up onto the saw table, and she let him, her mouth still pressed against his own. He pushed her crushed-silk skirt up to her thighs, then wrapped her legs around his waist. It positioned her hips intimately against the hot bulge of his jeans, and she rubbed against him instinctively.

He kissed her deeper, streaking her cheeks with sweat and tears. And still she didn't protest, only held him tighter. Her hair fell completely free, his large hands burying themselves in the fine strands. He combed through them as if they were as thick and luxurious as sable, and she felt her throat burn. He needed her. Garret Guiness needed her.

She wrapped her tongue around his own, drawing him into her mouth and reveling in the tangy taste of salt and sawdust. His hands clutched her shoulders, and he rotated his hips suggestively. She thought she might spontaneously combust.

He trailed kisses down her throat, and now he was the one whispering soft words of encouragement. His head slipped down, his silky, damp hair brushing against her chin as his tongue dipped between the valley of her breasts. She arched her back, knowing already where she wanted his lips, where she needed his touch. He pulled down the scoop neckline of her blouse, freeing her breast. Slowly, almost tenderly, he drew the nipple between his lips and sucked hard.

She cried out, her legs tightening fiercely around his hips as ribbons of desire spiraled all the way down and exploded deep within her. He sucked again, laving the rigid nipple with his tongue and lips until her blood roared wildly in a maelstrom of sensation.

She whimpered low in her throat and felt his thick words of encouragement against her neck. Her hands gripped his forearms, drawing upon his strength. She splayed her fingers across his chest, reveling in the hard contours and rippling muscles. Experimentally, she drew her hands down and felt him suck in breath. For a long moment, her hands lingered at the edge of his jeans, wanting and suddenly afraid of the need.

"Please," he whispered hoarsely, his lips suddenly stilled against her cheek. "Suzanne..."

Her fingers slid over the stiffness of new denim and pressed around his rigid length. He arched against her touch, and she felt the first rush of sensuous power.

But then his fingers drifted up the inside of her thighs, drawing heated little circles as he went. Breathless, she stiffened, suddenly unsure. His forefinger reached her damp panties and rubbed hard.

Her back bowed unconsciously, her hips arching to meet his touch. Her breath caught in her throat, and she could no longer breathe. The intensity was overwhelming, the need washing over her like a thunderous wave.

And all of a sudden, she was frightened. She could feel the burning outline of him against her hand, powerful and large. And his fingers moved against her, experienced and knowing, like a musician playing an intimately familiar tune. But she didn't know the music and she didn't know the chords.

He was the one who traveled with three condoms in his wallet, and he was the one who obviously knew more about the female body than she herself had even guessed. For him, the knowledge was a tiny part of the universe he roamed. For her, it was everything.

And she just couldn't bear to give him so much. Not when, for him, the need would end with the moment, while for her it would go on for all the lonely nights and endless years to come. And this time, he wouldn't even be whispering "Someday" under the soft cover of rain.

She pushed at his chest with one powerful surge, catching him off guard.

"I can't," she gasped out. "I just can't."

He reached for her, but she was already scrambling down from the table, half-tripping as she tugged at her skirt and blouse.

"Suzanne…" he tried to say, but the words were too thick in his throat. She caught his eyes, black and glittering with raw need, while the sweat and sawdust streaked down his cheeks.

He made another attempt to hold her but she simply couldn't bear the pain. She grabbed the door and thrust it open upon the sultry July dusk.

She fled toward the house and never looked back at the wordless hunger in his eyes.

Upstairs, she stripped off yet another ruined skirt and blouse, figuring if her emotional wreckage wasn't enough, she should at least consider Garret's impact on her dry-cleaning bill. But the watery smile the thought brought to her lips still wasn't enough for comfort.

She took a long shower, scouring her skin as if that would remove all traces of his touch. But the pounding spray only tortured her swollen breasts and overwrought nerves. In the end, she shut off the old faucets with more force than necessary, cursing Garret Guiness under her breath.

She should have just left him on her porch half-dead a week ago. All he'd ever brought her were fragile hopes that died bitter deaths, and she was too old to need him to beat up Tank Nemeth anymore. These days, she fought her own battles.

But as she drifted through her closet, trying to find something new to wear, she wondered how many of the wars she'd actually won.

She still lived in the same house she'd grown up in. Still fell asleep in the same room, with the same hand-sewn comforter, looking at the same white cotton curtains. She could follow the years of her life in the tiny notches she and Rachel had made in her old dresser until they'd finally outgrown it completely.

Rachel's room still remained untouched and waiting for a homecoming that would never happen. Down the hall, her mother's room was also the same, except empty gin bottles no longer neatly lined the closet.

She'd grown up trying to save her mother and, in the end, could only hold her hand and listen to her soft groans as she lay dying. Now she stockpiled money on the off chance her sister might actually leave the lout who was her husband. And she taught other people's children, counseled other married people and assisted with other people's lives.

And for what?

She found no answers in her closet, just a long line of dresses. Well, at least her taste in clothing had improved. Her lips twisted wryly as she pulled on a simple cotton dress, the yellow-and-green flowered fabric flowing gently over her rounded form. She walked back into the bathroom to blow-dry her hair, but found herself staring at the woman in the mirror instead.

She was thirty-two years old now. There were lines crinkling the corners of her eyes, and fifteen pounds around her hips that she'd always meant to lose but never quite had the incentive. She was growing old, she thought suddenly, and she was growing lonely.

She lived by herself in a seven-bedroom house she would one day leave to the church because her sister would never come back to Maddensfield, and there were no other Montgomerys left.

She collected dolls for a daughter she would never have and slept alone in a bed that had never seen company.

What had ever happened to all those dreams she'd had so long ago? When had all the days suddenly rolled into months, and the months into years? She'd thought that after her mother died, she would work on her personal life. But then, money was so tight she'd had to work three jobs to survive the medical bankruptcy. And somehow, time had just slipped away, each year turning into another year. Until she was no longer young and fresh and spirited. She became a serious, practical, efficient woman. And the town spinster.

She rested heavily against the sink, feeling her heart thunder suddenly in her chest. And she knew what she was going to do.

She wanted her moment. She wanted one moment of selfishness, one moment to know all the things other people whispered of. She wanted the intensity; she wanted the passion. She wanted Garret's lips on her own, his fingers running down her body and making her feel all the things she'd never felt before. She knew he wanted her, and after all these years, she knew she still wanted him. Who better to give her her moment than a man who traveled with three condoms in his wallet?

Her hands clenched and unclenched the folds of her skirt while she let the thought take hold.

Garret still wouldn't stay. She needed to remember that. But she wasn't sixteen anymore, and she didn't whisper silly words in the rain. What she wanted from him was his experience. It would be an even transaction, a sharing of mutual desire and satisfaction.

Once more, practical. She felt a wry smile twist her lips and wondered at the sudden burning in her throat.

There were so many things about herself she would never tell him. So many nights so long ago when she'd needed him and he hadn't been there. So many dreams he'd started, never to come back to fulfill. So many times she'd lain dry-eyed in her bed and wondered if the loneliness ever got any easier to bear.

So many moments when she'd looked at him and known that she loved him.

She took a deep breath and willed the tightness away. She wasn't a silly girl anymore; now she looked at the world with a woman's eyes. She didn't need a hero. She just wanted a couple of warm days and passionate nights. Time taught compromise.

She reached for the dusty compact of forgotten eye shadow and felt her hand begin to tremble.

* * *

When she walked down the stairs thirty minutes later, she thought her intentions must show in her face. She'd spent far too long on her hair, trying valiantly to style it to reflect some sort of glamour. In the end, she'd settled for a loose French braid, and she could already feel the fine strands slipping free. But after a few false starts, she'd managed to highlight her eyes nicely with the soft brown eye shadow. An additional touch of green emphasized the golden flecks in her hazel eyes.

Now, she simply held in her stomach, wondered if she'd dabbed on too much perfume and tried to keep a smile on her face.

She stopped in front of his bedroom door and took a last, deep breath. She raised her hand and rapped gently. The door flew open, and her smile froze.

"What?" he growled. His hair was damp from his own shower, and she could smell the fresh, tantalizing fragrance of soap and shampoo. Once again, his shirt hung unbuttoned, revealing the crispy black mat of his chest hair.

"Hungry?" she ventured softly.

His black eyes raked up and down her figure, lingering for a moment on her new hairstyle. "What are you offering?" he asked, his voice low.

Coffee, tea or me, her mind singsonged. "S-steak," she stammered out instead. Her hands crushed her skirt.

He nodded curtly, but his eyes remained considerately on her face. "All right. Anything I can do to help?"

She shook her head. If she had to move around with him in the kitchen, she'd lose her nerve completely. She was beginning to wish she could serve wine with dinner to loosen herself up, except she didn't buy alcohol. Ever.

"Forty-five minutes?" she suggested, her gaze falling down onto his chest until she caught herself at the last minute and forced it up.

"Fine."

"Fine."

She stood there a minute longer, her nerves wound tighter than she'd ever anticipated. Kindergarten teachers didn't receive training in slow seduction. She took another deep breath.

"I'll go fix dinner now," she announced. He looked at her strangely and nodded. "Okay," she said.

"Okay," he replied.

She turned and marched back down the hall to the safety of her kitchen. More of her hair slid free to wrap around her cheek.

She put on the potatoes, prepared the steaks for broiling and readied a tossed salad while they cooked. At the last moment, she realized she didn't have anything for dessert, then remembered the raspberries they'd picked. She also recalled the way he'd plucked the raspberry from her fingers with his teeth. And the way his mouth had felt on her breast.

She whipped up some fresh cream, layering it with the raspberries in a simple parfait, hoping the berries might bring back memories for Garret, as well. Her stomach began to tighten with anticipation, and her hands shook as she set the old, warped dining room table.

At the last moment, she lit two slender vanilla candles, lending the room a soft, mysterious glow and adding a final, delicate fragrance. She took another deep breath and pressed her hand against her stomach as she looked at her old dining room suddenly transformed into an intimate scene for two.

She could do this.

She would do this.

The timer went off in the kitchen, and she retrieved the steaks. She was just pulling them out of the oven when Garret walked into the kitchen.

"Are we ready?"

Probably not. "Yes."

"Is there something I can do?"

Toss me over your shoulder, carry me upstairs and make me forget my own name. "Salad's ready for the table."

"Got it. Anything else?"

Kiss me. Please. "No, that's all."

He disappeared into the dining room, and she dragged in a deep lungful of air and resolutely squared her shoulders. She put the steaks and mashed potatoes on serving plates and marched into the dining room.

They sat down and, after a short, awkward silence, began passing the food between themselves. Garret didn't say much as he forked the larger steak and placed it on his plate. He simply watched her intensely, while her nerves bunched tighter and tighter.

She didn't eat during dinner. She moved the food around on her plate and watched him. The way he moved, the way he ate. The way his foot tapped restlessly throughout the whole meal. The way his partially unbuttoned shirt revealed the sprinkling of dark black hair waiting to be touched.

She'd run her fingers through that hair, flatten her palms against that chest. She'd press her lips against his throat and taste his salty, tangy skin.

He sat back at last, taking a long, finishing sip of iced tea. His gaze went to the candles and then to her plate of carefully cut and completely rearranged food. But still he didn't say anything.

"I made dessert," she whispered. His dark eyes rested on her flushed cheeks, and he nodded.

The plates trembled in her hands when she picked them up, but she managed not to drop anything. At the last minute, he stopped her with a hand on her arm. He looked her straight in the eye. "It's okay," he said quietly. "There's no need to be so nervous."

She nodded, but her hands shook harder at his words. In the kitchen, she dropped all the dishes in the sink and braced herself against the counter. She closed her eyes and took one last deep breath. This was what she wanted. With Garret. Garret, who filled her with fire.

She reached into the refrigerator and took out a single parfait. Then she walked back to the dining room. She froze in the archway, looking at the candlelight flicker over the high ceiling, her doll cabinet, her old, warped table.

She moved into the room, and each footstep seeming like a mile, walked over to where he sat. Her hands trembled on the parfait and her face was pale. But his dark gaze held her own and that gave her strength. Slowly, she swung one leg over his chair and sat down intimately on his lap.

For the first time, she allowed a small smile to tremble around the corners of her mouth. She held up the parfait, her hazel eyes shiny and beguiling by candlelight. "I brought you dessert," she said quietly.

His eyes never left her face. "You're beautiful," he whispered. Carefully, his hands closed around her waist and shifted her just enough to let her know her effect on him. She gasped softly, and color flushed her cheeks. But she didn't move away.

Instead, she dipped one finger into the parfait and scooped up a swirl of fresh cream and ripe raspberries. Then, delicately, she offered it to him. "Raspberries?" she asked.

He chuckled with delight. "My favorite," he assured her, and closed his lips around her finger. He sucked slow and deep, his tongue swirling around her finger. She shivered, and his eyes glowed his encouragement.

She removed her finger from his mouth and dipped it once more into the cool parfait. This time, she popped her finger between her own pursed lips, licking the last of the cream from her fingertip with meaningful deliberation. Garret's eyes flashed dark fire and narrowed intently.

He took the parfait from her grasp and set it on the table. His large hands smoothed up her back, his thumbs brushing the sides of her breasts. She watched him with tawny eyes, her breath heavy with the anticipation. Then slowly, he drew the rubber band from her braid and freed the delicate, silky strands of her hair. With his thumb, he followed the curve of her cheek, the elegant column of her neck.

And then he drew her forward and kissed her softly on the lips. "Tell me, Suzanne," he whispered against her skin, finding the indent of her lips with his tongue. "Tell me what you want."

"Need," she sighed, arching against his touch. He smiled, masculine and sure.

"So we're back to need." He kissed the other corner of her mouth, then the throbbing pulse at the base of her throat. "Then tell me what you need, sweetheart. I want to hear it from your lips."

"Make..." She had to moisten her lips, the words catching in her throat. She looked at him again, her eyes already molten gold and heavy lidded. "Make love to me, Garret. Please."

His lips consumed hers, his tongue plunging into her mouth, deep and slow and promising. He nipped her ear, her neck, then buried his face between her breasts, breathing in the warm, seductive scent of roses. Taking his time, he moved his head and tongued her nipple through the thin fabric of her dress.

She cried out at the electric touch, arching against him, her hands tightening fiercely on his shoulders.

He raised his head, his own eyes heavy and glittering with desire.

"Shall I take you upstairs?" he asked thickly.

She nodded, her arms tightening around him.

"No regrets?"

"No regrets," she agreed.

He swung her up into his arms, rising from the table and heading for the stairs. "Remember that, sweetheart. Remember that."

Chapter 8

Upstairs, Suzanne looked at the stark simplicity of her room, her virginal bed and childhood curtains, and knew a moment of uncertainty. But then Garret's mouth was upon her own, his lips sure and knowing, his tongue delving and plunging with a master's touch. He stoked fires deep down in her belly and ignited fantasies far more primal than an adolescent's dream.

She squeezed her eyes shut and trusted herself to this man she'd selected more than fifteen years ago.

His large hands smoothed down her sides, his thumbs curving over her breasts, around her hips. She shifted from side to side with restlessness, feeling at once voluptuous and empty. She wanted more, needed more, from him.

Her hands combed through his hair impatiently, her palm rasping over the shadow of his beard. Suddenly, she kissed him fiercely, earning a low chuckle from his throat.

"Easy, sweetheart. We have all night."

Her eyes narrowed at the smoothness of his words and she pressed the palm of her other hand against his rigid outline. His chuckle ended in a low moan, his hips arching against her touch, and she felt a measure of satisfaction. She didn't want to burn alone.

His fingers skimmed down her back, quickly finding and releasing the tie at her waist. Holding her hands above her head, she let him strip her dress up and off to lie in a puddle on the floor. The warm night wrapped around her, soft and sultry like velvet. For a long, burning moment, his gaze simply drank in her rounded form clad only in a thin pink slip, his dark eyes gleaming and honest with desire.

"You are so beautiful," he whispered hoarsely. She blushed all the way to her toes and thought again of the fifteen pounds she'd really meant to lose. But the minute she tried to cover herself, he grabbed her hand.

"No. Don't. Just trust me on this."

She wanted to. She wanted to be beautiful to him. She wanted him to look at her and feel the same hot, maddening desire that flared in her own blood every time she looked at him. But he was a purely, primal creation, muscles as well-defined and rippling as those carved on Greek statues. She reached out a trembling hand and ran it down his clothed arm with wide, guileless eyes. In response, he slowly began unbuttoning his shirt.

Her eyes drifted up to find his own hungry ones, and the passion in his gaze was unmistakable. She reached forward and slid his open shirt from his shoulders. His hands closed around her waist and jerked her against him. With a sigh, she relented, wrapping her long arms around his shoulders and arching her neck for his kiss.

His belt dug against the soft skin of her belly, but she didn't care. She just wanted his tongue, plunging and probing her mouth with luscious promise. She reveled in the taste of raspberries and fresh cream mixing with the dark, masculine taste that was purely Garret's alone. She felt his hands in her hair, his shadowed cheeks burning against her own, his iron chest flattening her breasts.

One hand scooped down to her knees, and he lifted her up a second time, carrying her over to the bed.

He set her down carefully on the mattress as if she was something precious and dear. She allowed herself to feel that way because this was the moment when she could be all the things she never would be by the light of day. So when his eyes caressed her figure once more, sliding down the sleek length of her pink slip, she didn't try to cover herself. She simply watched him with trusting eyes and took pleasure in the desire tightening his jaw.

He bent over her and kissed her lips lightly. Then he trailed his lips lower, finding the sweet curve of her neck as she sighed and arched up. His head drifted lower still, his tongue making languorous circles as he dipped between her breasts and inhaled the soft, delicate scent of roses.

He pushed down the slender straps of her slip with large hands just beginning to tremble. She lifted her hips willingly, and the slip slid off the side of the bed to the floor. Taking a deep breath, she reached up and unfastened his belt buckle with shaking fingers. The belt slithered down and landed with a soft thud.

Her hands rested on the waistband of his jeans; she could feel his heat just inches from her fingers. But at the last minute, she just couldn't. He was so large and so powerful, and she knew it was going to hurt just as she knew that the pain was also part of the experience. She closed her eyes, a tremor running through her, and wished he would kiss her again so she'd feel only the hunger and none of the dread for what had to come.

As if he was reading her mind, his warm palm cupped her cotton-covered breast and his thumb rasped across her nipple. She gasped, her muscles instantly melting and arching against the sensation. His thumb moved again, sending bolts of desire firing down into her belly. Then he lowered his head and took the turgid nipple into his mouth.

She moaned helplessly, tangling her hands into his silky black hair and pressing him closer. He pulled down her bra, finding and suckling her exposed nipple with exquisite hunger. Then he raised a hand to her mouth, and as he suddenly sucked hard, she sank her teeth into his thumb.

The bed sagged as he abruptly rolled onto it, then carried her up and onto his chest. His tongue plunged into her mouth, its exploration no longer gentle and probing, but fierce and explicit about his desire. His hips arched and rocked against her scantily clad core, making her gasp and moan. She ran her fingers down his arm, raking him lightly with her nails, and was rewarded with a devilish groan.

"You like to play tough, huh?" he teased gruffly. His eyes narrowing, he nipped at her neck, taking the tender skin between his teeth and sucking delicately. She arched her back and shivered against him.

Her bra disappeared, freeing her breasts so he could cup and roll them in his hands, bring the nipples to his lips and suckle them fiercely, then feel her hips twist and churn with restless anticipation. Then, to be sure, he slid a hand into her panties and cupped her intimately.

She whimpered low in her throat and his blood boiled.

Slowly, almost leisurely, he slid a single finger into her warm, wet core. She went wild against him, writhing at his touch, gasping against his throat. She had never wanted anything as much as she wanted this, never thought she could feel such fierceness.

His finger moved slow and steady inside her, and the tension built and built until her teeth sank into her lower lip and her neck strained with the gasping need.

"Give me a second, sweetheart," Garret groaned, his voice so thick she barely recognized it.

He rolled from her in one swift motion, rising up until she almost cried out her loss. But then as she watched, he stood before her and unfastened his jeans, pulling the uncomfortable fabric from his lean, sculpted legs until he stood before her, naked and powerful. With a low, muttered oath, he wrestled with the pocket of his jeans, finally producing his wallet and withdrawing a condom. Her eyes widening, she watched him roll it on, her body still trembling, her mind finally registering what was about to happen.

For long seconds, she simply stared and willed herself to swallow.

He was huge. Powerful, formidable, made of granite. He was going to rip her in half. How could he not? Unconsciously, she crushed the folds of the quilt in her hands.

Slowly, she forced her gaze up and met his hungry, passionate stare. This was Garret, the man who'd never liked to see girls cry. The man who'd taken on Tank Nemeth just for her. This was Garret.

She held out her arms.

His knee settled between her legs, and she opened them accordingly, accepting what was to come as her choice and her will. She wrapped her arms around his shoulders, closing her eyes as her panties slid to the floor. Her body stiffened, and at any minute, she expected to feel a horrible, renting pain. His fingers brushed through her curls and her hips jerked unconsciously. Then his thumb rubbed against her, and warmth flooded through her once more.

He made small, soothing circles that forced low, needful moans from her throat. The mattress shifted, and this time she wrapped her legs around his waist and offered herself completely to him. He kissed her deeply, and just as his tongue mated with her mouth, he plunged into her.

He knew instantly he'd done something wrong. Her whole body went rigid, her teeth sinking into his shoulder. She wasn't just tight, she was *tight*. All of a sudden, he knew. Damn, he'd expected her to be fairly inexperienced, but a virgin? A thirty-two-year-old virgin?

"Suzanne," he groaned, feeling at once helpless and on fire. His desire-soaked mind sought desperately what to do, while his body moved without his consent, seeking satisfaction, needing coupling. She shifted uncomfortably beneath him, and that only made matters worse. "Suzanne," he urged, his voice thick, his throat choked, "don't move, okay? Just don't move."

"No," she told him simply, and experimentally rotated her hips. Pain rocketed through her, but it wasn't as bad as before. Now, it was merely uncomfortable. She felt Garret shudder above her with the force of his need and held on to him all the more tightly. Once more, she moved.

He groaned, losing the war and hating himself for his defeat. He tried to be slow and gentle; he tried to make something of it for her. But her body was so tender and his passion so fierce. He buried his face in her neck, breathing in the scent of roses, and felt the satisfaction rip through him like a raging river.

He poured into her and felt her hands soothe down his back.

"It's all right," she whispered. "It's all right."

Afterward, he rolled off her and lay on his back, while she curled at his side, her legs coming together instinctively. She could still hear his ragged breath, still feel the ache between her legs, but more than all that, she was aware of the tension that still radiated between them. Suddenly, with a muttered curse, Garret shot off the bed and strode angrily across the hardwood floor.

She watched him go without saying a word, but her eyes began to burn.

Moments later, however, he returned. The condom was gone, and now he held a wet washcloth in his hand. Without asking, he sat down beside her and slowly eased her legs apart. He pressed the warm washcloth against her and she flinched from the immediate sting.

"You should have told me," he said flatly. She risked a glance to find all the warmth gone from his eyes. Instead, the black depths registered a tight anger.

"It doesn't matter," she said simply. He eased the wash-cloth down the inside of her thighs and her cheeks flushed.

"The hell it doesn't," he informed her curtly. "If I'd known, I could've—"

"Could've what, Garret? Could have turned away? Could have said no?"

He glared at her darkly. "Could have made it better."

She shrugged, having to look away. He was sitting naked by her side as casually as if he was suited up for tea. He had a washcloth pressed against the most intimate part of her body while the rest of her sprawled naked across her bed. And they were arguing. It wasn't how she'd imagined the "moment after" to be.

Maybe she should have told him, but there were things she just didn't want him to know, little pieces of herself she needed to hold back. That way, when he left in the end, the pain wouldn't be so bad. If she'd told him, perhaps he wouldn't have made love to her. If she'd told him, perhaps he would have thought it was something special. And she would never admit that to him.

"It's done now," she said at last, forcing herself to meet his eyes. "It's okay. I knew it would hurt. It's just the way it is for a woman."

He looked at her for a long moment, his eyes unread-able, but his jaw still rigid.

"Why, Suzanne? Why now? Why me? You understand, of course, that as soon as I remember enough, I'll leave. I'm still a SEAL, you know."

Her throat tightened, but she didn't look away. "Of course, Garret."

He stood suddenly, the washcloth dangling from his hand while he paced the room with unconcealed tension. "You should have told me, damn it. You should have let me know." He turned and pinned her with burning eyes. "I deserved that much at least."

She sat up, and trying to be as subtle as possible, began folding the old quilt up and over her naked figure. "I wanted you, and you wanted me. We made love. I didn't realize you wanted a narration in between."

He swore, hating the anger and confusion that gripped him. Mostly because she was partly right. If he'd known from the start she was a virgin, he definitely wouldn't have continued. Men like him didn't seduce virgins. Maybe because he was old-fashioned enough to believe the first time should be special, with someone who cared, with someone who would be around. Certainly she shouldn't have lost it to someone who was just passing through.

Standing naked in the middle of the room, he ran a hand through his hair, feeling uneasiness gnaw at his belly again. Why hadn't she told him? She'd just given him her virginity, something a woman could only give one man, one time. But she hadn't let him know. She hadn't let him truly get close to her.

He pivoted to face her, feeling angry and uncertain. "You should have told me," he said yet again. Then not knowing how else to explain the tightness in his chest, he turned sharply and stomped out of the room.

From under the cover of her old quilt, she watched him go, feeling a burning in her throat that matched the hollowness in her stomach. When she shifted her hips, she felt the new ache from the ancient act and had to squeeze her eyes shut with the intensity.

And she remembered the old saying, "When God punishes you, He answers your prayers."

He tossed amid the sheets, the thin white cotton tangling around his lean hips and muscled legs. Somewhere in the depths of sleep, old scars burned fresh and he writhed once more with pain.

* * *

Walking, the ax heavy in his hands. He neared the top of the hill, his footsteps slowing, dragging. He knew what lay waiting on the other side—unbearable sights of unimaginable savagery. He didn't want to look, he didn't want to see, but his feet carried him forward anyway.

The bodies, scattered across the ground like broken dolls. The ruins of the tents, smoking and black. The birds, circling overhead, guarding their gruesome feast.

A victim of his own dream, he had to walk through the scene of carnage time and time again, knowing already what he would find and that he was forever too late to halt the tragedy.

He kept walking through the ruins, the ax growing heavier and his chest squeezing tight. Until he was at the last tent and seeing her once more, her lifeless body cradled against Zlatko's brawny chest, her beautiful honey blond hair sweeping the ground.

Zlatko's hands that had torn wooden doors in half now tenderly brushed back his wife's hair. Shoulders that had once carried two full-grown men to safety now shook with the force of his grief. And from his cracked lips rose the heartrending keening of a tormented soul, wailing through the smoke-filled sky.

Garret looked at it all—the last stand by a bunch of peasants' wives, already chased to the edge of the city by the war. Here they'd tried to build a new camp amid the destruction. And here they'd died, alone and defenseless, while their men were off fighting the flames threatening to burn the city to the ground.

So much death, so much ruin.

He felt the rage inside him begin to grow. He wanted to find the men who slaughtered children. He wanted to corner each and every one of them and see the fear in their eyes as he personally demonstrated all the types of pain that could be inflicted upon a man.

The savagery grew, relentless and fierce. A warrior's blood, old as time, flowed strong and raw in his veins. He would find the butchers. He would hunt them down to the very ends of the earth. He would wrap his hands around their bare throats. He would make them pay for the blood spilling into the Miljaka River.

He awoke with a jolt, his breath still thundering in his chest, the anger still burning in his blood. The first rays of morning were peeking into the window, but he didn't notice. He just knew his hands were clenched at his sides, the adrenaline pounding loudly in his ears.

He had to go, he thought wildly, bolting upright. He hurtled out of the old bed and began throwing on his clothes. He had to go—today. He had to find whoever had done the slaughter and tear them apart with his bare hands. He wanted the satisfaction of slamming into fleshy faces with meaty fists. He wanted to hear the tearing of cartilage, the soft thud of hammered flesh.

The need, the savagery of it, was unbearable.

He slid his feet into shoes without putting on socks and, like a wild man, began buttoning his shirt. He grabbed the door when only halfway done, not caring anymore, and threw it open.

He ran face-to-face into Suzanne.

She came to an abrupt halt in the hallway, her face paling and her eyes growing wary as she self-consciously smoothed a hand over her walking clothes. He didn't say a word, but her gaze took in his burning eyes and haggard features, slid over his twisted shirt and sockless feet, and she knew.

Slowly, painfully, her eyes came back up to his face. "Would you like something to eat before you go?" she whispered softly, amazed by the calmness of her own voice. Her heart thudded unbearably in her chest, and for one horrible moment, the blood rushed from her head, leaving her dizzy and swaying.

Garret shook his head furiously, his fingers mangling his buttons. "I gotta go," he said hoarsely.

She looked at him sharply and, for the first time, noted the pallor of his skin, the sharp lines around his eyes. His dark hair was still rumpled and tousled. Long creases from the pillow marred his cheek.

Her gaze narrowed and she willed herself to take a deep breath. "Garret, if it's about last night—"

"I'm leaving," he growled. His fingers fumbled with the last button, then suddenly, with a vehement oath, he tore it from his shirt altogether and tossed it to the ground.

Her face paled; she closed her eyes and wondered for the tenth time why she'd allowed him back into her life. And why, oh, why, she'd ever thought she could just sleep with him and have it be that simple.

He twisted his shirt, trying to get the incorrectly buttoned cloth to hang straight revealing a purplish love bite on his shoulder. She had to look away. Even then, her eyes burned.

"You don't have to leave," she whispered, the words so hoarse she barely recognized them. She would not do this. She would not make a scene again. Damn it, hadn't she learned something all those years ago?

He gave up on straightening the shirt and began forcing the edges into his unbuttoned jeans instead. "Of course I have to go," he said curtly. "If they really thought they could get away with it . . . Damn it, where's my belt?"

His hands stopped suddenly and her cheeks turned crimson as she followed his thoughts. His belt still lay on her bedroom floor.

Slowly, his eyes rested on her cheeks, and for the first time, his frenzied movements calmed. He saw the shadows under her eyes, the tight line of her lips. All at once, though she didn't say anything, he understood how much he was hurting her.

He swore vehemently under his breath and wondered why the hell it wasn't raining. "Suzanne—" he began, but she cut him off.

"You don't have to explain," she said stiffly, her eyes refusing to meet his own. "We've always known that as soon as you healed ..." She shrugged, the motion at once feeble and vulnerable. "I just don't want you to go because of last night. That's all."

"I wouldn't leave because of that," he said quietly, his dark eyes resting on her face. "Damn it, Suzanne..." Once more he searched for the words and once more he cursed himself for never being able to express what he wanted to say. "Last night was special, Suzanne. At least, it should have been. You gave me your virginity. Hell, you can only do that once. But I didn't know. I couldn't...I couldn't make it right."

She blinked, feeling her throat tighten another inch. Because he had made it right. He'd made her feel things she'd never felt before: beautiful, desirable, feminine. He'd taught her how to kiss and be kissed, how to hold and be held. She'd waited fifteen years for last night, and she didn't care that it hurt. It was what she'd wanted it to be.

"Why...?" She had to stop and lick her dry lips. "Why are you leaving, then?"

His face grew somber, his jaw suddenly clenched. "I have to find the people who killed Zenaisa," he said simply.

Instantly, Suzanne stiffened, her hands curling into fists at her sides. Her gaze caught his warily. "Zenaisa?"

"Zlatko's wife. She held the camp together. She...she took care of people."

Slowly, Suzanne nodded, her fists relaxing slightly. "What camp, Garret? What people?"

For the first time, a puzzled frown creased his brow. "Sarajevo," he said at last. "We were in Sarajevo."

"Your team, then," Suzanne filled in, her eyes widening. He remembered. He finally remembered.

But the man in front of her was still frowning. He racked his brains, searching for Austin or C.J. or anyone at all that he should know. But he just saw Zlatko and Zenaisa and the broad Slavic faces of village people sitting around a fire. "Not the SEALs," he said finally, then shook his head. He was a SEAL, damn it. Of course there had to be SEALs. Assignments were done in teams of seven or fourteen. Where the hell was Austin?

Suzanne began to study him covertly, her face carefully composed. "Were you on a mission?" she probed quietly.

"Yes. No. I...I fought fires. The mortar shells were burning the city to the ground. The Olympic stadium, the government buildings. Everything." And there wasn't enough equipment and not enough time for proper training. He led the men into the flames, armed with axes and hoses, but unprotected from the heat and the snipers who whizzed bullets over their heads.

Why was he fighting fires? SEALs specialized in hostage rescue missions or deep reconnaissance behind enemy lines. Why the hell was he playing fireman?

"Garret," Suzanne said carefully, "you were shot in D.C. What can that have to do with fighting fires in Sarajevo? Perhaps you are just remembering something you once did or even heard of. Even I've read about John Jordan who's been leading some program to fight fires there."

Garret half nodded, puzzling over her words. John Jordan, Global Operation Fire Rescue Services. It sounded familiar; he understood the name and the program the Rhode Island native had started in Sarajevo. It was a seat-of-the-pants effort to help and to train the volunteers struggling to keep the city from burning to the ground.

He knew about it. Perhaps he'd once helped.

But then he saw Zlatko, felt the weight of the ax in his hands, and saw the ruins of the camp.

"The Miljaka," he whispered.

"What is that?" she probed calmly.

"The river. The river that runs through Sarajevo. And it was in the note, Suzanne. 'The waters of Miljaka still flow red.'" The ravaged camp, Zenaisa. He squeezed his eyes shut.

Suzanne watched him, slowly twisting the bottom of her T-shirt. She didn't know whether to go to him because he looked so stricken, or to run away because his memory was returning, and in a matter of hours, he could simply walk away.

Even last night, he'd reminded her that he couldn't stay. And she'd already given him the only thing she had to give.

"Garret," she said at last, willing her voice to be level, "even if the shooting was tied in with... this river... what does that mean?"

He shook his head, hating the gaps in his memory he couldn't quite fill. Why was he a fire fighter? Where was his SEAL team? How long had he been there? Would he really have deserted the SEALs? And why did the dread still sit low in his stomach? Did something worse still linger on the corners of his mind that he just couldn't grasp yet?

So many people dead. Such horror, and he didn't even understand why or what his role was. What if it had been his fault? What had he done to get himself shot in D.C.? And who had shot him?

He shook his head, pressing his palms against his temples while the questions swirled around with sickening uncertainty. "I don't know," he muttered in frustration. "I just don't know."

Suzanne took a deep breath and felt a small measure of control return. "Maybe you should give it a few more days," she suggested gently. "Until you know who's out there, you could be walking into some kind of trap. If things are starting to come back this fast now, just another day or two could make all the difference."

He scowled, but recognized the sense of her words. His body just rebelled at the thought of waiting even longer when the adrenaline in his blood already screamed for action. He flexed and unflexed his fingers, not able to get the pictures out of his mind. He was not a man who sat patiently. He was a man who did.

"Garret . . . ?"

"You're right," he snapped at last, whirling around in the hallway and staring down at his mangled shirt. His lips tight with annoyance, he pulled it out of his jeans and began to unbutton the twisted shirt and rebutton it properly. "A day or two, I suppose. To put it all together." He shook his head in frustration, his fists crushing the light cotton fabric.

Suzanne didn't say anything, feeling at once as if she'd won but lost anyway. So he wasn't leaving just this moment; she was only delaying the inevitable. His memory was returning, and now time poured through her hands again.

Unconsciously, she laced her fingers together. She'd told herself she would be strong; she'd told herself she wouldn't care. But she'd only had one night, damn it. And there was so much more she wanted. . . .

So many more days she wanted to keep him.

She turned away and walked into the kitchen before she made a total fool of herself. After his anger last night, he probably didn't want anything more to do with her. She wouldn't ask again.

She wasn't sixteen. She didn't whisper words in the rain and she absolutely, positively, would not miss Garret Guiness this time.

But somehow, she'd thought she'd have more than just one night.

Chapter 9

The high-pitched squeal of the router cut at last through his reverie. With a start, Garret realized he was holding the tool with one hand while the table leg remained untouched in its clamp. He shook his head, frowning, and turned his attention back to cutting a mortise in the top of the table leg for the mortise-and-tenon joint. He was supposed to be finishing the table, damn it, not woolgathering.

He adjusted the goggles over his eyes and managed to make a rough mortise with the router. Then he sanded out the cut until it was smooth, forming a tight fit for the tenon. One down, three to go.

He shook his head again. He should be done with the joints by now; he just wasn't concentrating well. His head filled too easily with scenes he didn't want to know. Too many times he saw the destruction. Too many times he saw Zenaisa and Zlatko and the others.

But he was no closer to understanding any of it. If anything, he fought the memories. Because the dread still lingered low in his stomach, and somewhere deep inside, he understood he wouldn't like what was to come.

Something terrible had happened. Something that had taken place outside a war-torn city and had followed him all the way to D.C. Something that had earned him a bullet in the back.

He found himself staring blankly at the router yet again and clenched his jaw in frustration.

Just focus on the table. The beautiful wood, the smell of sawdust and the buzzing hum. He cut out the second mortise.

The table was decent, but not everything he'd originally wanted it to be. He'd stuck with a simple pattern for the legs, not wanting to spend too much time at the lathe. He really wanted to finish the table today.

Finish it up, sand it down and stain it quickly with a water-based stain. After dinner, maybe he could present it to Suzanne, his small token for her generosity.

It seemed like the least he could do.

He moved on to mortise number three. He actually liked the work more than he'd expected. There was something simple and elemental about the feel of finely grained hardwood in his hand and the rich, warm scent of sawdust filling his nose. He liked watching the pieces come together. He liked the clean elegance of the design and found pleasure and satisfaction in seeing his own work develop. He was beginning to understand how his father could spend a whole life in a wood shop.

But even so, there was no adrenaline surge in making a table. No heated rush of right now at this microsecond of time in this place this act must happen or everything will fail. And exactly at the right instant, the roar in his ears, the thunder in his blood, his chute might rip open into the cloud-choked night or his MP-5 might explode with a clean burst of three shots.

Those were the moments that filled his blood with fire and sparked his dark eyes. Those were the challenges he lived for. He didn't look for simple pleasures or quiet moments. He lived to act, to master, to combat.

And right now, just waiting was beginning to get to him.

If he could only make all the pieces of his memory come together . . .

If he could only stop remembering Suzanne's pale face when he said he was leaving . . .

He shifted restlessly, feeling the uncertainty and doubt inexplicably swirl in his gut. He needed to get going, he thought with near savagery, forcing the last table leg into the clamp with more pressure than was necessary. Memory or not, he needed to move to figure out Step Two in his plan.

He adjusted his goggles, and resolutely blanking his mind, cut the last mortise.

When Suzanne walked out onto the back porch a little before eight, she found him on his hands and knees in front of a newly assembled table, staining a leg. For a long moment, she simply looked at his back while he brought the brush down with a smooth, steady stroke.

He'd put newspaper under the table and rigged some sheets along the open sides of the porch to enclose his work area on at least three sides.

"Looks like it's nearly done," she said at last, squinting at the piece in the failing light. She reached over and snapped on the bright porch light.

His brush paused, then resumed its work.

"I was hoping you wouldn't be out for another fifteen minutes or so," he said.

She shrugged, sticking her hands into her skirt pockets and admiring her white sandals as if she had no place else to look. "Well, I guess I can go back inside if you'd like."

"No. I just didn't want you to see it until it was done."

His brush completed its last stroke. With a small grunt, he rose to tower over the small oval table. He'd used a light, red-toned varnish to complement the cherry wood, and the table, rich and glistening, gleamed under the porch light. A thin seam of black walnut circled the table in a simple but effective design.

Still, Suzanne didn't say anything, and finally he looked at her with impatient eyes. "I know it isn't much, but I made it for you, you know. As a thank-you."

Her eyes widened, then slowly she nodded as she walked around the piece. Maybe he didn't think much of it, but it looked beautiful to her. The four legs were gracefully rounded, the tabletop shiny and elegant with its black beading. Certainly it looked better than anything she currently owned. She didn't even have chairs that would do it justice. On impulse, she reached out to touch the small treasure, then realized the varnish would still be wet. She pulled her hand back to her side.

"You must have learned a lot from your father." Her voice sounded quiet and thick.

Garret stared at her, shifting from side to side. He looked back at the table, then at her again. Well, he knew it wasn't a masterpiece, but hell, he'd thought it was worth more comment than that.

"I just wanted to thank you," he grated, gesturing to the table almost in dismissal. "For putting me up and everything. You know. You don't have to use it or anything. Hell, I don't even have time left to make some chairs."

She looked at him sharply. "A parting gift, then?"

He shrugged. "It's whatever you want it to be," he said at last. It must not have been the right thing to say, because her lips thinned into that narrow line he knew too well.

"Dinner's ready," she said shortly. She turned sharply, and not knowing what else to do, he followed her back into the house.

The tension remained through dinner, however. Suzanne seemed hell-bent on not saying a word, and for once, the silence bothered him. She wasn't happy with him; he was astute enough to realize that. Maybe what he hadn't anticipated was the fact he wasn't happy with himself, either.

His stomach kept knotting, the uncomfortable silence building. He liked it better when she fought with him. And he definitely preferred the seducing. Now, she just seemed uptight and withdrawn.

A lot of women had looked at him like that before. A lot of women had tried sobbing or arguing or carrying on at the last minute when they realized he really was going to leave. It never bothered him, because he was a man who spelled things out in the beginning and made sure the message remained consistent. If they wanted to try to manipulate him with tears or silent treatments, that was their prerogative but he didn't let it affect him. He always knew where he was going, and he always knew what he was doing.

So Suzanne's behavior shouldn't mean a thing. Except...except he couldn't imagine her ever begging him to stay, and he couldn't imagine her ever trying to manipulate him. Instead, it seemed as if her withdrawal worked to distance him before he even had a chance to leave.

He'd once made the assumption that she was simple and guileless; he was beginning to realize that he was wrong. In the end, she might be much better at holding things back than he was himself.

Hell, he hadn't even realized she was a virgin.

He found himself frowning again and rose to collect the dishes instead. Suzanne never said a word.

After dinner, he followed her onto the back porch, a glass of minted iced tea in hand. She didn't invite him, but he was feeling perverse. When she sat down on the first step and leaned back to look at the clear canopy of stars, he simply followed suit.

"Nice night," he said at last.

She nodded, sipping from her tea. "Nights and mornings are about the only bearable times during July." She fanned her face with one hand, the little wisps of hair framing her cheeks scattering nicely. "Even then, it's hotter than hell."

"Still, you've got to love the sound of crickets and the scent of roses in the North Carolina air."

She looked at him sideways with speculative hazel eyes. "You ever miss home, Garret? You ever think of Maddensfield when you're off playing your war games?"

He shrugged, examining his tea. "Sure I do. I grew up here. My family's here."

She nodded. "Dotti says you're pretty good at dropping postcards."

"Yeah, well, it seems it's the least I can do. I don't get much leave time."

"That's funny considering I heard there were some Navy training programs in the Carolinas."

She kept looking up at the stars, but she could feel him shift uneasily beside her. "There are," he said after a long pause. He rotated the sweating glass, then took a long sip of tea. "Training's not the same as a break, though. And I suppose . . . I suppose there's a lot more out there I'd like to do—"

"Than come home to Maddensfield," she finished for him dryly. "I never did understand that about you, Garret."

He stood abruptly, but she didn't shy away. Instead, she kept her head up and her eyes challenging as he walked to the railing.

"There's a lot out there, Suzanne. A lot I want to see, a lot I still know nothing about." He looked up at the night, turning his glass restlessly. "You know," he said pensively, "somewhere, in some country, right now there is a war going on. And right under these same stars, men are getting ready to fight men, and good is taking on evil, and by morning—though maybe not this morning—someone will win that war. I don't want to read about it. I want to be there. I want to be doing something."

"Why, Garret? It's not your fight."

He looked at her impatiently. "Sure it is. I've got ideas. I've got values. I can tell right from wrong. That makes it my fight. I fight for what I believe in."

"And you have to go to another country to do that?"

He looked at her warily. "What do you mean?"

She set down her glass of tea and looked at him with a level gaze. "I never understood men's concept of war," she told him, standing up so she could meet him eye-to-eye. "I never understood why you had to go to some foreign country to prove you were brave. Women fight all the time and we don't even have to leave home. We fight to balance budgets, feed our families and keep our marriages together. We fight to take back our communities from criminals and we fight to create a world worth raising our children in. The only difference is that we don't earn medals."

"That's not what it's about," he tried to say.

"Then what's it about, Garret? What's so important you haven't spent Christmas with your family for the past five years? What's so important that your idea of quality time is dropping a postcard?"

"The challenge," he fired back, crossing his arms and leaning against the railing, "is putting all of yourself on the line because you know you can do it and you can make a difference. I don't expect you to understand, Suzanne. You have your roses, you have your kindergarten classes. Well, I guess I have my demolition team."

Her lips thinned even tighter, and for one moment, her eyes burned so brightly he couldn't tell if she was furious or hurt. Abruptly, she spun around. Just as abruptly, he caught her arm and spun her back.

"You started this. Don't walk away now."

Her eyes narrowed, her jaw worked, but she seemed unable to settle upon an appropriate reply.

"There is so much more here," she protested at last, her voice low and raspy with the effort. "So much more you've given up because you're running everywhere else."

"Tell me what, Suzanne. Tell me."

Me. The word burned her throat so badly she had to deliberately bite her tongue to keep it back. The warm, salty taste of blood tingled forth, but it only reminded her of the taste of tears.

"People," she returned heatedly. "Sharing. Family and friends, people who understand your victories because they know your defeats. People who really know you."

"Trust me, Suzanne, you don't know anyone on the face of this earth as well as you know your teammates. Hell, Austin's like a brother to me."

Suzanne looked at him helplessly, shaking her head. She didn't care about his military buddies; she just wanted him to see *her,* damn it. She just wanted him to look once and really *see* her. Didn't he realize all the things she held back? All the stories she kept from him precisely because she wanted him to know? She wanted him to understand the defeats so he could understand her victories. So he could love her.

This time when she stepped back, he didn't try to stop her.

"It's getting late," she said, not looking at him anymore. She could still smell her roses in the air, but their fragrance no longer brought her any pleasure. "I'm going to bed."

"You're angry with me," he said quietly, his eyes level on her face. "I'm just telling you who I am, Suzanne. You understood fifteen years ago."

She smiled, but her eyes stung. "You're a fool, Garret Guiness," she said finally, her voice low and cutting. "You are a damn fool."

"Suzanne—"

"I didn't understand, Garret!" She whirled so suddenly her skirt whipped around and nearly tangled in her legs. She advanced forward in spite of the crinkled folds, her hazel eyes flashing golden fire. "How can you be so naive as to expect a sixteen-year-old girl to understand? I waited for you, you idiot. I waited each and every night for you to come back for me. And I woke up each and every morning all alone in the same damn house in the same damn room. I didn't understand, Garret."

He stilled against the railing, his dark eyes widening. She smiled at his expression, shaking her head with frustration.

"Ah...so now you're getting it. What did you really expect, Garret? You were young and wild and all the girls wanted you. You had everything and I had..." She waved her arms uselessly in the air. "I guess I had this."

"I didn't know," he said quietly. She still looked cynical and sad, and he didn't like seeing that expression on her soft face. He tried to step forward, but the look she gave him clearly halted the action. "Suzanne..."

She walked away from him, pattering down the steps and towards the soft embrace of her roses, while he looked on helplessly. Just when he was about to follow anyway, she turned.

"Don't say anything, all right, Garret? I don't want to hear any lines. I don't want you to make up platitudes on my account. You never meant any promises, and I really was just a fool."

She wrapped her arms around herself, staring out at the velvety outlines of her roses by night. The porch light cast her profile into a soft mix of shadow and light, emphasizing her high, rounded cheeks and the delicate curve of her neck. In a flowing crimson skirt and off-white poet's shirt, she looked unbearably lovely. And suddenly, he was struck by the image of her at sixteen, her hair long and fine, her shoulders thin and hunched. Nothing of that awkward girl remained, but her face had struck him even then.

He thought it might haunt him now.

He walked down the steps. "It must have been hard back then," he said at last. She still wouldn't turn and face him. "I don't think I used to appreciate my parents at all," he continued on casually, making a fist at his side to resist touching her. "We all grew up in such a . . . happy home, I guess. Our parents were always there for us. We just took them for granted. You didn't have any of that."

"No, I suppose not."

"Do you think about your mother much?"

Suzanne stilled, and he could feel uncertainty grip her. He reached out very slowly and laid one hand upon her shoulder.

"Suzanne?"

"I planted the first rosebush when she entered the hospital," she said suddenly, the words so soft he had to lean forward to hear them. "We'd tried before to get her into treatment, but she'd never go. Then she started hallucinating. I think sometimes she thought she was with our father. I was never sure. She never said much except that he'd died and left her alone. But then she was hallucinating he was alive, and it scared her enough to enter.

"I planted the first bush and told her she could watch it bloom when she came home."

She turned and looked at him, her eyes calm while his own throat felt tight. Slowly, she closed her hand over his on her shoulder.

"I never knew what to feel about her. She was never much of a mother, and yet she was the only mother I ever had. Rachel and I were so embarrassed by her. And there were days I hated her so much for needing the alcohol more than she ever needed us. But . . . but I think I really did want her to see the roses."

He nodded, his black eyes searching her own gold-flecked depths. "She kept drinking?"

Suzanne shook her head. "No. She died. Her liver failed, her kidneys collapsed. I buried her next to my father. I imagine she's happy with that. But then, she never said enough to be sure."

"I'm sorry," he said simply, the words feeling woefully inadequate.

As if she knew that, she cocked her head and looked at him with eyes that were suddenly sad. "Why, Garret? Because you got away from all that? Because you got to travel like you'd always wanted to travel, because you got to do all the things you'd wanted to do?"

"No." He shook his head. "Not that. But maybe I shouldn't have said anything at the bus stop. I don't know. I never meant to hurt you."

Suzanne took a deep breath and focused on the stars overhead. She could feel his hand, large, warm and strong beneath her own. And she wanted to take just one more step, until she could lean her cheek on his shoulder and feel his arms wrap tightly around her. So many nights, so many years ago, she'd dreamed of falling into his arms. Now he was here, and the tears were simply memories.

She'd grown up, and learned how to stand on her own two feet. But that didn't seem to matter. She wanted him anyway, and the longing scared her.

"I'm not sixteen anymore," she said at last. She looked at him through lowered lashes and shrugged. "I suppose you're not eighteen anymore, either."

He smiled, running a hand self-consciously through his hair. "No, I suppose not. But then, I wasn't good for much at eighteen."

She gave him a small smile. "You could beat up old Tank."

"Yeah, I could beat up Nemeth."

Suzanne laughed, then squeezed his hand and slowly took it off her shoulder. She brushed her skirt, picking at unseen lint and glanced back up at the lush July night. "I really should be going to bed."

"It's not that late."

"It is if you get up at five in the morning."

He shook his head. "You should be the one in the military."

"Being a kindergarten teacher is close enough."

"I bet you're good at it," he said softly.

She shrugged, still fidgeting with her skirt. "I try."

"I still remember you leading Rachel to and from school. You were the only one who could ever make her stop crying."

"She was my sister."

"Still. You really tried for her. You really tried to make things better."

"And we saw what that accomplished." Suzanne buried her hands in her pockets, and hated herself for the sudden weakness washing through her. She wanted his hand on her shoulder again. She wanted to throw herself into his arms and pretend that maybe she was sixteen and maybe he had come back.

If I close my eyes, can it just be once upon a time?

She turned toward the door, feeling her hands start to tremble.

If I close my eyes, can you just hold me forever?

"Suzanne?"

She half rotated, not able to see his face through the burning in her eyes. She felt his hands on her shoulders, the soft whisper of his breath as he drifted near.

"Don't go."

His lips brushed her forehead, teasing the corner of her eye. And all of a sudden, her hands were clutching his shoulders, her lips seeking his own with the flood of longing that made her pulse race and tightened her throat. His mouth slanted across her own and she welcomed him in, feasting on his lips, demanding his taste.

He brought her against him hard, and she wrapped her arms around his neck in response.

"Make love to me." Her voice was urgent; she didn't care. She pressed herself against him shamelessly, feeling his hardening length through the thin folds of her skirt. She rotated her hips suggestively and heard him groan. "I want you, Garret. Please."

"Sweetheart, you couldn't stop me if you tried." He swung her up into his arms, sweeping back up the porch steps and into the house before either of them could regain sanity. He could feel her trembling against his chest, her hands tight and demanding around his neck. The desire to touch her, the need to possess her, was so strong it scared him.

He barely made it to his room before she was sliding down his body while he was reaching for her blouse. They shed their clothes quickly, needing them gone so bare skin could press against bare skin. His tongue dueled with her own, drawing out faint gasps of hunger while her nails raked down his arms. The sensitive nubs of her breasts rubbed against his darkly furred chest, her smooth leg sliding up and down his muscled thigh.

He had just enough presence of mind left to find and use a condom, then he surrendered once more to the generous promise of her arms. He curved his large hands down her back, sliding back up the front to trace her lush, heavy breasts. She felt warm and full in his hands; he couldn't stop from bending down and claiming the first nipple with his mouth. He drew it in delicately, rolling it with his tongue while her hands tangled in his hair. He licked the nub, and she pressed him closer. He grazed it exquisitely, and she moaned her need.

He raised his head with knowing eyes and suddenly found himself pushed backward onto the bed. She didn't give him a chance to recover but climbed on top to kiss him passionately. Her legs tangled with his own, her hips pressed intimately next to his rigid length while her tongue traced his lips and flickered inside experimentally. He caught her head with his hands and, in slow, leisurely motions, stroked her mouth with his tongue.

Just as her body turned liquid, he shifted her over until her legs straddled his waist, pressing her against his rigid, demanding length. For one moment, she stilled.

Slowly, he stroked her back with his hand and looked at her with burning eyes. "It'll be better this time, Suzanne. Trust me."

For her reply, she bent down and kissed him deeply.

He went more slowly, wanting it to be good. He wanted to watch her eyes turn that iridescent gold. He wanted to see her skin flush and her neck arch with passion. He wanted his name on her lips, hushed and breathless. Slowly, with spine-tingling control, he rotated his hips against her. Her cheeks flushed, and her eyes darkened. He moved again, and felt her hands grip his shoulders.

"Like that, sweetheart," he whispered. "Just concentrate on the feel."

She arched back helplessly as he moved, her own hips restless against him. She felt achy and heavy, hungry and needy. She could feel his burning length so close, pressing against her, rubbing against her. She at once wanted him just to take her, but also to prolong the moment. She shuddered, leaning back and moving against him.

He cupped her breasts with his hands, rolling her nipples as he continued to rotate his hips. She gasped, and her eyes turned molten gold. He bit his lip at the effort for control, and at that moment, nothing meant more to him than watching her satisfaction.

He brought one hand down and found her warm, moist folds with his index finger. She cried out, her eyes closing and her hands squeezing his shoulders. He rubbed her again, watching her body bow while his teeth bit into his lower lip.

"Please, sweetheart," he whispered thickly. "For me."

He pressed his hand against her and watched her explode. Her whole body shuddered, the passion washing through her like a giant crest that crashed into his own burning need. Before the last wave had passed, he thrust into her, plunging deep and low as her name was wrenched like a plea from his lips.

She collapsed onto his chest, and he held her tight as they shuddered through the storm.

For a long, long time, he simply stroked the long, tangled mass of her hair and listened to her breathing return to normal.

"I told you I could do better," he breathed against the top of her head. Against his chest, he could feel her lips curve into a smile.

"Of course," she said sleepily as her eyes drifted shut. "I always knew it would be you," she murmured as she drifted away. "Somehow, it would be you."

Chapter 10

Suzanne awoke with the hazy sensation of sleeping next to a furnace. Hot and uncomfortable, she made a feeble effort to push away from the heat, only to discover it was rock solid and included a heartbeat. Her eyes popped open and she discovered herself half-sprawled across Garret's chest.

For a long moment, she didn't breathe. Then very slowly, she exhaled.

He didn't move, and from her position she could see the even rise and fall of his flat stomach. Realizing he was still asleep, she allowed herself another breath. Then, moving carefully, she brought up a hand and cleared the rest of her hair from her eyes.

So this was waking up with a man.

She imagined it was nicer during the winter, when the air was nippy and you could huddle close. Right now, the room's air conditioner was turned too low to combat the July heat, leaving her sticky and warm. Lying as she was, her right arm had fallen asleep wedged between them, she could feel a slight dampness against her hip.

Her cheeks abruptly turned red as she figured out what the moisture was: the infamous wet spot on the sheets. She'd heard other women whispering about these things.

She shifted slightly, not sure what to do, when suddenly, Garret moved next to her. With a sleepy mumble, he turned toward her, pillowing her head on his shoulder while his other arm curled around her hip. He sighed, muttered something and fell back asleep with his arms around her.

In spite of herself, she felt her eyes sting. She could hear his heartbeat, loud and strong, and his legs felt muscular and tantalizing tangled with her own. After all the years of simply waking up and getting out of bed, this felt right. She brought up one hand and lightly touched his cheek. Twenty-four hours of beard rasped against her fingertips and brought a smile to her lips. Very slowly, she slid her hand down his arm.

He'd definitely regained some of his weight. Running her hand down farther, she found filled-in strength versus the gaunt outline of before. He probably had another fifteen pounds to go.

Lightly, she traced the puckered path of the burn scar down his arm and found herself frowning. He'd fought fires in Sarajevo, he thought. It would explain so much. But what had he been doing there away from his team? And why did he get shot in D.C.?

The surge of protectiveness gripping her caught her off guard, and she found herself automatically snuggling closer to him. She liked her head on his arm. She liked the way he moved to accommodate her and she liked the way he wrapped his arm around her and held her close.

She gripped his shoulder firmly and willed the feeling to pass. He wasn't hers. Just the moment was hers, and she'd sworn she would be content with that. She stroked his arm and shifted more comfortably in his embrace.

This time, she tested out the thick matting of hair on his chest. It felt springy and rough, a unique texture she decided she liked. She followed the line of hair down and felt his stomach abruptly contract. Her hand stilled, and all at once she became aware of burning heat just inches from her palm.

The early-morning erection, a normal biological function, one corner of her mind registered—she'd read of these things. The rest of her flushed crimson all the way to her toes.

Her fingers beat a hasty retreat up to his chest and lay there in agonizing wait. At any second, she expected to feel his hand abruptly grasp her hip, or perhaps hear his gravelly voice rumble in her ear, "Don't you ever finish what you start, sweetheart?"

Maybe he was just waiting and, the minute she actually rolled away, he would grab her in a viselike grip and make fierce, passionate love to her until she melted into the sheets all over again.

Jeez, would he ever wake up?

The paradox of these thoughts didn't escape her, and a feeling of desolation swept through her. She didn't want one moment, damn it. She wanted dozens of moments, hundreds of moments. She wanted to wake up knowing she would wake up like this again and again and again.

He'd gotten to her last night. He'd showed her worlds she hadn't known even existed. And waking up in his arms like this... She'd never meant for him to get this close. She'd never meant to fall for Garret Guiness all over again.

She curled her hand into a fist and forced herself to take a deep, steadying breath. Then carefully, not daring to even look at his face, she crawled out of bed, picked up her clothes and left.

Garret found her out in the driveway two hours later, his eyes blinking owlishly against the bright sun. His shirt hung open, his jeans still unsnapped and his feet bare, as he walked out the front door.

For a moment he simply looked at her, armed with a crescent wrench and wearing old gray sweatpants with an oversize white T-shirt already streaked with grease and other older stains. She glanced over at the sound of the door opening, but didn't stop working on the exposed engine of her Ford.

"Car trouble?" he asked, his voice still raspy with sleep.

"You shouldn't be out here," she replied crisply, still bent over the engine. "Someone could see you."

He looked out at the empty road before him and the trees on all sides. "There's plenty of time to return to the house at the sound of a car." He walked down the porch steps to the driveway. "You got up early this morning."

"I always get up early."

"Did you sleep well?"

"Well enough."

"I didn't hog the covers? I didn't snore?"

"No. Could you hand me that screwdriver over there?"

He turned his head to see an open red tool case on the grass. Telling himself he wasn't disappointed, he retrieved a large screwdriver and handed it to her. As she bent under the hood, he could see the shapely outline of her butt through the soft fabric of her worn sweats. He grinned to himself, feeling better.

"Need some help?" he asked at last.

"No."

"What seems to be the problem?"

She glanced over sharply, looking at him directly for the first time. "You're in my light." Unperturbed, he reached over and wiped a smudge of dirt from her soft cheek. He didn't start frowning until she flinched at the gesture. "Please, Garret. I've got to get this fixed."

He stepped back, feeling a tightness in his stomach as she returned to her work. He didn't like waking up this morning and finding her already gone. Never mind that he'd done that a time or two himself. Never mind that he should be grateful she was handling this so well.

Whatever he wanted, this wasn't it.

"What seems to be the problem?" he tried again, pleased by the reasonableness of his voice.

She banged against something with the wrench and muttered a curse that sounded suspiciously like "tuna fish." "Won't start," she said more clearly. She straightened up, wiping her hands on her old gardening T-shirt, and glared at her car. "I've had problems getting it to turn over lately, so I guess I should have known."

"Sounds like the solenoid switch or the starter. Maybe I can help."

She turned to him, her face set. "I don't need your help, Garret. In fact, I just examined the solenoid switch and it happens to be fine. Now, I'm going to take out the starter and give it a look. I've been keeping this thing running for quite a few years all by myself, thank you."

He looked at her for a long, hard moment, his own dark eyes beginning to spark. "Since when is it a crime to offer assistance, Suzanne?"

"I can take care of it myself."

"I'm not disputing that."

"I don't need you, Garret."

"Sweetheart, that wasn't what you were feeling last night."

Her jaw opened, her eyes widening and her cheeks flaring a brilliant, furious red. "You...you..." She took a deep breath, then her eyes narrowed dangerously. "But we're not in the bedroom anymore, are we, Garret?"

He stiffened, not liking how sharply her words struck. Muttering an oath under his breath he snatched the tool from her hand. The silvery metal flashed in the sun, and just as he was about to say something else, his eyes caught the gleam and abruptly he stilled.

* * *

The fire in the sky...

It had taken them four hours to pile the bodies together. Four hours to find family and loved ones and heap their remains on top of the other. Then Zlatko stood, his massive shoulders straight, his eyes expressionless. He lit the torch and touched it to the funeral pyre.

And the men who'd spent their days fighting fire now let the flames carry their loved ones away.

He'd never seen flames burn so brightly as that afternoon, and the crackling of the branches sounded to him like weeping. The wood at least mourned. The men simply watched and were silent.

No one talked that night. No one gathered around the campfire to swap tales of the latest adventure. No one told stories of other times and other places. There wasn't even the heated sound of arguments from people who'd been cooped up in the little camp for too long.

They all just sat on toppled logs, enveloped in grief and rage, drifting helplessly without anchor. Finally, Zlatko stood in the middle of the camp. His eyes burning on Garret, he drew them all together.

"There must be vengeance for this crime. There must be retribution.

Tonight... Something must happen tonight...."

"Garret! Garret!"

He blinked rapidly, his eyes coming into focus to find Suzanne staring at him with concern. A frown crinkled her brow, and she looked at him intently.

"You remembered something?"

He simply nodded, still wading through the depths of his mind.

"Something useful?"

"I don't know. Maybe. I think." He looked at the car, blinking several more times. He was still gripping the crescent wrench and he had Suzanne pinned against the car. Belatedly, he took a step back.

"Are you leaving?" she asked straightaway, her chin coming up.

He just looked at her.

"I want to know when you go. I want you to tell me."

He shook his head, his own thoughts not keeping pace with hers. "I'm not going," he said at last. "I still don't understand...."

His voice trailed off and he squinted his eyes as if that would help him see the past more clearly. The slaughter, the funeral pyre. He understood quite clearly that he fought fires, though he didn't understand when he'd stopped being a SEAL. Still, he trained and led the men to fight the flames, until that one day when they'd returned to find the camp destroyed. And they'd built the funeral pyre, watched the flames soar to the sky. And then ... and then ...

He swore, and hurtled the wrench to the ground, where it jumped and clattered. Slowly, Suzanne bent down and retrieved the tool.

"You're almost there, Garret," she said softly. "Don't push yourself too hard." *You don't have to be that anxious to leave.*

"I just want to know," he said, his voice taut. He began to pace out a restless circle on the driveway. "Everything went so badly. Was it my fault? Did I do something that got those people killed? What the hell went wrong and what did I do? Suzanne, what happened?"

She looked at him helplessly, only able to shake her head. "I'm sure whatever happened, you did the best you could," she supplied weakly. He merely glared at her.

"People died, Suzanne. Women and children. And I can't even remember enough to know why. I see it happening in my mind over and over again. Maybe I don't have amnesia at all. Maybe I did crack up."

"Dr. Jacobs said you just needed time."

"Yeah, well, Dr. Jacobs isn't the one dreaming of red-flowing rivers." He ran a hand through his hair, closing his eyes for a long moment.

In front of him, Suzanne twisted the wrench in her hand. "Maybe you shouldn't try so hard," she said at last. "Maybe it will come to you just like it did now."

He nodded and glanced at the wrench in her hand. Slowly, his gaze came to rest on her face. She didn't look angry anymore. If anything, she seemed concerned about him. Without questioning the instinct, he stepped forward and pulled her into his arms.

He buried his face against her neck, breathing in the soft scent of roses. She wrapped her arms around his neck and stroked his silky black hair. A shudder trembled through his strong frame, and he pressed his lips against her neck. He needed the feel of her softness pressed against him; he needed to feel her close and know that at least here, there was shelter from the storm.

He held her even tighter and closed his eyes.

Then, just as unexpectedly, he pulled away, looking out at the distant horizon and all the things he couldn't see. His gaze settled back on her face, and he tried to ignore the sudden sheen in her eyes and the ache in his own chest.

"Maybe I can get that starter out," he said gruffly.

She nodded and handed him the wrench. Without another word, he bent down and crawled beneath the car.

When Cagney pulled into the driveway six hours later, the car was gone. Frowning to himself, he walked through the house, searching for signs of Garret. Just as he was beginning to get worried, he stepped onto the back porch and heard sounds of clanking from the shed.

After glancing idly at the new table sitting on the porch, he walked down the steps to the workshop. "Garret, it's Cagney. Open up."

The clattering suddenly stopped. He heard a muffled oath and then the door was pushed open. Garret's rumpled head appeared, his eyes blinking owlishly at the bright daylight.

"Something happened?" he asked curtly.

Cagney shrugged. "Nothing really happened. But I just got off the phone with my old partner from D.C."

Garret nodded and let Cagney in.

As the door closed behind them, Cagney also found himself blinking to adjust to the dim light in the shed. He glanced around. For all intents and purposes, Garret appeared to be packing up the tools.

"Leaving?" he asked sharply.

"I don't know," Garret said levelly. "You tell me."

Cagney leaned against one wall and folded his arms across his chest. "Couple things," he started to say, keeping his voice curt enough to match his brother's. Even as he listened, Garret was packing up more equipment. "I actually called Melissa nearly a week ago, wanting to get more information about the shooting in D.C. and ask her to be on the lookout for anything strange. Well, it took a bit of doing, but just two days ago, officers were called by some neighbors to report a possible break-in. Window broken, but best they could tell, nothing stolen. It was Mitch's house, Garret. And I had Melissa check it out. There was another note there, addressed to you."

Garret stiffened, his hand momentarily stilling over an assortment of sandpaper. He forced himself to pick up the sheets and add them to the box. "And?"

"Same words as the note at Mom and Dad's."

Garret nodded. "They don't know where I am."

Cagney nodded back. "Exactly. Looks like someone is leaving the notes in all the logical places, trying to draw you out. Do you know what it means yet?"

Garret began to slowly wind up a long extension cord. "Yes. No." He shrugged his shoulders, keeping his eyes on the thick orange cord. "I think I was in Sarajevo, working as a fire fighter. Something happened . . . the camp was destroyed. I don't remember much after that.''

"What does that have to do with D.C.?"

"Well, there you go, brother—the million-dollar question."

"Melissa had some details on the shooting," Cagney said quietly.

Garret looked up, his eyes suddenly wary.

"They have you down as a John Doe, but it's in the files because there were two witnesses who called the ambulance. Of course, your pulling a gun on the ambulance attendants also made quite an impression."

"Yeah, well, we all have our charm."

"Witnesses said the shot came from up high. Police couldn't find any shells, but on the roof of one of the buildings, there was a small pile of fresh cigarette butts. From that height and distance, we're talking at least a high-powered rifle. Melissa says it looks like a professional job."

"Professional job?"

"Yeah, Garret. A hit man. And the police aren't the only ones interested. The navy just demanded copies of the reports, and all of a sudden, they're taking care of the matter. Mom's already gotten two calls from navy officers trying to track you down."

"Has she said anything?" Garret asked sharply.

"Of course not," Cagney snapped back. "This is Mom we're talking about. But she's damn worried about you. And at this point, I don't blame her. A hit man, Garret? Just who the hell did you tick off?"

Garret clenched and unclenched his hands restlessly. "I don't know," he growled at last. "I just don't know."

Cagney watched his older brother for a minute longer, feeling his own tension growing. He was worried, damn it. And he wasn't used to being worried about Garret. The past two nights he'd remained awake with his fiancée Marina, pacing the abandoned lot while she continued painting the huge warehouse wall. While she might be capable of maintaining her strange sleeping schedule, it was beginning to take its toll on him.

Finally, Cagney sighed and ran a hand through his hair. "Well, the good news is, no one seems to know where you are yet."

"Yet," Garret emphasized. He finished wrapping the extension cord and threw it into the box without looking at it. He paced the room a few more times. "Simple process of elimination," he said shortly. "They'll keep checking and narrowing down the possibilities. Let's see, if I were them, I'd check my place, then Mitch's, then local hospitals. Airports, as well."

"You used an assumed name, right?"

"Of course. Which sooner or later, they'll anticipate. It's been a week and I haven't materialized in D.C. It's a pretty safe bet that I've left somehow. Next stop, Maddensfield."

"I have my deputies keeping an eye out."

"What did you tell them?"

"Not much. Just that people were looking for you, and since this was your hometown, they'd pass through, so we'd better keep our eyes open. Anything they hear, they should pass along to me."

"Did they ask if I was actually here?"

"Give 'em some credit, Garret."

"Yeah, well..." He tried to take another step, but there was really no room for decent pacing in the tiny shed. He raked his fingers through his hair instead, a gesture that unconsciously mirrored Cagney's. "I don't know whether to go or to stay," he said at last, his voice low.

Cagney simply looked at him with his steady gray eyes.

"I mean, sooner or later, pressure will be applied here. And if it's a professional, maybe more than a mere note. But even if I'm not here, they'll still go through that process. If I left, I'd probably be unable to do anything. Let alone figure out where I'd go. Hell, I've got the navy and a hit man looking for me and I have no idea what to think of either. And my brain is so damn fickle it won't give me an answer."

"Aren't you get forgetting someone else?" Cagney asked quietly.

Garret looked up impatiently. "Who?"

"Suzanne," Cagney said in a steely voice. "You know, the woman who's putting you up."

Garret looked startled, then wary. "Suzanne knows I'll leave sooner or later."

Cagney shook his head, his eyes narrowing. "Does she, Garret? You look me in the eye and tell me you're not involved with her."

Garret straightened up to his full height, looking down on his younger brother. "That's none of your business."

"Like hell, it isn't," Cagney countered levelly. He shook his head. "You are sleeping with her, aren't you? You bastard."

Garret stiffened, his hands balling into fists at his side. "I'm telling you, Cagney," he warned softly, "it's none of your business."

But Cagney stepped right up to him, his eyes an unusual and dangerous shade of gray. "Why, Garret? Why drag her into all this? Wasn't leaving her fifteen years ago enough for you? Did you have to return just to break her heart all over again?"

"Damn it," Garret growled, "Suzanne can take care of herself." But Cagney's words were striking uncomfortably close to home.

"Yeah, Suzanne can take care of herself," Cagney agreed. "And she can take care of you, and her sister, and this whole damn town. But who takes care of her, Garret? Just this once, who takes care of her?"

"She doesn't need me," Garret said slowly.

Cagney looked at his older brother and shook his head in disgust. "You're sleeping with her and you still don't understand her at all. But then I shouldn't be surprised. You always were a selfish bastard."

"Cagney, I'm telling you, I'll handle it."

"Yeah, right."

"Who do you think held her up the last time you left, Garret? Who gave her the shoulder to cry on when suddenly you were gone and she was trying to believe in that damn fairy tale you left her with? Who drove her to visit her mom in the hospital? Who held her hand while she watched her mother die? It wasn't you, Garret. It was never, ever you."

"I checked up on her," Garret said stiffly.

Cagney just laughed. "How charitable of you, Garret. And did you check up on her when she used her baby-sitting money to catch a bus to Charlotte so she could bail Rachel out of jail? Did you check up on her when she declared medical bankruptcy to cover her mother's hospital bills? You are some piece of work, brother."

"She did just fine."

"Of course she did fine. When did she have any other choice?"

"Damn you, what do you want from me?"

Very slowly, Cagney jabbed his brother with his index finger. "I want you to stop toying with her. I want you to stop thinking about yourself and start thinking about her for a change."

"I do think about her," Garret countered gruffly. Not knowing what else to do, he pointed toward the back porch. "I made her a table."

"A table, Garret?"

"Damn it," Garret practically roared, "I do care!"

"Like hell," Cagney countered just as fiercely. "You're a selfish son of a bitch who knows nothing about love."

"You have no right!"

"I have every right. So help me, God, Garret, if you break her heart yet again..."

At Cagney's unfinished threat, Garret's eyes narrowed, the pulse at his temple pounding dangerously. He felt frustrated and angry and guilty, and hated feeling any of these things. "You'll do what, little brother?" he challenged softly.

Cagney looked at him long and hard, then felt something snap inside him. Without any warning, he drew back his fist and slammed it into his older brother's eye. Caught off guard, Garret took the blow squarely, staggering back a couple of steps.

Almost in slow motion, he brought his hand up to his face. Before him, Cagney shook out his fist, his gray eyes wary.

"You've had that coming for a long time," the younger Guiness said levelly.

Garret just looked at his imperturbable brother, the one he'd never been able to provoke, though God knows he'd tried when they were younger. With light fingers, he felt around the top of his cheekbone, already beginning to swell. "When the hell did you learn to fight?" he finally asked, his voice gruff.

Cagney looked down at his bruised knuckles and winced. "Never really did, actually." Though he'd done a decent job with Bennett Jensen only a month ago. Of course, that monster had insulted Marina. He looked at his brother once more, not willing to back down though Garret outweighed him by twenty pounds.

Garret, however, was still checking out his cheek and staring at his brother as if he'd never seen him before. Abruptly, the shed door was yanked open, blinding sunlight leaping into the dim shed.

"So here you are," Suzanne said. She peered in, her eyes focusing on them one after the other, Garret still touching his cheek. All of a sudden, she stiffened, her lips thinning as she took in the scene. Garret felt himself flush, and beside him, Cagney began to shift uncomfortably. "And exactly what happened in here?" she demanded crisply.

"I fell," Garret said immediately.

Cagney nodded. "And I was just helping him up," the younger brother filled in.

"And I'm the Queen of France," Suzanne informed them curtly. "You two were fighting."

They both looked away, two guilty kids caught in the act.

"What is going on?" Suzanne demanded to know. They still wouldn't meet her eye, but Cagney's cheeks were turning beet red. Abruptly, her eyes opened wide. "Cagney Guiness," she breathed softly, "please tell me you didn't."

"I didn't," he said weakly.

"So help me God," she stormed, "if you interfere with my business again, I'll... I'll... I'll tell Marina about little Mary Maple who punched you out when you were nine."

Cagney paled nicely. "Suzanne—"

"Cage, I can take care of myself. Though, God knows, Garret doesn't make it easy."

This time, Garret flushed, looking down at the floor as if he suddenly had a keen interest in his shoes.

"Brothers shouldn't fight," Suzanne said sternly in her best schoolteacher's voice. They both nodded obediently. After another awkward moment, Cagney cleared his throat.

"I'd better be on my way now. I'll, uh, check on you two later." He dipped his hat at Suzanne, already beating a hasty retreat toward the door. She stepped back, allowing him to pass into the bright July sunshine. She could see him limp more than usual, and her hazel eyes returned to Garret with dangerous intent.

"Whatever Cage said," she uttered stiffly, "I'm sure it was true."

Garret didn't say anything, but his jaw clenched.

In the awkward silence, Suzanne's gaze swept around the shed, taking in the half-packed boxes and dismantled tools. Her lips thinned, but her look met his squarely.

"We'd best get some ice for your eye," she said shortly.

He nodded, and after a moment followed her from the shed.

Chapter 11

With a groan, Garret sat up in bed, the sheet already twisted around his waist. It was too hot for sleeping, the old air conditioner no match for the intense heat. Not to mention that his eye throbbed and he could barely see a damn thing. Garret used to spend half his waking moments trying to provoke his quiet younger brother into fighting, and all those moments had come to nothing; Cagney had simply stared down Garret's raging temper with cool gray eyes.

From the current state of Garret's face, Cage had picked up some of his older brother's talent after all.

Garret rolled out of bed, standing naked and sweaty in the middle of the room.

He opened the bedroom door and crossed the hall to the bathroom. There, he splashed cold water on his face and looked at the nice black-and-blue mess that his eye had become. For a moment, he allowed genuine admiration for Cagney's blow. Not bad for a kid who'd spent his whole life with his hands behind his back. Seemed like everyone in Maddensfield had grown up nicely while he was away.

Cagney was now engaged and, from what Garret could tell, a fine sheriff. And Suzanne... Suzanne was just plain beautiful.

He stilled for a moment with his hands on the sink. And then he swore again.

She was back to being distant. Oh, she was polite enough. She fed him dinner, made small talk and was unbearably cordial. He hated very minute of it.

He supposed he couldn't blame her. To hear Cagney talk, all he ever did was hurt the woman. And yet she'd taken him back in and asked nothing from him. When he needed her, she was there.

But if she needed him?

He turned away from the sink and padded back into his room. It was too damn hot. He fumbled with the air conditioner's controls, but was afraid if he cranked it much more the miserable thing would explode. He settled for standing directly in front of it, and felt the cool air whisper across his stomach.

The sound of sirens cut through the air, and he looked up, senses alert. The sirens kept on wailing. Fire engines.

He peered out the window, but couldn't see any sign of flashing lights. Working on instinct, he retrieved his jeans from the floor and pulled them on. He'd just walked out into the hall again when he ran into Suzanne.

"Fire engines wake you, too?" he asked gruffly. She was wearing a white cotton gown that came discreetly to her knees. But the material was thin and virginal, and he knew she was naked beneath it.

"Yes," she lied. She walked to the back door, opening it to the porch so she could peer outside. "Sounds close," she said presently, "but I don't see anything."

Garret walked up behind her, standing close enough to catch the scent of roses. She immediately stepped away.

"My parents' house isn't too far from here," he said quietly, not pursuing her... yet.

She looked at him sharply, and he could tell by the sudden lowering of her eyes that it had been her first thought, as well. "I'm sure it's nothing serious," she said. "Probably just a routine call. You know how it is when some of those systems get set off these days—the fire department has to arrive at the scene."

"Could be," Garret acknowledged, but both their eyes looked out toward his parents' house. The night was too dark to see much.

Idly, Suzanne walked over to the table still sitting on the porch, running one finger across the dry finish. "We should take this inside," she said absently.

Garret nodded, still peering at the horizon. Was it his imagination, or did he smell smoke? It should be impossible to smell anything at this distance.

"It's really beautiful," Suzanne remarked. "The table, I mean. I don't think I ever thanked you properly." He looked back at her, his eyes unable to stop from drifting over her thinly clad form. She shifted a little under the intensity of his gaze, the color rising becomingly to her cheeks. Stiffly, she brought her chin up. "You have a nice touch with furniture, Garret," she said levelly.

He stepped toward her. "With furniture?" he drawled. She backed up lightly against the table, but that didn't stop him.

"Bored again?" she quizzed ruthlessly.

He traced a finger down her cheek. "Hungry again?" he retaliated just as softly. He trailed the finger down her bare arm, his body already hard for her.

"You don't play fair, Garret Guiness," she whispered, turning her face away.

For one moment, he looked at her pale, luminescent profile. She looked like a cameo portrait, round and soft and feminine, and everything he'd never wanted in a woman until he'd found it in her. "Do you really want me to?" he demanded bluntly now.

"Yes. No. I don't know."

He let his hand slide down to cup her breast through the thin fabric of her gown. She arched back a little, filling his hand. In response, he rubbed his thumb over the sensitive nipple. Her eyes drifted shut, and he saw her teeth sink into her lower lip with the sensations.

"I can make it good again," he promised. He cupped her other breast.

"I know," she whispered. Her eyes fluttered open, and there was an anguish there that caught him off guard. Her mouth opened, her eyes beseeching him to let her be even as she arched against his touch and a moan escaped her lips as a fluttered sigh.

He could take her, claim her body, please her senseless. But her gaze told him how much he hurt her anyway, giving her so much, but leaving her in the end.

"Suzanne—"

The phone rang, cutting through the silence with shrill demand. Instantly, she pulled away, her eyelids shuttering down.

"I'd better get that," she whispered. Not looking at him, she fumbled with the door and disappeared down the hall. Shaking his head in the darkness, he followed.

He'd just walked into the kitchen when she picked up the receiver.

"Suzanne? Cagney. Don't let him out of the house, you hear me? No matter what he says or does, do not let him out of the house."

She nodded, glancing at Garret instantly. He caught her look, and his eyes narrowed.

"It's my parents' house, isn't it?" he growled.

She shook her head, clutching the phone tightly. "I'm sorry," she muttered primly. "But you have the wrong number." Then not knowing what else to do, she slammed the phone down.

Garret shook his head. "You're not very good at this, Suzanne."

He headed off down the hall. After a shocked minute, she went after him.

"Garret? Garret, what are you doing?"

He didn't say anything, but in the dim light of his room she could see him pulling on his shirt. Her lips thinned, her arms folding tensely in front of her. She straightened her shoulders and, ignoring the tightness in her chest, prepared to do battle.

"I'm not letting you out of this house, Garret."

"Sweetheart, I'm not asking permission."

She stormed toward him, her hazel eyes turning molten gold. "Darn it, Garret. If you leave this house, I'll... I'll—"

He cut her off with a simple, harsh look. "You'll do what, Suzanne?" He turned his face a little. "Blacken my other eye? You Maddensfield people need another form of retaliation. I'm growing bored."

"You can't go out there," she persisted, refusing to be derailed by his black humor.

Garret merely pulled on his shoes.

She began to seriously contemplate ways of knocking him unconscious. Maybe she could lure him into the kitchen. Would a frying pan really work, or was that only good in the movies? Her hands slowly crushed the folds of her nightgown.

"Why are you doing this?" she asked at last, the frustration raw in her throat. "You know it's probably a trap."

"It's my parents' house," he said levelly, tying the last shoe. He rose, and the fear crept up her throat like bile.

"Damn you, Garret. Can't you trust Cagney even a little bit?"

"It has nothing to do with that," he said, already striding to the door. At the last minute, she flung herself in the doorway, earning herself a droll raised eyebrow. "Sweetheart, you don't weigh much more than a sack of potatoes. I could fight that fire with you flung over my shoulder. And I will if I have to."

She glared at him, and at that moment, seriously wished she did have a frying pan in hand. He could use a sharp blow to the head.

"Cagney is taking care of everything," she said yet again. "And the fire department here does fine. There's nothing you can do, Garret, but get yourself in a whole lot of trouble. And your mom won't give a fig about the house if she loses you instead."

He leaned down, his lips so close she could almost feel them on her cheeks. "Give me a little credit, Suzanne. I'm a professional. I've been trained just for these occasions. And what good was all that training, if I can't use it to help my own family?"

"Cagney has training, too," she replied stubbornly. "And so does the fire department."

"Goodbye, Suzanne." And true to his word, he physically lifted her up and moved her out of the way as if she wasn't any more nuisance than a small child. He strode down the hall while she rubbed her arms and searched desperately for some other way to make him stay.

Darn it, she thought with a sigh, and scurried to the kitchen for the frying pan. But by the time she was at the entryway with cast-iron skillet in tow, the front door was already open. She stormed out to the porch, but it didn't make a difference.

For all intents and purposes, the night had swallowed Garret Guiness alive.

He could smell the acrid odor of burning fabric as he came closer. Thick clouds of smoke billowed up, the humidity-swollen wood putting up a good fight. But there hadn't been a decent rainfall for weeks, so the clear winner of the battle was never in doubt.

He crept along the perimeter and kept his senses tuned.

He had to come tonight, if only because he was meant to come. Of course the fire was a trap. But he'd been playing mole for over a week now; he wanted this matter resolved. So Mitch and Jessica could return to D.C. and have their children in peace. So his parents could sleep at night without wondering what was about to happen. So Suzanne could get on with her life.

He eased around to the front and saw his parents standing in their bathrobes in the front yard. Dotti had her head on her husband's shoulder, Henry's arms around her, as together they watched their home of thirty years burn. Just a few feet away, Cagney stood with his hands on his hips, his sheriff's badge gleaming on his chest, his black cowboy hat pushed back on his forehead. His face was grim as he watched the flames.

They'd all grown up in this house. Doorways still had pencil marks tabulating the years of their growth. Garret's room still had a dent in the wall from the time he went to punch out Jake, but the quick-thinking boy had ducked at the last moment. And then there was the cupboard under the counter where Liz always used to hide when they played hide-and-seek, and the attic with its treasure trove of limbless G.I. Joe dolls, cracked water guns and broken wooden horses. When they were younger, the house had been their universe. But even as they grew older and traveled and built their own lives, the house remained home.

And standing here now, looking at his parents and Cagney, he knew there was nothing he could do to save it.

Already water streamed onto the blaze, targeted toward the roof. The house itself was beyond hope, but there were plenty of water-starved trees just waiting to be seduced by the fire. If that happened, the situation could get out of hand pretty fast. Firemen began to climb up the ladder toward the roof of the house, and Garret could almost feel the weight of an ax in his hands.

So much fire, crackling at his skin, licking his hair. The searing heat, the choking smoke. But they drove into it anyway, man versus fire, a drama replayed time and time again in a war with only battles and no victory.

He led the men into the blaze because he wanted to, because after the churches of Rwanda, the streets of Haiti, he needed to do something real. He needed to feel alive.

And he led the men into the blaze because he had to.

He continued around the perimeter, not knowing what he was looking for, but certain he would find it anyway. At the periphery of his vision, he caught a faint movement and he instantly stilled.

There, to the left.

He slunk down low, and moving with the slow, agonizing pace only a pointman can truly appreciate, he journeyed over. The shadow shifted again, then suddenly seemed to melt into the darkness.

He moved faster.

But suddenly the tall grass was still, the night consumed by only the crackle of flames and thunder of water. He frowned, peering carefully and wishing he had his infrared goggles. SEALs generally had good toys; he wasn't quite as well versed in the old-fashioned ways.

He came to a matted spot in the border grass and sank to one knee. Big, heavy man, judging by the depth of the depression. He rustled through the trampled grass and shortly came across the cigarette butt. He brought it up and sniffed it. American made. Marlboro, maybe.

And somewhere in the back of his mind, that fitted.

He shook his head and began to follow the trail through the grass. The other person was good, he concluded after he lost the trail for a second time and began backtracking once again. So D.C. thought a professional hit man. His mind turned it over and dismissed it without any logical reason. He would dwell on it more later; for now he just wanted to pick up the trail. But suddenly he was at the edge of the field, wide open road materializing before him and not even a decent moon for light.

He sat down hard on his heels. Damn.

And heard something crackle to his immediate right.

He fell back abruptly, falling flat on his butt as he sought the cover of the grass. He tried scrambling up again, but his hand slid out from beneath him. He went down hard, feeling the pain in his wrist. Then his head hit the rock, and he didn't feel any pain at all.

The water lapped against the shore, peaceful and rhythmic. Leaning closer, he could feel the light spray against his face and looked at the waves with something akin to longing.

He hadn't dived for a year now. Instead, he'd studied the mastery of rock and fire. Still, he missed the water. And these days, he found himself suddenly missing his home.

He shook the thought away and focused on the man beside him. They'd been crouched on the shoreline for two hours now. It was cold out, and the night an inky black that didn't set well on a man's nerves. Garret could feel the ripples of hypersensitivity snaking up and down his back, but Zlatko didn't look tense or nervous. He just loomed large and grim, the way he'd looked for the past three days now. Since the time they'd found the camp.

Garret looked away and watched the water once more.

Any time now, a boat should appear—if it had gotten through all right.

"How long do we wait?" Garret asked at last.

"As long as it takes."

"There's no guarantee that it'll get through."

"It'll get through."

"And then, Zlatko?"

"Then we launch our own war."

Garret shut up, mostly because he didn't have an answer for that last statement. He'd helped pile the bodies of the

*people who had kept him. He'd closed the eyes of the
women who had cooked his food and teased him about
finding a wife. He'd lived with them, laughed with them and
shared with them for a year.*

*In the beginning, he'd helped them set up the camp es-
tablishing a new home after their village had been destroyed by the Serb forces. And he'd watched as they'd sent
their children away, hoping they could at least find a future
far away from the land that promised none. And he'd risen
with their men each morning, going off to the city to save
what could be saved, to fight when they could fight, because it was their land and they did still care.*

In the past year, he'd learned to care, too.

"They come from Kazakhstan?" he whispered, and hated
himself for the question.

Beside him, Zlatko simply nodded and lit a new cigarette.

"It's a long way from Kazakhstan to here, my friend,"
Garret continued. "And with the embargo..."

"They'll get here."

"How? Down the coast? Do you know how many miles
that is?"

"What does it matter? All that we care is for them to arrive."

Garret stiffened, but managed to shrug his shoulders casually enough. "I just like knowing the big picture," he
grumbled after a bit. "I didn't believe in Santa Claus as a
kid, either—there was no way you could convince me a 250-
pound man with a stack of toys was gonna fit down the
chimney."

"Italy," Zlatko said, impatiently crushing out the barely
lit cigarette. "I think they go to Italy, then down the coast
from the border and upriver from there. Takes a bit, but it
can be done."

Garret made a show of glancing at his watch while he
tucked that piece of information away. Kazakhstan to Italy,

through the border, down the coast, up the major tributaries. Intelligence would want more details than that.

The funeral pyre burned in his mind, and the self-loathing passed through him like a wave.

The sound of breaking water penetrated the silence. Beside him, Zlatko stiffened. Moving quietly, both men drifted down to the shore. They exchanged looks and nodded to each other in wordless communication. Zlatko went forward while Garret held back with his hand on the Ruger at his waist.

While he looked on, Zlatko helped pull the small boat ashore. Two men stepped out, holding a rough crate between them. After a few words, they opened the case for Zlatko's inspection, revealing a cache of AK-47s. One of the men's hands moved beneath his jacket, and immediately Garret's hand tightened on the Ruger. He slipped it out and dropped the safety. But the man simply produced a piece of paper, which Zlatko examined with interest.

Garret relaxed his shoulders, and as he did so, the sound of a second boat broke the silence. Zlatko reached immediately for a gun, and even as Garret watched, one of the "deliverymen" yanked out a pistol from the small of his back and pointed it at Zlatko's head. Garret rose and fired off three rounds. The man fell without even a gasp.

The second man pivoted, a gun materializing in his own hands. But just as he raised it up, Zlatko charged with a low roar. The burly man slammed the deliveryman to the ground, catching him with one succinct blow. Shots came from the river, and Garret jumped down to the shoreline.

"Grab the case," he yelled, spraying covering fire the best he could with a pistol. His gun suddenly clicked blank, and with a cry of fury, he threw the gun at the approaching boat.

"This way," Zlatko roared out, and shots targeted the sound. Garret saw his friend lumbering along with the case and sprinted toward him. Bullets whizzed past, and he heard

a low grunt as one found its mark. But Zlatko didn't stop moving.

They tumbled into the underbrush, Zlatko dropping the case once and the weapons spilling out. Garret grabbed one, but the light feel indicted no bullets. He swore softly, tossing the weapons back in and grabbing the case from his friend. He hoisted it onto his shoulder and kept moving.

"Through here," he directed, stumbling over the rocky terrain with his burden. Zlatko stumbled behind him. And the sound of bullets tore through the air.

They ran along the twisting goat trails, scrambling and tripping and falling, but gaining ground from sheer knowledge of the territory. Finally, they came to a myriad of caves, and Garret ducked into the third one. Zlatko followed.

They collapsed against the wall halfway down, pressing themselves against the cold, damp stone. They could hear the sound of their labored breaths, and it was loud and conspicuous in the echoing cave. They heard the thud of footsteps, the sound of falling rocks and scrabbling feet. Garret heard swearing, then abruptly, the scraping of boots faded.

They sat in breathless silence for another few minutes, then Garret slowly eased out a sigh.

"Traitorous bastards," Zlatko mumbled. "The country dies for passion, and they kill for greed." He changed position, and Garret could hear the sound of his sharply indrawn breath.

"How bad?" he whispered.

"Arm. Clean through, I think. Not bad."

Garret nodded, automatically ripping off a strip from the bottom of his shirt. Zlatko presented his right arm, and Garret felt out the wound in the dark, tying the bandage accordingly.

"We still have a ways to go," he said quietly.

"We'll make it. We have to. We have the guns."

Yes, the guns. Garret remembered the crate at his feet and felt the loathing once more. Moving his fingers around, he found one of the AK-47s and picked it up. Cold, solid weight. Effective.

They could wage a nice war with these. And suddenly, he could see the bodies all over the camp. The women and children, completely defenseless because he'd led their men away to save buildings. *Buildings.*

His hand tightened on the grip. He could train the men again, not to fight silly fires, but to seek, to destroy. One band of men, and they could win this bloody war, SEAL-style.

He knew how.

He could feel Zlatko's eyes in the darkness, and the heavyset man laid a hand on his shoulder. "In time, my friend. In time. Together, we will avenge her, no? Together, we will make them pay."

Yes, Garret's mind agreed savagely, the raw, passionate need to act as pure as it had ever been. The Serbs had destroyed his friends, and he knew, he'd studied, he'd learned and he'd mastered the art of just how to make them pay.

He thought again of the crate of guns next to his feet, and the temptation was so strong it sent a shudder up his spine. To unleash the beast he'd been trained to be. To avenge his friends.

Except he couldn't do it.

He wasn't just a volunteer fighting fires. He was a SEAL on a covert mission, deep reconnaissance to trace the arms flow into Sarajevo. A SEAL who had to think of his country and his duty first.

And not the friends he'd made along the way.

He set down the gun and turned to Zlatko, his heart heavy, his shoulders slumped.

"Zlatko," he whispered in the damp stillness of the pitch-black cave. "There's something you should know."

* * *

Garret's eyes peeled open, and he looked at the smoke-filled sky for a full sixty seconds. He blinked twice, taking a mental inventory and discovering that he was indeed alive and back in Maddensfield.

He sat up slowly. His wrist hurt, and there was a dull throbbing at the side of his head. At this point, he either had an unusually thick skull, or his brains were simply so scrambled it didn't matter anymore. He felt the growing lump and winced.

After another few minutes, he determined that no one was around anymore. Zlatko had left the area, but Garret would bet there was a note at the house. Moving slowly, he crept back through the grass.

The fire still burned, though not nearly as fiercely as before. His parents were sitting down now, a few neighbors in attendance. His mom had tears on her cheeks; he hadn't seen her cry since Nick's shooting four years ago.

He turned away and went looking for Cagney.

He found his brother behind the house, staring at the smoke-filled sky with his arms around a beautiful woman. She had long black hair with the most startling gray streak he'd ever seen. So this was Marina. He was about to step forward when a fireman came walking by.

He flattened himself against a tree, hearing the low murmurs of conversation. Then the fireman walked past again.

He slipped into the yard, and Cagney's head immediately swiveled. Before Garret could say a word, Cagney's eyes turned a dark, stormy gray. Even Marina carefully stepped back from her fiancé.

"So what did you do? Lock Suzanne in a closet?" Cagney growled.

"Not quite," Garret replied evenly. The smoke stung his eyes, and looking at the burning remains of his childhood home, he didn't feel up to a fight.

"You shouldn't be here," Cagney said flatly, "but that goes without saying."

"He's gone."

"Who?"

"Zlatko. The one who set the fire."

Cagney looked at his brother, then shook his head. "I gather your memory is returning."

Garret nodded.

Cagney gestured at the house. "Too bad it wasn't a little sooner, don't you think?" The words were harsh, and gingerly, Marina placed a soothing hand on his shoulder. Garret saw the gesture, and it reminded him of Suzanne.

"I wish..." he began, searching for the words. "I wish..." He looked at the ruins again. "It was my home, too," he said at last.

Cagney's shoulders seemed to relax a fraction and he sighed. "So where do we go from here, brother? Is Suzanne's house next?"

Garret shook his head. "I'm leaving. Zlatko wants me, and he'll keep searching until he finds me. I think it would be easier if I found him first."

"What did you do?" Cagney asked curiously.

"I betrayed him," Garret admitted simply.

Cagney scoffed at that. "Hell, Garret, you're the most loyal person I know."

Garret nodded, a grim smile playing at the corners of his lips. "Precisely the problem."

Cagney looked confused, but for some inexplicable reason, Garret didn't feel like explaining. He didn't want to talk to Cagney about it. He wanted Suzanne.

"I'll take care of it," he said shortly. "Sooner or later. I suppose there's a note."

Cage nodded, reaching into his shirt pocket. "Mom handed me this. She's crying, Garret. Do you know the last time Mom cried?"

Garret nodded, wondering if he could feel any worse. He accepted the note and stuck it in his own pocket. "Was anything saved?"

"Couple of things. Your "friend" must've intended this only as a warning, because he woke Mom and Dad by throwing a stone tied with this note through the window. Of course, he'd already started the fire by then, but at least they were able to get out of the house. You know Mom—she made Dad grab Grandma's rocker and she snatched her jewelry box. I pulled a lot of the living room stuff out.

"But I don't think that's what Mom's worried about, Garret. She hasn't seen you for nearly a year. And now she's getting notes on her dining room table and someone sets her house on fire. They have insurance, so they can rebuild the house. What she really wants is her son."

"Tell her I'm all right," Garret said. "Tell her I get out of trouble now as well as I ever did and that I'll see her in a week or two."

"Garret, I don't want to give her messages. I want to find this guy, Zlatko, so I can simply give her you."

"No."

"No? Garret, I'm your damn brother. And in case you haven't noticed it yet, I have a star on my chest. I can do a thing or two, you know."

"I know," Garret said levelly. Then he grinned and pointed at his eye. "You've got a good right hook, too." Then he sobered. "This is personal, Cagney. I need to take care of it myself."

The sound of footsteps reached them, and Marina nodded toward an approaching fire fighter.

"It's nice to finally meet you, Garret," she said softly, "but I think you'd better leave now. Don't worry. Cagney and I will take care of things here."

Garret looked at her, taking in her exotic beauty, and flashed his brother a knowing grin. He nodded to her, then crossed quickly back to the bordering field of grass, seeming to disappear before their very eyes.

Marina looked impressed, but Cagney simply shook his head and swore.

Chapter 12

Garret couldn't find her in the house, though her car was still parked in the driveway. Her bedroom was empty, the living room, the kitchen. His room was empty.

He felt the first twinge of foreboding and began to search in earnest. Not the first floor, not the second floor. Maybe on the third? But the house only rang with the sound of her name, the rooms revealing no one.

He came downstairs in a flurry, wondering how he could have been so stupid. Zlatko had left the site of the fire, meaning he could have easily come here.

Garret felt the beginnings of panic and fumbled for the note he'd stuffed in his pocket. With trembling hands, he unfolded the thin paper.

Do you still remember the flames, the way they licked at your skin, before I pulled you from the building? I remember, prijatelj. I remember the flames and I remember the fury. Tonight, I fed the fire a snack. Tomorrow, it will be a meal.

He stared at the paper for a long time and felt the dread ripple like a snake down his spine. Suzanne. God, not her. He began tearing through the house with a vengeance.

But still there was no one.

He was about to put his fist through the wall in frustration when he suddenly noticed a thin beam of light in the backyard. Adrenaline pounding, he raced for the back door.

Suzanne.

She was on her knees in the garden, her white cotton gown now smeared with rich dirt as she worked the soil by the light of an upturned flashlight. She'd knotted her hair up, revealing the long, graceful column of her neck. As she bent down and tended her roses, she looked beautiful and ethereal.

His steps slowed and he swallowed hard. With the softness of a cat, he approached. She didn't look up until he blocked her light.

"The fire?" she asked softly, her gaze falling back down to the mixture of ash and loam she was mixing into the soil around her roses. She continued kneading the ground with her pale fingers.

"The house is gone," he said hoarsely. Her hands stilled, then dug back into the earth.

"Your parents?"

"They're okay, I guess. For people who just watched all their belongings burn."

She simply nodded and kept working. "Your parents are very strong."

"They shouldn't have to be this strong!"

She didn't say anything at all, but moved on to the next bush. He remained standing, feeling the raw ache in his chest and wishing she would stop tending her damn flowers and really look at him.

"Suzanne, the fire was my fault, directed at me. And until I find Zlatko, things will only get worse. I remember, Suzanne. I know what happened."

Abruptly, her hands stilled and then just as abruptly, dug deeply into the dark pungent earth with a harsh, compulsive motion. "So now you know everything?" she whispered, still not looking up.

"Yes, damn it." He continued staring at the back of her head, but even with the full force of his glittering black gaze he could not make her stop. He squatted beside her, needing her to look at him, needing her to understand what he was about to tell her. "I was in Sarajevo," he said hoarsely, his eyes intent upon her. "I went first on my leave just to volunteer as a fire fighter and maybe do some good. But then Intelligence approached me. Despite the embargo, weapons were still being smuggled into the country, fueling the war. They wanted to know how and by whom this was being accomplished. Then, if the UN or the U.S. became more involved, we would know where to start. So instead of going back to my team, I stayed, fighting fires during the day, making contacts and doing some probing at night."

"I'm sure you did the right thing," Suzanne said stiffly, her eyes still on her roses. They smelled sweet in the night air, soft and comforting. When all else failed, she still had her roses.

"Suzanne, I lived with these people for a year. I ate with them, I talked with them. I trained the men to fight fires. And they shared with me when they had so little to share. Food, medicine, laughter, it didn't matter." His voice was low and intense, but she couldn't bring herself to look up.

"And then one day," he whispered behind her, "one day, we came back from the city, and they were all dead, scattered like fallen leaves all over the camp. The women, the children . . . Zenaisa."

His voice broke and she felt her eyes sting. Vehemently, she dug her fingers into the ground. It wasn't her war and it wasn't her story and she didn't want to get any more involved. Garret would do his own thing anyway. He'd been taking care of himself for a long time, and now that his memory had returned ...

"I'm trained to fight," Garret said quietly behind her. "I'm trained to kill. But I didn't protect anyone in that camp. Instead, I led the men away so the butchers' job was that much easier to do."

The raw self-condemnation in his voice tore at her. The first tear trickled down her cheek, but she didn't, she wouldn't, look up. She just bent over her roses, watering the ground with her tears as she had done so many years ago.

"Suzanne?"

She stared hard at the ground.

"I wanted to kill them, Suzanne," he whispered hoarsely. She could feel his eyes burning into her neck, raw and needful. "So help me God, I wanted to find every last one of the men who'd destroyed the camp and kill them with my bare hands. And then Zlatko got up and said he knew how to get revenge. He knew how to get weapons if we could just get the cash.

"All of us chipped in, myself included, to buy the guns. Because we all wanted revenge, I, as much as the others. Except it wasn't my war and it wasn't my job. My job was to observe, not to participate. Even now, I'm not allowed to participate."

He turned away, and she was grateful for the respite. Her cheeks burned with her tears; her stomach ached with her need. She wanted so badly to go to him and hold him against her. But he was leaving, and she'd already given him so much. She didn't know how to hold him without loving him even more. And she didn't know how to bear that kind of pain. God, she just wanted it to end.

She wiped her cheeks fiercely, smearing long smudges of soil across her face. "I'm sure you did the right thing," she said at last. Ruthlessly, she picked up the pruning shears and attacked the first bush. Behind her, she heard his mirthless laugh and her hands trembled.

"The right thing? The right thing? And what would that be, Suzanne? Go AWOL to help my friends, or serve my country?"

She flinched at the vehemence in his voice and clipped off an entire branch.

"Damn it, Suzanne! Would you just look at me!"

"No," she muttered defiantly. "What do you want from me, Garret? What do you want me to say? I don't know what you want."

He grabbed her shoulder and forcefully turned her around, the shears falling to the ground. His dark eyes blazed, his jaw rigid with intensity. "I couldn't do it, Suzanne. I looked at Zlatko, wounded in that cave, and I knew I couldn't help him, but I knew I couldn't betray him, either. So I told him I was an undercover naval officer on a mission. And then I turned and walked away. From everything."

She looked at him in anguish. "It was the best you could do."

"No, it was the worst. Zlatko went nuts. He jumped me, hitting me and calling me every traitorous name he could think of. I had to knock him unconscious to get away. Now, he's gone off the deep end, convinced I'm the root of all evil. And maybe I am. I let my friends down. I let my country down. What's left after that? Suzanne, tell me what's left!"

She couldn't bear it anymore. She wrapped her arms around him, feeling him shudder in her embrace. He buried his face against her neck, his large shoulders shaking from the doubts and the strain. All his life, he'd lived by a few simple maxims. And suddenly black and white were gone, and he lived now in a wasteland of grays.

"You did what you had to do," she whispered in her ear. "It's all right now, Garret. It's all right."

He held her tighter, and she felt the tears on her cheeks once more. She hated the fact that he had to feel such pain.

Why couldn't she just soothe it away? Why couldn't she just keep him?

His head came up, and he kissed her hungrily.

"I need you," he whispered, delving his tongue into her mouth. "I need you, Suzanne."

"I know, I know," she said, kissing him back just as fiercely. Her hands tangled in his hair, smoothing around his corded neck. "Garret...I..." She couldn't bring herself to say the words, so instead, she kissed him harder.

"Zlatko will find you sooner or later," Garret warned her starkly. "I have to go and find him first. You understand that, don't you?"

She nodded, feeling her eyes burn even more. "In the morning, okay? Just give me until then."

He answered by swinging her up into his arms and carrying her upstairs.

In the velvety black-and-white shadows of her room, he ripped off her thin gown, and she yanked his own shirt free, throwing it to the floor so she could smooth her hands down the rippling muscles of his arms. He looked so strong and sculpted in the dim moonlight. More man than she could ever have wanted.

And she liked the way he felt and the way he held her. She liked the morning when she'd awakened in his arms and he'd rolled over and snuggled close.

Remember this, she told herself as she caressed his lips with her own. Remember this touch, this smell, this taste. Remember the way his hair feels in your hands, the way his cheeks rasp across your own. Who knows when you will ever feel such things again.

She closed her eyes and pressed her body against his. Then her hands found the waistband of his jeans. This time, there was no hesitation when she unsnapped the denim. She tugged the rough material from his hips as her right, because she was his lover and she wanted him.

When his hands cupped her breasts, she arched back freely, offering herself to his touch. His rough thumbs sent shivers down her spine, and she moaned, her cry low and encouraging. "Yes, Garret. Like that. Just like that."

He took her nipple into his mouth, and she wanted to weep from the pleasure. Instead, she raked her hands through his hair and held him close. He was so beautiful to her. Everything she'd ever wanted, ever dreamed of all those nights so long ago.

She dragged his head back up and kissed him deeply, her nails raking fiercely down his back. In response, he drew up her leg and wrapped it around his waist, pressing her intimately against him. She didn't shy away, but rubbed against him suggestively. He groaned roughly from the movement and she took pleasure in the sound.

With open, honest eyes, she caressed his chest, explored his arms. His own gaze was black and intense, boring into her. He reached up and plucked the first hairpin from her hair. Two more, and the long, silk strands of her hair cascaded down, caressing her shoulders. He plunged one hand through, massaging her scalp as she arched her neck in appreciation.

He picked up a handful of her hair, then released it to sweep back down once more. "You have beautiful hair," he murmured gruffly. "Shiny and silky and...beautiful."

She shook her head, but reveled in his touch anyway. She moved her hips, feeling his hard, thrusting length so close. Shivers raced up and down her spine, goose bumps popping up on her arms. She stood on tiptoe, positioning him even more intimately. Suddenly, he lifted her up from beneath the arms, wrapping her other leg around his waist.

With slow, muscle-flexing control, he eased her down onto him, watching her eyes turn molten with the heat. She enveloped him completely, tight and warm and moist. Thighs rippling with the strain, he rolled his hips and heard her gasp. It was a beautiful sound on her lips.

Her eyes darkened, her hands gripping his shoulders. He could see the throbbing blue pulse on her neck, watch her bend back with the building passion.

Her nails dug into his upper arms, moisture beading her brow. He thrust deeper, faster, and the look on her face nearly drove him over the edge.

At the last minute, he pulled out completely, hearing her cry out her disappointment. "The condom," he grated. "Just give me a minute, sweetheart."

His hands were trembling so badly, his body coiled so tautly, he could barely get the foil packet out of his jeans pocket. In the end, she took it from his shaking fingers and tore the wrapper open herself.

In contrast, her hands were amazingly steady as she grasped him with one hand and rolled the condom on. Then she gripped his shoulders and drew him down onto the bed, her shapely, voluptuous legs wrapping around his waist once more.

He thrust into her without preamble and it happened for her with one gasping cry, her teeth biting into her lip. He thrust again, then again, then again, and tumbled over the precipice with a roar.

He buried his face in her neck and she wrapped her arms around his shoulders, holding him close. She refused to relinquish her grip when he tried to take his weight off later, and after a moment, he gave in with a sigh.

Still buried deep within her, he fell asleep. But Suzanne remained awake far into the night. Stroking his back and hoarding the memories.

Eight miles away, the sound of shattering glass tinkled through the silent night. The large, dark form cleared the rest of the jagged edges from the window and climbed easily inside. Then starting with the appointment book, he worked his way through Dr. Jacobs's office.

* * *

Suzanne opened her eyes as the mattress unexpectedly sagged. Strong, muscled arms left her as Garret climbed out of bed. She didn't say anything, simply remained lying on her side and staring at the window as she heard him stop and pull on his jeans. Quiet footsteps, then the sound of the house's old pipes groaning to life.

She sat up in bed. Judging by the sun shining through the window, it was later than her usual 5:30 rising time. Her eyes still felt heavy, and her thighs sore. She ignored both as she climbed out of bed.

Her bare feet settled on the hardwood floor and she took in the sight of their clothes scattered messily across the room. Leave it, she told herself. She had the rest of her life to spend cleaning.

She found her old terry-cloth robe, belted it around her waist and then pattered downstairs. Behind her, the pipes groaned more loudly as the shower came to life. In the kitchen, she opened the refrigerator and methodically went to work.

When Garret came down fifteen minutes later, still buttoning his shirt, she was flipping over the fifth piece of French toast. He stopped in the doorway, taking in her tangled brown hair and thick, fuzzy robe. She threw another piece of egg-soaked bread into the frying pan without looking up.

"You didn't have to do this," he said at last, the words husky.

"You should eat," she said simply. "You'll need your strength."

"Suzanne?"

The spatula froze in the air, and for one moment, he could see her hand tremble. "What, Garret?"

"I'll go get the table," he found himself saying. They weren't the words he wanted, but he couldn't seem to find any others. She nodded, the spatula moving again, and he headed down the hall to the back porch.

He took down the protective sheets without allowing himself to think. He laid them over the railing, then picked up the shiny table. He should have made chairs to match. Or maybe a leaf. He didn't know.

He carried it into the house awkwardly, slowly easing it through the narrow doorways.

"In the kitchen?" he asked from the hall.

She shrugged. "Sure, the kitchen."

He looked at the old, rickety wooden table sitting in the corner now. "What should I do with that?"

"The third floor, if it's not a problem. There should be room for it somewhere there."

"It's not a problem." Already beginning to sweat with the morning heat, he carried the old table upstairs. He found a half-empty bedroom on the third floor and deposited the table there. By the time he came back downstairs, Suzanne already had the new table set up with the old chairs and was putting down place mats.

"I would've moved it for you," he said after a minute, frowning. The old chairs, scratched and gray, definitely didn't go with the rich cherry wood of the new table.

"I know," Suzanne said softly, glancing up for a moment. Her gaze was immediately drawn to his chest exposed by the half-buttoned shirt. She looked away. "There's plenty of French toast," she said.

He sat down, not knowing what else to do, and felt the tension stretch even tighter. Moving in the quick, efficient steps he knew so well, she set the table and placed a heaping plate in front of him. It was followed by warmed maple syrup, a shaker of cinnamon, confectioners' sugar and fresh butter. Then she brought the sliced melon and orange juice.

She stood there expectantly until he dished up the first piece. Finally, she took a seat.

"It's very good," he said after taking a bite. "Fresh bread?"

"Challah bread," she told him. "It works the best. And I add a hint of cinnamon to the eggs."

He nodded, chewing another mouthful. "I'll have to remember that," he said presently. She gave a little smile and dished up some fruit.

"Do...do you know where you're going to start looking?" she stammered out after a few minutes.

His fork stilled, then he finished stabbing another piece. "The airports," he said. "I need to figure out how he got here and if he's still around."

"Do you really think he wants you dead?"

"Yes."

She paused, then gave up on eating altogether. "Maybe you should take Cagney with you," she suggested softly, but he shook his head.

"It's personal, Suzanne. Between Zlatko and me. I don't want anyone else involved, and I don't think he'll tolerate it."

"But why?" she persisted, trying to keep the worry out of her voice. Beneath the table, her hands nervously twisted the belt of her robe.

Garret looked at her for a long time. "Zenaisa was his anchor," he said at last. "His home. His heart. When she died, he lost everything. War does that, and men, well, I guess we just have our own way of dealing with things. Vengeance. The vengeance sustained him. Me, too, for a while. I really did want to fight. I really..." He looked down at his plate. "Zlatko needs someone to hate. When I announced who I really was, that someone became me. The hatred is all he has now."

"What will you do?"

"Find him, talk to him. What else can I do?"

She looked at him intensely. "What if he's determined to kill you, Garret? What then?"

For endless seconds, he just looked at the shiny new tabletop. Then slowly, his eyes came up to meet hers. "I can't hurt him, if that's what you mean. I saw those bodies, Suzanne. Women and children . . ." His voice faded away into a whisper. "What was done there never should have been done. And if I could have, I would have stayed and fought that war myself. Even now, I want to."

She pushed her chair back, and unable to look at him anymore, she carried her plate to the sink. She didn't doubt his dark eyes at all. He was a man trained for war, a warrior. What could she give a man like that? Roses? Dolls? French toast? She twisted her lips and began rinsing the plate mindlessly. She could feel his gaze on her back.

The phone rang, and both of them started. With a weak smile, Suzanne picked up the receiver. "Hello?" she said tremulously.

"Suzanne? It's Mitch. Is Garret there?"

She glanced over at Garret, a sudsy hand still clutching the phone. "Sure he is, Mitch. Don't any of you Guiness boys ever say hi?"

She heard Mitch sigh at the other end. "Sorry. Just got a lot on my mind, I guess."

"No problem. Here he is." She held out the phone, and with a questioning eye, Garret rose and took it.

"Yeah?"

"Garret, I got that twitchy feeling again. Tell me you got your memory back."

Garret half smiled at the sound of Mitch's voice, then sobered. "It's okay, Mitch. The situation's under control. I was just a little late."

"What happened?"

"Mom and Dad's house burned down last night."

There was a long silence, then Mitch swore. "Everyone okay?"

"Yeah, they're fine. Cagney's taking care of things."

"You're sure?"

"Yeah, Mitch. Give it a rest."

"Then why are my shoulder blades still suffering from the heebie-jeebies?"

"Mitch, it's only four a.m. your time. Anyone's bound to feel strange at four a.m."

"I suppose. Can Jessica and I return from exile yet? For God's sake, she's due to give birth in just two weeks and she's not very happy with me."

Garret considered his request for a minute, a frown rippling his brow. "Give me one or two days, okay? Just to be sure. I have to find Zlatko yet, and he always was smart."

There was a moment of silence. "You sure you know what you're doing?"

"Yes, big brother."

Mitch ignored the sarcasm in the tone. "Maybe you ought to talk to Cagney. Hell, maybe I should come help out."

Garret's voice became very firm. "Look, Cagney's got a new fiancée and you've got Jessica to look after. And, well, I've just got..." He paused, looking at Suzanne, who was scrubbing the dishes with more vigor than was necessary. "I've got duty," he finished at last. "Look after your wife, Mitch, and give her my best. I'll call you in a day or two."

Mitch muttered something about "bullheaded" and "hot tempered," but finally hung up the phone. Garret put down the receiver a little more slowly.

He walked back to the table, then carried the rest of the dishes and food over to the counter. He gazed at Suzanne a minute longer, but she kept her eyes on the glass she was washing. After a moment, he returned to his room and retrieved the rest of his stuff.

He had a wallet full of cash and a fresh ID he could still use. Hopefully, the airlines could provide him with enough information to let him know if Zlatko was still in the area, and then he would proceed accordingly. How hard could it be to find a man who was built like an ox and spoke heavily accented English? The real trick would be what to do once he found him.

Shaking his head, he laced up his shoes. After securing the cash and IDs in a belt wrapped around his waist under his shirt, he was set.

He returned to the kitchen to find Suzanne placing the last glass in the drying rack. This time, she at least looked up when he entered. Her gaze went to his shoes, then journeyed up to meet his face squarely.

"Do you want to take some food with you?" she asked. "In case you don't find a good place to stop?"

He shook his head. "I'll be all right."

"A coat?"

"Suzanne, it's July."

Her lips thinned for a moment, then she seemed to relax. She leaned back against the counter and crossed her arms in front of her as casually as possible. "Well, if you do need something, you can always call."

"Right." He shifted restlessly in the doorway, his hands jamming into his jeans pockets as he looked at the glossy table. "Thank you," he said finally. "Thank you for everything."

She shrugged. "Neighbors ought to help each other out."

He looked at her, grinning, but the grin had a sardonic twist. "Well, I guess we're that then."

"What?"

"Neighbors."

Her gaze fell, and just for a moment, he could see the strain around her eyes. Then she slowly looked up.

"Be careful, Garret," she said quietly.

"I will be." He remained standing in the doorway, one foot tapping restlessly. At last, she pushed away from the counter and approached him.

"You should get going so you can find this guy."

He nodded, his eyes resting heavily on her face. There were dark smudges under her eyes from the sleepless night, and her hair was still tousled from making love. He didn't know how many kitchens he'd walked out of in his life, but he'd never found leaving quite so difficult before.

"Suzanne," he said at last, searching for the right thing to say and, as usual, finding none. He shook his head in frustration. Mitch always had something reassuring or rock solid to say, Jake something witty and clever. But Garret never could find the right words. Why couldn't he find the words just once? His hands clenched in his pocket, then he forced them to relax. "Suzanne, it was really good of you to let me stay here."

She nodded, looking down at her cracked linoleum. She should strip it down and rewax it soon. Or if she ever won the lottery, replace it altogether.

His thumb suddenly touched her cheek and she flinched. But slowly, his hand moved to cup her chin and tilt her head up. "You're something else," he whispered with dark eyes.

She could only stare at him and hope her gaze didn't reveal too much.

"You should leave," she whispered hoarsely.

He pushed away from the door frame, his hand falling down to his side. Then abruptly, he grabbed both of her shoulders and kissed her passionately. His tongue delved into her mouth while her hands gripped him with equal fervor. Just as suddenly, he pulled away and, without stopping to look back, headed down the hall.

She stood there in her kitchen as she heard the front door open and shut. She stood there, her hands still clutching at the air.

"Goodbye," she whispered to the silence, and finally her hands sank to her sides in the empty house. "I love you."

Chapter 13

Suzanne had a lot of things to do. Those mailings for the parade committee still needed to go out. She was sure she was due at the Y, never mind how far behind she was in her women's group. She should wash all the linens now, and the downstairs bathroom needed to be cleaned. She hadn't dusted in two weeks nor vacuumed in three. Oh, yes, she should strip and wax the linoleum in the kitchen.

So much to be done.

And yet here she was in her garden—properly clad, at least—staring at the roses as if they could tell her the meaning of life. A branch still lay in the grass where she'd accidentally cut it off. She picked it up apologetically, admiring the beautiful pink blooms of the Damask rose. Idly, she held the branch to her face and inhaled the soft scent of roses.

She should dry the petals for a potpourri, or maybe even make them into tea. She'd read somewhere you could make rose jelly. Perhaps she'd try; it was never too late to do something new.

She walked through her garden.

Such beautiful colors, the rich contrast of crimson and cream, the soft highlights of pink and white and red. Green and lush and flowing, tended well enough for a North Carolina postcard or summer retreat. She'd done well with her garden. She'd planned and planted and tended, and the roses had rewarded her accordingly. She hoped that someday, when she'd passed on and left the house to the church, someone would keep up the garden. Of all the things she'd tried, all the things she'd given herself to, the garden at least had repaid her.

A shadow fell across her path, and for a moment, she froze.

Garret. He'd missed her after all. He'd come back...

But as she turned slowly around, it wasn't Garret's face that she found.

The man before her was huge, as big as an ox, like a comic-book hero. Except his face wasn't chiseled and handsome. Instead, his features were battered and worn, the nose crooked, his cheek scarred, his forehead permanently wrinkled. A torn and stained white shirt could barely cover the massive shoulders, the sleeves shredded to reveal dark-haired arms and gnarled, bloody fists. Stained jeans ended in dust-covered feet. Here and there, she could see darker spots of what could only be blood.

Slowly, her eyes came back up, wide and staring with fear. She'd thought Garret could be dark and dangerous. But this man made him look like Peter Pan.

"Please," she whispered hoarsely. He only scoured her with a burning, rage-filled gaze.

"You will come here," he said thickly in his accented English. Almost impatiently, he held out his hand.

She shook her head, her hand going to her throat instinctively as she took a step back. If only she could just get through the wall of rosebushes, she thought vaguely. Her heart beat so rapidly that for one moment, she worried she might be having a heart attack.

The man's forehead furrowed, his huge hands clenching until the fear tasted like bile on her tongue. "Suzanne Montgomery, come here. Now."

"Who... who are you?" she stammered out, though she already knew the answer. She took another small step back, hoping he wouldn't notice.

"I am Garret's death," the man before her said. "And you will come here or I will kill you, too."

"Zlatko," she whispered.

The man stiffened, shaking his head with sudden vehemence. "I am no one," he corrected harshly. "I am a man with no family, no people. I am no one."

She tried another step, but this time he spotted her. His massive jaw clenched, his eyes angrily firing sparks. Oh, God, no. He charged forward.

With a small cry, she turned and ran, the terror powering her legs. If she could just get through the roses and run to Cagney. If she could just get—

A meaty fist swiped at her shirt, snagging the small loop in the back. She threw herself forward with all her might, her feet digging into the rich soil as she lurched for her roses. The worn loop gave, ripping away. She dropped to the ground. She scrambled forward on her hands and knees, diving desperately for the bottom of the bushes.

Tiny thorns scraped her tender cheeks, snatching her hair. She pushed forward relentlessly, her eyes on the light ahead, her pulse pounding with terror. Her head and shoulders emerged, her hands clawing at the grass for traction as she heard the man bellowing behind her.

Abruptly, a thick hand wrapped around her ankle, yanking her backward. She lost her balance and fell on her stomach hard, her breath leaving her in a whoosh. Zlatko pulled her back through the roses.

She grasped desperately at clumps of grass, searching weakly for one last barrier. He pulled harder, and the thorns tore into her cheeks.

"No, no, no," she cried, tears trickling down. One last desperate time, she grabbed the base of a rosebush, feeling the sharp little thorns dig deeply into her palms. He kept pulling, and her fragile skin simply tore away. She slid helplessly through the bushes, her hands wet with blood and her cheeks damp with tears.

He finally released her ankle, leaving her lying there like a grounded fish. She could taste dirt and blood in her mouth, but nothing quite blocked out the terror.

She found herself hoping that Garret had reached the airport and was now flying far, far away from this man.

"I didn't want to hurt you," Zlatko said. He leaned down and wrapped his hand around her long, loose hair. Dismissing her tearstained cheeks completely, he pulled her up and dragged her into the house.

Garret checked with the last airline, learning only that no one fitting Zlatko's description had boarded in the past twenty-four hours. He must still be in the area. But where?

A farmer, Zlatko had lived his life outdoors. Chances were he was camping out in the woods or at the pond near Maddensfield. Someplace not far from his parents' house.

He would just have to do it the old-fashioned way, Garret thought grimly as he walked out of the airport. No fancy satellite photos telling him the exact location of the target. Hell, they used to get reports telling them even the thickness of the door and composite materials so they knew what kinds of explosives to bring.

His missed his team, he thought vaguely. What was Austin up to these days, and what about C.J.? How many bars and brawls had he missed in the past year? How many dives and jumps and how much deep reconnaissance?

He wondered if he would be allowed back. If he could go back. And then he found himself remembering Suzanne and the way her hazel eyes turned gold when he was about to thrust into her. He should have made her chairs to go with the table. And maybe a doll case. He bet she would've liked that.

With a start, he shook his head, his forehead crinkling with consternation. He needed to focus, damn it. Zlatko was out there, his old friend turned into beast. And if he didn't find him soon, there was no telling how dear the price might become.

He requested a cab from the airport service, placing the charge on the new Visa, and returned to Maddensfield.

The clothesline cut into her arms, leaving welts she could feel every time she tried to move. One corner of her mind found it sublimely ironic to be held prisoner in her own house by her own clothesline. The rest of her watched Zlatko pour gasoline on her curtains and felt nothing but terror.

He was going to burn her house down. The house she'd fought so hard to protect because it was the Montgomery house and had been so for over one hundred years. The house she'd worked three jobs to keep, even though there were no Montgomerys to pass it on to. Her old, rickety, expensive, beautiful home.

Her hands struggled vainly up to reach the ropes once more, but the pain had stiffened her fingers while the blood had made them slick. She strained her shoulders, but the clothesline simply dug a little deeper.

She sagged in the chair, her head falling forward, and fought the instinct to weep.

Zlatko emptied out the last of the red can on her love seat, then turned to look at her with his flat eyes. "Are you Garret's woman?" he asked tightly.

She shook her head, biting her lip to hold back the hysterical laughter at the thought. "I'm just a friend," she said. She looked at him with pleading eyes. "Please don't do this, Zlatko. Please don't burn my home."

He turned away from her. "Garret has no friends," he said harshly and lumbered over to the entryway.

"Wait!" she cried out behind him, hating the desperation in her voice. "I know you hate him, but he's just a man, Zlatko. He has nightmares from Sarajevo, you know. It hurts him."

Zlatko turned enough to rake her up and down with scathing eyes. "He knows nothing of pain. He isn't human."

She simply looked at him, silently imploring him to let her go. Finally, his massive shoulders rolling uncomfortably, he glanced away.

"What... what are you going to do?" she asked at last, licking her lips nervously. "I'm just a neighbor. Garret won't care if you burn my house down."

"He'll come," Zlatko said shortly. "He'll come, and then he will understand pain." He looked back at her for a long, stark moment, then sharply turned away as if he couldn't bear the sight. "Zenaisa," she heard him whisper, and then he stalked from the room.

She sagged against the clothesline, drawing in a ragged breath that instantly seared her throat with the sickening stench of gasoline. She had time, she reminded herself, trying to fight back the raw terror. She had time before Garret came and Zlatko sparked the first match. Surely she could come up with something.

But as the gas fumes began to scorch her thoughts and the sun climbed high into the afternoon sky, she began to forget what she was supposed to do with that time. The room became very hazy, the curtains floating in waves of gas and heat.

She dreamed she was twenty-two again, stroking her mother's bloated cheek in the hospital, and whispered her mother's name.

* * *

When Garret found himself standing in the rose garden again, he had the uncomfortable sensation that fate was toying with him. How many times had he tried to walk away now, only to find himself back with this woman?

Worse, no matter how many times he tried to tell himself he was doing the right thing, he appeared to be too late. He'd scoured the area around his parents' house. He'd scoured the woods. And the only tracks he'd found in the sunbaked earth led him right to this place.

He looked at the mangled rosebushes, the scuffed ground and the trampled grass and knew his worst fears had come true. *Tonight, I fed the fire a snack. Tomorrow, it will be a meal.*

Garret faded back against the roses and contemplated his options. He had only his pocketknife and no other more lethal weapon. Then again, could he actually level a gun against a man he'd once considered a brother? Zlatko had saved his life. He'd pulled Garret from the flames and carried him back to the tent for Zenaisa to tend.

Garret closed his eyes for a moment, then looked down once more at the ravaged ground. Suzanne. He squared his shoulders. He would kill Zlatko if necessary.

On his belly, he crawled to the house. Peering up through the bottom of the bay windows, he found his worst fears confirmed: Suzanne was tied to a chair, slumped over. His hands balled into fists, clenching and unclenching with unconscious ruthlessness. And Zlatko? Where the hell was his "friend"? He eased along the outside of the house.

At last, he caught sight of the huge man sitting in the middle of the entryway. Next to him appeared to be a red can. Gasoline, Garret realized, and the first beads of sweat appeared on his brow.

He couldn't confront the man in the house, he thought immediately. Zlatko wasn't sane anymore; his hatred had made him unpredictable. At the first sight of Garret, he'd probably drop the match and torch them all. He had to get the man out of the house. Away from Suzanne.

The shed.

Dropping back down, he made painstaking progress to the shed. Sliding inside, he contemplated the boxed-up tools and determined what to do next. He pulled out the table saw and found the extension cord; at least it was still plugged into the house's outside outlet. Grimly, he plugged in the saw. Then he set wood scraps all around it to hold it in place and flipped it on.

He dived for the door, whipping around to the side of the shed. Sure enough, within seconds, Zlatko stood on the back porch, his dark eyes burning into the shed. The hulking man lumbered down the steps, walking toward the shed with slow, heavy steps.

He stopped halfway across the yard.

"I know it is you, Garret," the man said simply. "But you are too late. I have the woman and she is mine now."

Then, he turned and began to walk back toward the house. Garret felt his heart sink and swore vehemently.

"Zlatko!" he roared out, seeing the man freeze. "You want to fight, I'll fight you. You want revenge, well come and get it."

"I have my revenge," Zlatko said ominously, never turning around. "She is tied to a chair in the living room." Once again, he started walking.

With an enraged bellow, Garret charged. He could not let Zlatko back into the house; he had no other choice. The large man turned easily, standing like an oak to meet the attack. But at the last moment, Garret ducked low, driving his shoulder into the man's stomach. They went down in a thunderous crash.

Always the faster one, Garret scrambled first to his feet—only to be struck by a massive fist across his cheek. His head snapped back, stars dancing before his eyes. He almost went down, but years of experience had taught him that fighting wasn't about clarity. It was about adrenaline and instinct and a primal thirst to kill.

He fired back a blow while his head still rang and felt the satisfying pain of his knuckles connecting with flesh. He followed with his left and blocked just in time to keep a fist from burying itself in his stomach.

Zlatko roared his frustration, and Garret's cheekbone abruptly exploded from a powerful left. He swung back, a glancing blow to the shoulder, then was walloped again from the side. His feet flew out from under him, and he went sprawling. Dimly, he saw Zlatko turn and, shaking his head, stagger toward the house.

"No!" Garret yelled, and scrambled forward to grab his ankle. With a savage pull, he toppled Zlatko to the ground, then scrambled up himself. Abruptly, he became aware of the smell of smoke.

The house, the house was somehow on fire. *Suzanne!* He began to run.

On the stairs, Zlatko caught him again, sending them both crashing down to the yard. This time, Garret clipped his friend twice in short succession, wanting only to get the man away from him. He had to get to the house. He had to get to Suzanne.

Zlatko reached out with a meaty hand, but Garret slammed his foot into his gut. Zlatko staggered back and Garret leaped up the porch stairs.

Through the window of the door, he could see the hazy smoke starting to roll down the hall. He stripped off his shirt, tying it around his mouth and nose, then wrenched open the door. Behind him, he could hear Zlatko lumbering up the stairs.

Garret turned sharply, pinning his friend with raging black eyes.

"What would Zenaisa think?" he demanded hoarsely. "What would Zenaisa say to see this? *Prijatelj*, my friend, I loved her, too."

He had a momentary impression of Zlatko's face going pale, then Garret rushed down the hall. The smoke was thick in the entryway, rolling out of the living room in choking waves. His eyes stung, the smoke searing his throat even through the filter of his shirt. Waving a hand in front of him to clear the air, he rushed into the living room.

The curtain around the window danced with the flames, the fire leaping higher and higher to lick hungrily at the ceiling. He grabbed the heavy fabric even as the fire scorched his skin. Ripping it down, he stomped the blaze out with a fast, heavy foot. But the other curtain was already burning, the fire prancing along the trail of gasoline. Even as he yanked at the second curtain, the love seat flared up with a triumphant roar.

Tears rolled down his cheeks from the smoke and his lungs began to burn. He could not pass out. He could not.

He stomped on the second curtain and watched the fire suddenly whirl around him, lapping eagerly along the gasoline trail. His exposed skin began to prickle from the heat. He needed a fire extinguisher.

There was none in the living room.

He couldn't win, he thought vaguely, his foot stamping on the love seat. He couldn't beat the flames anymore. Through the haze, he found Suzanne. Then he turned and saw Zlatko.

Their eyes locked, and for one moment, Garret thought he saw tears on his friend's cheeks.

"Get the woman," Zlatko said thickly. "I will get the fire."

Garret nodded, jumping across the barrier of fire, feeling it lick at his jeans. Then he was beyond it, pulling at the clothesline with clumsy fingers. Suzanne sagged lifelessly, her head rolling from side to side.

He abandoned her restraints, and picked her up with the chair instead, his muscles bunching tightly. Behind him, he could hear the sharp tearing as Zlatko ripped down a cur-

tain from the entryway and threw it over the circle of fire.
Garret didn't dare look back, but rushed Suzanne down the
back hall toward the door.

They exploded into the hot July afternoon, Garret filling
his lungs with huge, gasping gulps of fresh air. He carried
her all the way out to the safety of the garden, his muscles
beginning to burn from the strain. He set her down with a
bit of a thud and began pulling on her bindings in earnest.

"Suzanne," he cried hoarsely. Her head lolled forward.
"Suzanne!" He slapped her cheeks lightly, but she didn't
respond. He untangled the last knot and yanked the
clothesline from her. She sagged into his arms.

He laid her on the ground, finding a faint pulse with
rough fingers. He slapped her hard, and was finally rewarded by a gulping, fluttering breath. Slowly, her eyes
opened and she peered at him groggily.

"Gasoline," she murmured.

"I know, I know," he told her. Unable to help himself, he
gathered her up in his arms and rocked her against his chest.
She rested her head on his shoulders and it was the sweetest
weight he'd ever felt.

Behind him, he heard the tinkling sound of shattering
glass, followed by the whoosh of rejuvenated flames. He
stilled, his eyes growing bleak.

Once the oxygen met the gasoline-fattened flames...

He looked at her for one last moment, then lowered her
to the ground. "Wait for me, sweetheart," he whispered.
Still looking at her, he grabbed his shirt and tied it once
again around his mouth. She watched him blearily, then her
eyes widened in shocked comprehension.

She reached out a hand, but before she could say anything, he was already turning away from her and rushing
back toward the house.

An explosion of glass filled the air, and after it, the first
wail of the fire engines cut through the afternoon.

He had to crawl to get to the kitchen now, the smoke so thick, the heat so searing. Next to the refrigerator, he found what he sought: the reassuring red canister of a fire extinguisher. Thank God Suzanne was so practical about these things. Holding it tight against him, he crawled into the dining room, seeing the first teasing flicker of flames in the entryway.

Where was Zlatko?

He couldn't make it more than halfway across the dining room, the heat so intense his skin tried to curl back from the touch. He held the fire extinguisher out and released the foam in a steady spray, relentlessly cutting a trail into the living room. Vaguely, he heard the sound of fire trucks pulling into the driveway.

He saw the dark form of a man lying in a circle of flames. And beneath the acrid odor of smoke, he caught the scent of burning skin.

He swathed the flames with the fire extinguisher, pushing forward with desperate and dangerous determination. The extinguisher gave out just as he reached Zlatko's body, and he could see the dark, crinkled mess of burned flesh down Zlatko's side. He grabbed Zlatko beneath his arms and struggled to drag the two-hundred-and-fifty-pound man toward the door.

Sweat rolled through the soot on his cheeks. His eyes stung with the smoke, his lungs burning with the effort. He had to get Zlatko out. He had to get them both...

The fire seared closer and the room began to spin. He was so dizzy, the fire so close, beguiling, mesmerizing. How many times had he fought the beast? And now it looked him in the eye and blazed in triumph.

He staggered, falling to his knees, and saw the fire jump in anticipation. He struggled back only to feel his hair begin to curl from the intensity of the flames.

He wasn't going to make it. They weren't going to make it.

Suzanne.

He pulled one last time, throwing his weight and what remained of his strength into the movement. They fell back against the front door, Garret's hand fumbling for the scorching doorknob.

"Over here," a voice shouted. He looked up to see a yellow-suited, oxygen-masked man approaching through the haze. "We got two over here," the muffled voice cried out.

Garret could see the figure only dimly, before passing out against the door, his hands still fastened beneath Zlatko's arms.

"Please tell me you're all right."

Garret opened his eyes slowly, squinting immediately against the harsh afternoon sun. He was alive, he determined. Alive and lying flat on his back in the grass. He tried to move, but his muscles responded only sluggishly.

"No, don't," Suzanne's voice told him. "Just lie there for a minute. You inhaled a lot of smoke."

She bent over and her face came into view, pale and covered in scratches. The hair framing her face was a long tangled mess of leaves and twigs, while her hazel eyes had darkened with worry. She shifted slightly, and Cagney's head appeared.

"How do you feel?" Cage asked, concern furrowing his brow.

"Fine," Garret croaked.

"You're suffering from smoke inhalation," Cagney retorted sharply.

"I said I was fine," Garret insisted hoarsely. A wobbly hand reached up to caress Suzanne's cheek. She flinched slightly, then smiled at him.

"Just a little bruised and battered," she said in reply to his unanswered question.

"Bruised and battered?" Cagney snorted. "You've both fried your brains."

But they didn't seem to be paying much attention to Cage. Garret's hand slid down the rest of Suzanne's cheek to cup her chin lightly. He could hear the sound of the thundering water from the hoses, the clamor of fireman yelling to fireman.

"The house?"

Suzanne's face stilled, then she mustered a small smile. "The living room is gone, the entryway, too. What isn't burned is covered in soot and destroyed by water." She shrugged a little. "I'm insured." But she looked at Cagney with worry in her eyes.

Garret's gaze swept to Cagney, as well. "Zlatko?" he asked at last, though he already dreaded the answer.

Slowly, Cagney shook his head. "They tried everything they could," he said softly. "He was burned pretty bad."

Garret simply nodded, feeling the tightness in his chest. They'd pulled each other from the flames so many times and laughed about it later with Zenaisa by the bonfires. It all seemed so far away now—the camp, the people who'd made their lives there, the women and children who'd died.

With Zlatko gone, who was left to remember them?

And he wished he could reach over and lay a hand on his large friend's massive shoulder and say that he understood. He'd been there in that camp, and he understood.

Suzanne's hand brushed back his hair; he shuddered at her touch.

Cagney looked up, his gray gaze fastening on something in the distance, then turned back to his brother and Suzanne. "They're ready to take you to the hospital now."

Garret shook his head.

"Garret, you need medical attention. You've been seriously injured."

"I'm fine," Garret said stubbornly, latching his gaze onto Suzanne. She smiled at him softly, and in that smile, he thought she might know what was going through his mind. He reached up and found her hand, then held it tight.

"It's okay, Cagney," she asserted. "I can take care of Garret."

"You? You're injured, too. No, you're both going to the hospital."

"A hotel?" Suzanne asked Garret. "With room service, of course."

He smiled faintly and nodded.

"Damn it, Garret..." Cagney began.

"You heard the woman," Garret said simply. "And you know you can't win an argument with Suzanne."

Cagney looked at both of them and shook his head. "I don't know why I bother."

"Because you care," Suzanne told him, then flashed him a reassuring smile. "It's all right now, Cagney. The damage is done, and now the healing begins. You did your part. Now go home to Marina. Aren't you supposed to meet her parents soon?"

Cagney looked stricken, then clutched his black cowboy hat, mumbling about damn condos and damn cappuccino machines and what was wrong with coffee.

"Little brother," Garret rumbled out, "thank you."

Cagney stopped mumbling and looked at him squarely. "Call Mom, Garret. She really needs to hear from you."

Garret hesitated for a moment, then slowly shook his head. Suzanne kept her hand in his, but her hazel eyes grew wary.

"I have to go to D.C.," Garret whispered, his eyes never leaving Suzanne. "I have to tell them what happened in Sarajevo. I don't know..." He hesitated, then shrugged weakly. "I don't know what will happen."

"Can't you just call it in?" Suzanne asked, not quite able to keep the pleading out of her voice.

Garret shook his head. "I'm a SEAL. I have to do this."

For one moment, Suzanne looked at Cagney as if somehow he could stop the madness. But looking at her beseeching eyes, Cagney could only shake his head. "Maybe you both ought to go to the hospital," he repeated quietly.

Suzanne looked down and shook her head. Slowly, she caressed Garret's hair once more. If she only ever got four nights in her life with him, she'd take them. She knew better than to be too greedy.

"Can you walk?" she asked Garret.

In answer, he grinned at her, and she felt her heart constrict in her chest all over again. "Sweetheart, I can practically dance."

Cagney looked at them both in disgust. "At least get first aid," he called out.

But Garret was getting to his feet with Suzanne's help, and neither was paying any attention to him.

Chapter 14

They checked into the local hotel, without bags and looking like refugees. But Garret paid cash up front and spent so much time looking at Suzanne the hotel clerk never had his questioning eyebrow answered. Still not glancing toward the man, Garret accepted the key and led Suzanne upstairs.

The hotel wasn't anything special, meant more for traveling salespeople and the like. The room was small and had that stale, stuffy smell of a hotel room. The beige carpet was worn in places, the furniture brown and nondescript. The bed, though, was soft and king-size with a rust-colored bedspread.

Garret sat down on it without preamble and drew Suzanne onto his lap. She went willingly, resting her head against his shoulder and wrapping her arms around his neck. He held her close and with one hand began to slowly work the tangles from her long, silky hair.

"You smell like smoke," he said at last.

She nodded against his borrowed shirt, moving carefully

so she didn't aggravate the host of minor burns that criss-crossed his torso. "So do you," she said.

"We should shower." But neither of them moved.

"Does . . . does it feel over?" Suzanne finally asked. She heard the weight of his answer in his silence. Then he sighed and rested his cheek against the top of her head.

"He was my friend," he said simply. His hand stroked her cheek, resting lightly on the scratches. "I could tell you things about Sarajevo, Suzanne, and you would nod your head and look at me with understanding. But you wouldn't understand, you *can't* understand. There are some things you have to be there for. Things I guess only your other buddies ever really know."

Suzanne thought about her mother dying in the hospital and nodded.

"Let's shower," she said, raising her head to look him in the eye. Maybe if they washed away all the smoke and soot, the past would be rinsed away, as well. Maybe he'd stop thinking of Zlatko and she'd stop thinking of her burned-out home, her ruined dolls. Maybe they could just think of each other and find some sanity there.

She rose and Garret followed her with dark eyes.

She undressed him slowly on the cold bathroom tiles, taking care not to pull his pink-tinged skin. He returned the favor just as slowly, his hands lingering on her scratched arms and tortured hands.

He looked at her intensely. "I would have killed him for this," he said quietly, then drew her into the shower.

They both winced as the water hit raw flesh, then laughed at their own pain.

"We're like two old people," Suzanne said, leaning back to let the warm water rush through her hair. Garret's eyes strayed over her creamy, voluptuous body and managed to arch an eyebrow. He unwrapped the tiny bar of soap with hands that were suddenly trembling, and swallowed against the tightness in his chest.

"May I?" he whispered hoarsely. She blushed slightly, then nodded as her mouth parted slightly in anticipation.

He soaped the front of her body leisurely, taking time with each curve and indent. He massaged her breasts, kneaded her belly and let his hand slide slowly between her legs. Her arms found his shoulders, and she leaned against him trustingly as he slowly melted her muscles and filled her with need.

"My turn," she whispered. Her hands weren't steady, and she dropped the bar of soap twice. But finally, she smoothed it down his hair-sprinkled chest, wincing at the myriad of burns from the popping flames. Garret didn't say anything as she soaped his chest, massaged his arms. His eyes simply bore into hers, and from time to time, the muscle in his jaw would clench.

"You could have been killed," she said softly, soaping the back of his neck. Her hands tangled in his singed hair and she pressed her slick, soapy body against his. His eyes drifted down to her lips, then met her gaze once more.

She rose on tiptoe at the open invitation, sliding her breasts up his chest, and kissed him. He opened his mouth for her, welcoming her tongue in warm, moist strokes. It was slow and tender and brought tears to her eyes.

At long last, she pulled back. "We should rinse off."

He simply nodded.

They toweled dry with the same mixture of grimaces and grins, moving slowly but steadily. Suzanne could smell the fresh fragrance of soap and shampoo, and it did make her feel better. The fire was over, gone, done.

But Garret remained.

She knew what she wanted when she led him over to the bed. She knew what she needed as she let the towel slip away. Life didn't come with promises, and Garret didn't give guarantees, but she'd take him anyway for as long as she could.

His dark eyes raked over her naked body and she arched toward him shamelessly.

"We shouldn't," he said, but his hand was already reaching out to caress her breast. "You must be tired by now."

She shook her head, arching her neck back and sighing as his rough fingers found her nipple. She flattened her open palm on his stomach, feeling the washboard ripples of the toned muscles. She traced her hand down and felt him contract the muscles tightly.

With a woman's knowing smile, she found him. He growled low in his throat as she wrapped her hand around him. But his hips arched forward, hungry for her touch. She stroked him tightly, bringing beads of sweat to his upper lip.

Suddenly, fiercely, he grabbed her shoulders and pushed her back onto the bed. She fell willingly, watching with golden eyes as he followed her down, then claimed her mouth with his own. It was savage and sweet, needy and demanding. He thrust his tongue into her mouth with bold promise, plundering the depths, capturing her tongue.

Then he kissed the corners of her mouth with near tenderness, nipping at her chin, then journeying around to capture her earlobe. She gasped; her hands clutching his shoulders as the desire shot like sparks through her veins. Her hips arched up to press against his, her leg rubbing against his suggestively.

He rolled onto his side, supporting himself with his elbow while his other hand smoothed down her beautiful body. He traced her breast again, found the indent of her waist. He caressed her rounded belly, then slid one finger down to find her.

She parted her legs for him, staring into his eyes as he slipped into her. She gasped, her eyes so molten they threatened to burn, and his body became so hard he felt near pain. He leaned over and, with exquisite slowness, captured her breast with his mouth.

He sucked hard and she cried out, her hips arching, her throat contracting. For the first time, she recognized the primality of her own nature, the savage need that held her captive with the force of the emotion. She did not just want this man; she needed him. Needed him in her, filling her, completing her.

Her hand found his hard length once more and guided him toward her. At the last moment, gritting his teeth, he pulled away.

"No, sweetheart," he groaned. "We can't. Just let me do this."

Her eyes widened with shock, and for one moment, the fire retreated as she looked at him with hurt confusion.

"I don't have another condom," he explained. "I can't protect you."

She shook her head, pulling him back over her. "It's okay," she whispered. "Just once is okay."

He refused to budge, the strain knotting his jaw. "We're not teenagers," he countered roughly.

She looked at him, entreaty in her eyes, feeling her heart constrict. With one hand, she cupped his cheek, and her eyes peered into his own with honest emotion. She wanted him inside her, without any barriers. She wanted to feel him explode inside her, pouring himself into her as man had been doing with woman since the beginning of time.

And maybe, just maybe, she wanted the consequences, as well. Would a baby be so bad? Maybe a tiny girl to hold on to long after Garret had left. Someone to love and to raise. She could teach her about dolls and roses and following her heart. She had so much to give. She wanted so much more....

"Please," she whispered hoarsely. "Please Garret."

He groaned, knowing he shouldn't succumb, but unable to ignore the golden need of her eyes. He fought so hard for self-control, but it meant nothing around this woman. He shifted and she wrapped her legs around his waist while her lips curved into the saddest, sweetest smile.

She pulled him inside, and he arched his neck as he sank into her warm embrace. Her eyes closed, the first tear tickling the lashes.

He pulled back slightly, then plunged again, deep and needful. She held him close, biting her lower lip as the pressure built.

Please, give me something more.

He thrust again and again, his neck corded, his back arched. She clung to him, her body slick with sweat, her hair tangled and wet. Yes, just like that. Yes.

Just give me something more.

He came with a roar, his bowed body emptying into hers with the force of a hurricane. And she cried out her own release, wrapping her legs so tightly around him it nearly hurt. He was hers. This instant, this one instant, he was hers and she loved him.

He collapsed in her arms and she stroked his back with trembling arms. She did not let him go for a long time.

When she awoke in the morning, he wasn't beside her. For a moment, she felt panic, then she spotted him sitting at the small round table by the window. He was naked still, his eyes peering out to some sight she couldn't see. She watched him for several minutes before he noticed.

"Good morning," he said. His voice sounded hoarse, and she imagined his throat hurt as much as hers did. She felt dehydrated and stiff. Slowly, she rose onto her elbows, the sheet sliding down slightly to balance precariously on her breasts.

"You're awake early," she said. He nodded, his gaze turning back the window.

"Did you say you're insured?" he asked suddenly. Her brow crinkled warily, but she nodded. "Did Zlatko light the fire?"

"I don't know," she told him honestly. "Maybe the fire department will be able to find out more."

"Will the insurance cover everything?"

Now she was worried. She sat all the way up, pulling at the sheet until she could wrap it under her arms.

"I think so," she said at last. Then she couldn't take the waiting anymore. "You're leaving, aren't you?" she asked flatly.

He hesitated, having the decency to at least look guilty, then he nodded. "I've been away for a long time, Suzanne. The navy has me listed as a deserter. I have to go back and deal with that."

"And then?" she asked stiffly. Her heart was pounding in her chest and she hated the pain of its beating.

He couldn't meet her eyes. "I don't know."

"What do you mean, you don't know?"

"Just that," he said almost impatiently. "I don't know what the navy will do when they find out how I handled Sarajevo. And I don't know what I want them to do. For God's sake, Suzanne, I've been a SEAL for fifteen years now."

She looked at him, feeling guilty for wanting so much when he was going through such a difficult time. "Let me go with you," she offered.

He shook his head. Her eyes narrowed dangerously. "Why not, Garret?"

"It's my business. I'll handle it."

"When isn't it your business?" she snapped back fiercely. "You ran to my place alone. You went after Zlatko alone. And yet all of us were dragged into it. Your parents lost their home. I lost part of mine. When are you going to get it through your thick skull that you're not the Lone Ranger?"

He stood, looking perplexed himself. He ran a hand through his hair, unconcerned by his nudity. "I don't know what will happen and I don't know how long it will take. I just want to take care of it by myself."

She stared at him, and his words wounded her so deeply she couldn't begin to repair the pain. She twisted the comforter in her hands, searching to relieve her despair.

"Suzanne..." he began, but she turned her face away. She didn't care about her dignity anymore; she didn't care about appearing cold. After everything they'd been through, everything they'd shared, he was still leaving her just like that. He was going to shut her out even though she had so much to give. It hurt.

He crossed over to her, raising her head with his hands. The anger in her eyes stung him.

"I'll come back, Suzanne," he whispered.

"When?" she demanded, her voice uncommonly brittle. "In another fifteen years? I don't want to wait fifteen years, Garret."

He touched her cheek, but she flinched away. "Soon," he said. "I promise."

She could only look at him with bleak eyes. "Another promise in the rain, Garret? God, I'm too old for this."

The first tear spilled over. He tried to wipe it away, but it was followed by another.

"Trust me," he could only say. "Please, Suzanne, just trust me."

But she couldn't. She'd spent so many nights he'd never know about needing him so badly and he hadn't been there. So many nights.

She began to weep in earnest, the hot tears streaming shamelessly down her cheeks as her heart tore into pieces.

"I hate you, Garret Guiness," she whispered brokenly.

In response, he pulled her against him, stroking her hair while her salty tears rolled down his chest. "I hate you, too," he whispered back and held her close.

He didn't return in the first two weeks. She told herself it was okay, because there was so much to do. The fire department determined the fire had started from the sun heating up metal, which ignited the gasoline-soaked material. Whether Zlatko had actually lit the fire or not it was considered arson and her policy covered all damages. She'd had to sort through the entire first two stories, sending soot-stained rugs, drapes, clothes, linens, everything, out to be steam cleaned.

After estimates were given, contractors arrived to put up temporary supports while ripping out the wreckage. In six weeks or so, they thought they could restore the living room, dining room and entryway. Really, what with getting new floors and windows, she was coming out ahead. Then there was the new furniture and TV.

But it was hard to sort through the ruins, trying to salvage what she could when so much had been lost. All the pictures of past Montgomerys, which had sat on the mantel, were gone, including the one faded photograph of her father in his military uniform. She tried to call Rachel and tell her sister what had happened, but Rachel sounded wary and defensive at the first sound of her older sister's voice. After ten minutes of a painstakingly awkward conversation, Suzanne had given up and hung up the phone.

It didn't matter, she told herself. She'd been taking care of things alone for a long time now. At least her roses still looked beautiful.

The damage done to the dining room hurt her the most. Sure, the table had been warped and old, but it had been a Montgomery table, handed down from generation to generation. She felt she'd failed her great-great grandmother in some inexplicable way, and in the years to come, she was sure to be known as the Montgomery woman responsible for the loss of the table.

She allowed her hand to rest hopefully on her stomach, then made her way to the hutch that held her dolls. It was covered in soot and warped from all the water. The windows had exploded from the heat, and as she picked carefully through the glass, she found blackened pieces of porcelain. She'd promised herself she wouldn't weep, and now she focused her attention on the four dolls she could salvage.

Their dresses were gray with soot, their carefully coiffed hair flattened by the water. She took them out gingerly and held each one like a child.

For the next two days, she bathed them in bleach water while their clothing was dry-cleaned. Then she dried their hair, and with slow, meticulous care, reshaped it into the elaborate styles her own hair would never be able to maintain.

She moved them to the new hotel where she was now staying and they brought her a degree of comfort. Until the morning she woke up with cramps and a headache and knew her castle in the air had just been vanquished.

She sat on the edge of the bed, rocking back and forth while she stared at a phone that refused to ring. She was strong, she told herself again and again and again. She could handle this.

Then she got up and took a long shower.

She began preparing for her kindergarten class, which would begin soon, and managed to pull together the August Maddensfield parade at the final hour. And she even felt genuinely happy when Cagney told her Mitch's wife, Jessica, had given birth to twin boys, William and Jamie.

The Maddensfield Fair came and went and then September arrived.

She had dinner with Cagney and Marina and Dotti and Henry Guiness. Dotti and Henry's new home was coming along, as well, smaller this time, Dotti said, since the five kids were gone. She hoped to fill it soon with grandchildren, though, and gave Cagney and Marina a pointed look.

It was a nice dinner until Dotti finally set down her fork and asked if Suzanne had heard from Garret. Her pale face must have been answer enough, because Cagney muttered something fierce under his breath while Marina gave her a sympathetic smile. Suzanne squared her shoulders, picked her own fork back up, and said she imagined he was doing fine. Then she resumed eating food that now tasted like ashes on her tongue.

Classes started, the weather became bearable and the repairs to her house were completed.

And she never heard a word from Garret.

In mid-September, the church held its annual bazaar, and Suzanne went through her attic to find things to donate. She couldn't seem to come up with much until she went back downstairs and found herself suddenly standing in her new dining room. Garret's table, small and round and freshly varnished, now sat in the middle; she hadn't had a chance to buy anything else yet. On the table sat her remaining dolls.

She stared at them for a long time. Then she put them in a box, and not allowing herself to think about it, she took them to the sale.

Her hands trembled a little when she put them on one of the card tables. She arranged their fresh dresses nicely, tucking in their hair here and there.

"Why, Suzanne," came the Reverend Talbot's voice in her ear. "Surely you can't be giving away your dolls."

She nodded, not able to meet her minister's eyes for the first time in her life. "They're just sitting around my place," she said as briskly as possible. "I thought they might need a little girl who would really love them."

She felt the solid weight of the Reverend Talbot's hand on her shoulder, and her hands stilled in the soft pile of lace and cotton. "You're a strong woman," he observed softly. "But don't think you have to be too strong, Suzanne. The Lord knows we all need a helping hand now and then."

"I'm fine," she whispered, and went back to arranging her children so they'd be beautiful enough to buy.

And they were so beautiful, all white porcelain, black lashes and tumbling blond and brown hair. Bows and tucks of lace and dainty parasols turned them into ladies, soft and feminine, making every little girl's eyes shine with delight.

She sold every last one of them to one bright-eyed girl after another. She handed each and every one of them over, placing the money firmly in the tin box on the table. By the end of the afternoon, she'd raised eight hundred dollars for the church, and everyone thanked her for her generosity.

That night, Mitch called, wanting to know how she was doing. She said fine and he said once he got his hands on Garret, he'd give him a beating such as he hadn't experienced since he was twelve. She said she was doing fine again and hung up the phone.

Another night passed until she found herself up again Friday morning, walking, dressing and going to school. She stood before the children in the class, staring at trusting eyes, and realized she couldn't remember what letter came after *N.*

"*O,*" Jeff filled in for her at last, and she nodded her head thankfully. She did her best to make it through the morning.

When she walked out at one, she realized she just couldn't take it anymore. She might say she was fine, she might even act as if she was fine, but she was going through the motions on autopilot, simply waiting for Garret to return.

Well, damn it, she thought to herself as she got into her car, but she wasn't sixteen years old anymore. She didn't have to wait. Garret might not want her in D.C., but she was allowed to make up her own mind. If he wouldn't come to her, if he didn't have the courage to even call, then she'd just find him and tell him a thing or two.

She drove straight past her house and headed for the airport.

An hour and a half later, she pulled into the long-term parking lot, her hands shaking. She'd get a ticket for D.C. Why not? She didn't have to teach again until Monday and it wasn't as if she had any dependents. If she missed a choir practice or two, the universe wouldn't come to an end.

She was going to D.C.

She fumbled in her purse, digging out her credit card with shaking hands. Her stomach knotted and unknotted as she walked to the airline counter, but she didn't allow her feet to hesitate. Her cheeks finally had color, and that warm glow of determination was beginning to wash through her blood. She was going to do this!

She'd just stepped up to the waiting attendant when she saw him. Not thirty feet away, he walked past the end of the ticket counters, heading for the escalator leading to the baggage claim. She simply stood there and stared at his retreating back.

"Ma'am?"

She looked at the patient airline attendant with a pale face, then abruptly turned and walked away. Her hands tightened on her purse and she walked faster and faster toward the escalator. Garret stepped on and disappeared from sight. She began to run.

"Excuse me, excuse me," she mumbled breathlessly, pushing her way through the line of people to run down the escalator. At the bottom, she caught him. "Garret?" she whispered, barely trusting herself to speak.

Slowly, he turned, already recognizing her voice. His face looked pale and haggard, his eyes darker than she remembered. For a long time, they simply stared at each other while thin waves of people broke around them.

"Suzanne," he said, his voice a deep rumble. "I—I . . ." He didn't know how to get the words out. "I should have called."

Wordlessly, she nodded.

"I wanted to," he said, rushing out. "I thought of it, even reached for the phone so many times, but...but I just didn't know what to say." He took a deep breath and looked at her with his dark, honest eyes. "I'm a civilian now," he said quietly.

Her eyes widened, with shock? with horror? He didn't know. But then she stepped forward and clasped his hands. It wasn't enough. He pulled her into his arms, burying his face against her neck.

After fifteen years of service, it hurt him to say those words. Ever since he'd made the decision, it seemed he was swamped with memories of being an enlisted man, his SEAL training, his stint in Officer's Candidate School. He remembered the men he served with, the teams he served on. Austin, C.J. Jogging along the beach in his T-shirt emblazoned with the eagle, anchor and trident emblem of the SEALs.

Five years from retirement, and suddenly he was just a man.

Suzanne shifted in his arms and he slowly let her go. His eyes stung and he hated himself for the weakness. He'd done what was right.

"What happened?" she asked at last.

"I was debriefed about Sarajevo," he said. "Filled out some reports. There was a small trial over my conduct, the fact I told Zlatko who I was. Finally, given my past record and the 'extenuating circumstances,' they gave me a reprimand and a mark in my file. But...but I was burned-out before I ever went to Sarajevo, and really burned-out once it was over. It seemed best for me just to take a break from things, try out something new. I had a lot of leave time saved up, and only a few months left on my current service term. I'm a civvy now."

"You should have called and told me," she whispered, but there was no heat in her voice. He looked as if he was hurting, and she never could stand to see Garret Guiness in pain.

"I know. I didn't know what to say. For a while, I didn't know what I wanted." He paused for a long time, and she found her stomach suddenly twisting into knots. "I have something for you," he said abruptly.

He turned and, without preamble, walked to the baggage conveyor belt. Luggage was already gliding along the slow twisting belt.

"I wanted to give you a better present," he said, glancing at her with an intense, unreadable expression. "How's your house?"

"Fixed," she said, hating the nervousness shivering through her. A present? Were they back trying to even the slate? A long, rectangular box appeared, and Garret looked unsure. As he pulled it off the belt, she could almost have sworn he looked nervous, as well.

"I wanted to sneak in and set it up," he said, "to surprise you. I'm not sure it's the same to simply hand you a box."

She looked at it numbly. It was tied with rope and was taller than herself. "What is it?" she asked, finally finding words.

"A doll case. Cherry wood. I thought it would go with the table. It has glass shelves that are adjustable. Of course, I need to put it together." He looked at her expectantly.

She couldn't say anything. She tried, but each time she opened her mouth no sound came out. Her throat tightened unbearably.

"I made it for you," he said, "over the past couple of months."

Oh, he was definitely nervous, his eyes more uncertain than she'd ever seen them. Slowly, she pulled herself together enough to lay a hand on his arm.

"I'm sure it's beautiful," she said thickly.

He looked at her strangely. "Are you going to cry? I didn't mean for that, Suzanne."

She shook her head furiously, rubbing at her eyes. "I gave the dolls away," she whispered, "to the church."

He looked startled, then suddenly paled. "Your dolls, Suzanne?"

She shrugged miserably, her hazel gaze asking forgiveness for her lack of faith. "It had been so long, and you hadn't called. I wasn't sure...I just didn't know what to think anymore."

He reached out and slowly stroked her cheek. "I should have called," he said. "You are so strong and I've hurt you so much. Forgive me, Suzanne. Forgive me." And then, without warning, her eyes widening in shock, he fell to his knees before her. "I don't want there to be any more doubt, Suzanne," he said intensely. Squaring his shoulders, he swallowed, took her hand in his and then said in a voice loud and clear enough to slice through the airport chaos, "Will you marry me, Suzanne Montgomery? Will you be my wife forever?"

People stopped and stared, then a few encouraging claps broke out.

Suzanne looked down at his intent, blazing eyes, his serious, somber face. And she saw him in rain and she saw him in fire, but mostly she saw him waking up in her bed, morning after morning after morning.

She saw her future and the love she would finally be able to call her own.

"Yes," she whispered, and the scattered clapping exploded into serious applause. All around them, passing strangers stopped and smiled and looked on with goodwill.

Suzanne leaned down and kissed him, his strong arms around her waist, and it was right.

Epilogue

They all sat in the backyard, the picnic table overflowing with Guinesses. Mitch and Jessica each held one of the twins, while Liz Guiness Keaton's stepson, Andy Keaton, pushed his baby sister with rapt attention on the toddler's swing. Cagney lounged against the table, one arm around Marina, who was talking to Jessica about teaching. Suzanne would have taken part, but she was showing off her engagement ring to Liz. Garret looked on, still maintaining an indulgent smile despite all the ribbing he'd received from both Mitch and Cagney on finally settling down.

"So when is Jake gonna be here?" Garret asked in hopes of changing the topic.

"I'm sure he'll be in any time now," Mitch said lazily. William had a solid grip on his finger, and Mitch admired the baby's strength with a father's enthusiasm.

"Does he have himself a woman yet?" Cagney piped up.

"Nah," Garret answered. "Jake's too smart for that." Suzanne gave him an arched brow, and he caught her in a quick kiss.

Mitch rolled his eyes and shook his head. "When are you guys getting married, again?"

"December 15," Suzanne said, giving her simple ring another admiring glance. "It's going to be a Christmas wedding. Besides, we wanted to get all the good presents before everyone spends all their money on Cagney and Marina's wedding."

Cagney smiled, waving a mocking finger at his older brother. "Pretty sneaky, you two, getting engaged after me, but married before." Cagney and Marina had finally set a date in May for a garden wedding.

"I'm older," Garret said, "therefore I should get married earlier. Besides, I like presents."

He grinned roguishly, and all the women exchanged glances at the quintessential Guiness expression.

"Have you talked to Jake about your furniture shop yet?" Mitch asked seriously.

"We talked about it last week. He likes the idea. I'm just not sure I want him to be the one financing the operation. Dad and I have enough plans of our own."

Mitch nodded, understanding. Jake handled his wealth politely, not making it an issue, but making it available when necessary. Of course, none of them had ever approached him for money, either, and Mitch could understand Garret's need for a certain degree of independence now that he was putting together his furniture shop. Their father couldn't be happier that *someone* was finally taking up the family craft.

"So what are we going to do for Mom and Dad's forty-fifth anniversary?" Mitch said, returning their attention to the original matter at hand. "They're due back home in less than an hour, so we'd better make some decisions."

"The trip to Las Vegas," Liz said immediately. "They fell in love there and have never visited it since. I think they'd love a sort of trip down memory lane. Can you imagine, meeting and getting married in just four days, especially back then?''

Jessica looked up from Baby Jamie to give Mitch a slow smile. ''So that's where you get it from.''

Mitch colored slightly, earning himself a great deal of teasing from his assembled siblings. Liz's husband, Richard Keaton, coughed discreetly, earning everyone's glances and bailing Mitch out.

''Liz and I can provide the hotel suite for a week,'' Richard said quietly, his hand on his wife's shoulder. She looked up at him and smiled, then, in unison, both of their gazes turned to their children. Andy was still pushing baby Melinda on the swing. The beautiful girl's dark coloring was a perfect foil for Andy's golden looks, and the boy was clearly enraptured with the new addition to the household. Melinda had only to point to something, and he'd trot off and get it. He'd even taken up children's stories so he could read to her.

''Marina and I will supply the limo,'' Cagney said.

''Suzanne and I will cover the romantic dinner.''

''Which leaves Jessica and me supplying tickets to a few shows,'' Mitch said. ''Jake will cover the airplane.''

''Speaking of which...'' Garret said.

Mitch looked at his watch, then shrugged. ''He's usually on time. I don't know, maybe he does have a woman. Remember the actress from last year?''

They all obediently suppressed smiles. ''She was a little much,'' Cagney finally said as diplomatically as possible.

Garret arched a wicked eyebrow. ''A little?''

''At least she was better than the poet,'' Mitch said.

Garret couldn't keep from laughing this time. ''He does like 'em wild.''

Cagney shook his head. ''Face it,'' he said with a shrug. ''Marina and I are the last wedding Mom and Dad will get.''

''Yeah,'' Garret agreed, ''but as long as Jake continues to supply the champagne, who's complaining?''

"Where's he flying in from?" Liz asked, a smile still tickling her lips as she recalled the poet. The woman had been breathtakingly beautiful—all of Jake's women were— but when their mother had served barbecued ribs, the woman had actually climbed onto the middle of the table and recited an impromptu poem "in memory of" the dead animal.

"He was in Poland," Mitch said with a shrug. "He's having some labor problems at his new plant, I gather. But I thought he was going to be back in Virginia a few days ago. Then again, who knows with Jake?"

"Uncle Jake is coming?" Andy piped up. For once, he pulled his attention from his baby sister and looked at them all with rapidly blinking eyes behind his thick glasses. Liz smiled at him.

"Andy worships Jake," she said dryly, and even Richard had a hint of a smile.

"Uncle Jake went to Harvard," Andy said.

"Yes, dear, we know." Andy looked at Liz with such longing eyes she gave in with a smile. "All right, Andy, tell us once more about Uncle Jake and the big, bad bully."

Andy nodded fervently, his blue eyes lighting up with enthusiasm for his favorite story. "In eighth grade," he began with hushed tones, "the big, bad bully, Ted Michaels, stole the kids' lunches, eating them all." Andy's eyes grew round. "He was *so* big, and *so* bad, no one could stop him. Then Uncle Jake decided that he'd had enough." Andy leaned forward, and despite the fact they'd all heard the story a dozen times before, everyone around the table leaned forward, as well. "Uncle Jake got all the kids together and said if they paid him one dollar each and gave him their lunches, he'd make sure they were never bothered again, or their money back. The whole eighth grade agreed.

"So the next day, Uncle Jake came to school early and gathered up all the lunches. Then he filled all the food with diuretics. At lunchtime, he gave the food to the big, bad bully, Ted.''

Andy leaned back with a satisfied smile. "And the big, bad bully, Ted Michaels, spent three whole days in the bathroom, because brains can beat brawn anytime." He looked at his father for confirmation, and Richard nodded agreement.

"And Jake," Garret finished for him dryly, "made fifteen bucks profit, because brains can make big bucks, as well."

The phone cut through the silence and Garret whistled in appreciation.

"Speak of the devil, I bet."

Cagney got up and walked into his parents' new house to answer the phone.

"Jake," he said loud enough for everyone to hear, "we figured it was you."

"Get me Mitch," his older brother growled. Cagney frowned. Garret growled and stormed, but Jake simply grinned and got even.

"Everything all right?" he asked sharply.

"Sorry, Cage, but I only have thirty seconds left. Get me Mitch."

Cagney's frown grew a little deeper, and when he called out for Mitch, his voice rang with genuine concern. Mitch looked at the group with startled eyes, then slowly got up from the picnic table and walked into the house.

"Hey, Jake. What's up?"

"I'm in jail," Jake practically snarled at the other end of the line. "*Your* Bureau people have me under arrest. For God's sake, Mitch, get over here and talk some sense into these people."

"Okay, okay," Mitch said immediately, his brow furrowing in confusion. "You in D.C.?" At Jake's grunted confirmation, Mitch glanced at his watch. "I think there's a four o'clock flight out of Winston-Salem. Give me three hours and I'll be there. Who's in charge?''

Jake mumbled something explicit and uncomplimentary.

"Now, Jake, I thought they taught you Harvard boys bigger words than that."

"Agent Regina O'Doul," Jake grated out.

Mitch repeated the name. He hadn't heard of her, but the witness protection program was its own division anyway.

"Jake," he finally said, "I'm sure it's all a mix-up, but to be safe, you'd better call your lawyer."

"Yeah, yeah," Abruptly, Jake sighed. "Mitch, have I told you yet today how much I hate bureaucrats?"

Mitch smiled, relieved to hear his brother sound a little more like himself. "See you soon, Jake." Mitch walked out to find eight pairs of eyes fixed upon him. He finally shrugged. "Jake seems to be having a few problems with the FBI." They all looked startled, and Mitch couldn't blame them.

"Want me to come with you?" Garret asked immediately.

Mitch shook his head, giving Jessica an apologetic look. "I'm sure I can take care of things in a day or so." He rested a hand on his wife's shoulder. "Jake and I'll be back before you know it."

Jessica nodded at him, trying to keep the concern out of her eyes. After a moment, Mitch disappeared back into the house, and a minute later, the conversation resumed.

Suzanne looked at Garret with troubled eyes, though. "You sure he'll be all right?"

Garret grinned at her, his hand stroking her cheek the way it was prone to do. "Jake's like a cat," he told her. "He always lands on his feet." He pulled her onto his lap, kissing her again for everyone to see.

"So, sweetheart," he whispered in her ear, turning his attention back to more pressing matters, "where should we honeymoon?"

She smiled and rested her head briefly on his chest. "Someplace cold," she told him. Then whispered in his ear, "I have plans."

Garret grinned, that wonderful, wicked grin, but his brothers and sister were too busy with their own families to notice. It was just as well, because he had plans of his own.

He held Suzanne closer and slowly began to outline them in her ear while she turned a nice shade of red.

Dotti and Henry Guiness were going to have more grandchildren before they knew it.

*   *   *   *   *

FORTUNE'S Children™

In July, get to know the Fortune family....

Next month, don't miss the start of Fortune's Children, a
fabulous new twelve-book series from Silhouette Books.

**Meet the Fortunes—a family whose legacy is greater than
riches. Because where there's a will...there's a wedding!**

When Kate Fortune's plane crashes in the jungle, her family
believes that she's dead. And when her will is read, they
discover that Kate's plans for their lives are more interesting
than they'd ever suspected.

Look for the first book, *Hired Husband,* by *New York Times*
bestselling author **Rebecca Brandewyne.** PLUS, a stunning,
perforated bookmark is affixed to *Hired Husband* (and
selected other titles in the series), providing a convenient
checklist for all twelve titles!

FREE
Keepsake
Bookmark

Launching in July wherever books are sold.

Silhouette®

FCT

This July, watch for the delivery of...

An exciting new miniseries that appears in a different Silhouette series each month. It's about love, marriage—and Daddy's unexpected need for a baby carriage!

Daddy Knows Last unites five of your favorite authors as they weave five connected stories about baby fever in New Hope, Texas.

- **THE BABY NOTION** by Dixie Browning
  (SD#1011, 7/96)

- **BABY IN A BASKET** by Helen R. Myers
  (SR#1169, 8/96)

- **MARRIED...WITH TWINS!**
  by Jennifer Mikels
  (SSE#1054, 9/96)

- **HOW TO HOOK A HUSBAND (AND A BABY)**
  by Carolyn Zane
  (YT#29, 10/96)

- **DISCOVERED: DADDY** by Marilyn Pappano
  (IM#746, 11/96)

Daddy Knows Last arrives in July...only from

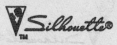

DKLT

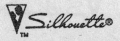

Alicia Scott's

Elizabeth, Mitch, Cagney, Garret and Jake:

Four brothers and a sister—though miles separated them, they would always be a family.

Don't miss a single, suspenseful—sexy—tale in Alicia Scott's family-based series, which features four rugged, untamable brothers and their spitfire sister:

THE QUIET ONE...IM #701, March 1996

THE ONE WORTH WAITING FOR...IM #713, May 1996

THE ONE WHO ALMOST GOT AWAY...IM #723, July 1996

"The Guiness Gang," found only in—